D1117264

THE ASHTABULA HAT TRICK

THE ASHTABULA HAT TRICK

A MILAN JACOVICH/ KEVIN O'BANNION MYSTERY

LES ROBERTS

GRAY & COMPANY, PUBLISHERS
CLEVELAND

Gray & Company, Publishers
www.grayco.com

ISBN: 978-1-938441-71-4

Printed in the United States
First printing

To Holly—
Always, To Holly

THE
ASHTABULA
HAT TRICK

PROLOGUE

MILAN

You think murders don't happen in small towns? You believe they only take place in cities—in "bad neighborhoods" replete with indolent loungers, poverty, sexual jealousy, and violence? Not quite. Maybe if you grew up watching sitcoms like *The Brady Bunch* and *Father Knows Best*, you think the world is really like that. I'm a big-city guy—lived in Cleveland, Ohio, all my life. I was a cop there first; then I turned private, and naturally ran into some pretty wicked people in my line of business. I discovered that bizarre crime happens not only on the mean streets of metropolitan cities, but in quiet, peaceful towns and villages, too.

Supercities like New York or Los Angeles are too big for my taste—too expensive, too crowded, too much crime, too much crap. Cleveland? Just about perfect. Good people, great restaurants, the best symphony orchestra in America, the Rock and Roll Hall of Fame, and three major sports teams. The teams usually stink, but they are *our* teams.

My blood runs a bit faster whenever I'm downtown—when I can see the lake, the changing skyline, and busy Clevelanders sharing sidewalks with each other. Older people retire and move to Florida. Me? When I finally leave Cleveland, it will be in an urn.

Like any city, we have our share of crime, which keeps me working. I'm a private investigator—just like actors Bogart and Mitchum and Alan Ladd, who used to be called movie "private eyes." When I opened my one-man company I designated it Milan Security, because that's what I hoped I'd spend my lifetime doing—solving security problems for local companies. I gave it my first name, the American version of an Eastern European one I pronounce MY-lan, instead of my surname, which hardly anyone can pronounce. It's Jacovich, which is Slovenian, as it happens, and you pronounce the *J* like a *Y*. YOCK-o-vitch.

You know what they say about best-laid plans. Security is the least of my worries. People get cheated or kidnapped or killed, and sometimes I get dragged into a case whether I like it or not. I've asked a ton of questions. I've interviewed some who didn't want to talk to me. I've been shot, or shot *at*. Stabbed. Punched around more than I want to remember. Scars, broken bones, concussions, and busted knuckles come with the territory.

What led me to a small out-of-the-way town in the northeast corner of Ohio started out as a romantic mini-vacation, with some business on the side. I have a significant other. After more than twenty years as a divorced man, and a string of disappointing re-lationships with women, Tobe Blaine entered my life—a surprise to both of us, happening more quickly than we had imagined. She pronounces her first name "Toby," but doesn't spell it that way. She's the only woman I've ever known who's as tough as I am.

She's a cop. Homicide Detective Sergeant Tobe Blaine chooses not to work with a partner, and answers only to her immediate supervisor, Lieutenant Florence McHargue.

My own history with McHargue has been contentious. She never accepted that I turned my back on police work, resigned from the force, and went into the shamus business, and I never really got over that her job was replacing my best friend, the late Lieutenant Marko Meglich, who was shot to death while he was watching my back.

I don't follow the rules that stifle the police; McHargue lives by them. We're of different races and genders All those things doomed our friendship from the start.

Tobe Blaine and I are also of different races, but that doesn't slow us down. You might have dated for decades, as I have—but just one look at a special person and you're in it for the long run.

Homicide detectives don't work nine to five—some murders happen after the sun goes down—so we're flexible in terms of spending time together. But thanks to McHargue and her boss, the chief of detectives, we had a few quiet days—working days for Tobe—in a dot on the Ohio map called Queenstown.

Queenstown is in Ashtabula County somewhere between Ashtabula itself—a harbor city on the shores of Lake Erie struggling to become a tourist spot and not a dying community—and another harbor town, Conneaut, just a spit and a holler from the Pennsylvania border. It's a quiet little town, population 3,026, and most of its residents are lovely people.

Most of them.

The houses are older and interesting in appearance. The three-man police department rarely makes any law-enforcement decisions beyond issuing citations for speeding along the road overlooking Lake Erie, or chasing teenagers back home to their parents after curfew.

The first homicide in Queenstown's history, during the last week in April, shook up the populace. The second came sixteen days later. Two murders were too much for the local constabulary to handle, so the part-time volunteer mayor contacted an old acquaintance, the mayor of Cleveland, with whom he went to college decades before at Ohio State. The mayor of Cleveland called the chief of police, who called the chief of detectives, who descended upon the Homicide Unit and ordered McHargue to assign a detective to temporary duty in Queenstown. McHargue had to look no further than her most recent department acquisition, Tobe Blaine, for someone to spend a few days in Ashtabula County to catch the villain.

Tobe suggested I come and keep her company in a small town where she knew precisely nobody. I thought but didn't say that the killer might now be several states away, but it wasn't my business—not then, anyway.

A year earlier I might have turned her down, as my work never stops. But I'd recently hired a young associate who could "watch the store" while I was gone. His name is Kevin O'Bannion—known as "K.O." to almost everyone—and he's surprisingly good at his job. He's also mean-tough, despite being five inches shorter than my six foot three. He's in his mid-twenties, an angry young man who's survived three tours of Iraq and Afghanistan, after three years in juvenile detention for half-killing two teenaged torturers and murderers of a stray dog. Don't get K.O. started on cruelty to animals—any animals. He's mellowed, though, since falling in love with the terminally cute Carli Wysocki, who takes such good care of him that he's moved into her apartment full-time.

Well—he's mellowed a *little* bit.

The good news is that in May we had a warm and mostly rain-less spring. The bad news is that in a murder case, people poking around where they don't belong sometimes get hurt.

CHAPTER ONE

MILAN

"Not exactly the world's most luxurious vacation resort," Tobe murmured as we pulled into the parking lot of the little motel just off the I-90 exit toward Conneaut after an hour's drive from her place on the near West Side of Cleveland.

We've maintained separate residences. We love spending time together, but each of us needs privacy, our "alone time." I've been married, though she has not, but each of us independently decided we didn't want an every-moment love affair. We're committed and monogamous, but we're individuals, and we like it that way.

The motel where the Cleveland P.D. had made a reservation for us—or rather, for Tobe, as I was just along for the ride—looked like those that appeared in many films noir of the 1950s. It didn't seem run-down, and was apparently clean enough, but it was hardly a honeymoon resort, either. I'm not even sure it had a swimming pool.

"Not that I expected a Ritz-Carlton," I said, "but couldn't your department afford a nicer hotel?"

She rolled her eyes to the spring-blue heavens. "There aren't a lot of hotels in Ashtabula County."

I laughed; she pronounces the name of the county and city incorrectly. She says Ash-ta-BOO-la, but it's really Ash-ta-BYEW-la. She also says LEE-ma for Lima, Ohio, as though it were the capital of Peru, instead of how all other Ohioans pronounce it—LIE-ma, like the bean. But then, she's from Raleigh originally, by way of Cincinnati—I guess they talk funny down there.

Side note: I loathe lima beans.

"We should have brought Herbie," I said. Herbie was my recently acquired dog. I had never had an animal of any kind, and Herbie was a surprise. His name wasn't Herbie, either; he was *Booger*, thanks to his original owner, who didn't survive my last murder investigation—but I refused to call any living creature Booger. Tobe and I together named him Herbie, after a courageous dog rescued and cared for until his death in a western suburb of Cleveland by a cop who was all heart. Despite my having to stay upwind of him, he'd grown on me—and my changing his diet from the dirt-cheap generic dog food he'd been fed all his life to a decent brand had minimized but didn't completely stop his noxious gastric problems.

K.O. was keeping Herbie while I went out of town with Tobe—and probably his girlfriend, Carli, was less than thrilled about that. Life changes—but we get used to it.

I said, "Aren't there any bed-and-breakfast inns around here?"

"There are cabins by the lake you can rent by the week—but McHargue wasn't sure how long we'd be here and didn't want to nick the department for a few extra days. Geneva-on-the-Lake has several bed-and-breakfasts. But if the owners saw some black, gun-packing female cop investigating a double homicide show up with her Caucasian boyfriend, you think they'd give us the key to the city?"

The clerk at the motel was caught off guard when he got his first glimpse of us. There must be interracial couples in Ashtabula, but they probably don't check into this particular establishment. He immediately stopped looking at us, but studied the reservation as if memorizing it. Finally circumstances forced him to talk to me. Not to Tobe, mind you, but to me. "Are you with the Cleveland Police Department, sir?"

"*I'm* with the police department," Tobe informed him, flashing her buzzer. "He's a private investigator, also from Cleveland. Milan, show him your license."

"That's not necessary," the clerk said too quickly. "So—do you wish adjoining rooms?"

"My department only booked one room, isn't that so?"

"Well, yes—but . . ."

"Then one room is all we'll need," she said.

The clerk's eyebrows rose to nearly meet his hairline—if he'd had one. His eyes were large and bulging, his nose upward bound and pointed, making him resemble a puppet that, like Pinocchio, had been magically brought to life. As he studied us both, dirty pictures stoked his imagination. "I'll have to charge you extra." He looked down at the countertop, fiddled with his clipboard, examined his fingernails, checked the weather outside the window. His job was to interface with the public; perhaps he was only comfortable interfacing with white people. "The reservation is for one. For two, it's a different rate."

"Then I'll pay the extra in cash," I said, "and you collect the regular fee from the Cleveland Police Department."

Sniffing, he pushed the clipboard toward me. "You'll have to sign in, too. I'll have to see some identification from you," he said.

"You said about sixty seconds ago it wasn't necessary. Oh, well . . ." I flipped open my wallet so he could see my driver's license, and fished out my P.I. license, too. He laboriously studied my name, Milan Jacovich, as though it were written in Farsi. Then he tried it aloud: "Mee-LAHN Ja-CO-vich."

"Not even close." I counted out five twenties and pushed them across the counter at him.

"How many days will you be here?" he demanded.

"It depends," Tobe snapped. She signed the registration card with a flourish. "May we have an extra room key, or should we just break in through the window?"

He pursed his lips as he handed her two electronic cards that would open our motel room door. "I'm just being careful," he said.

"Well, my friend here will watch to see I don't steal any of your towels." Tobe glanced at his cheap name plaque on the counter. "Feelo Ackerman, is it?"

"It's Philo!" he said, offended. "Long *i*. Philo!"

"I'm Tobe Blaine. Long *o*. *E* sounds like *Y*, but isn't. Long *a*. And a long memory." She spun quickly and marched from the office.

I leaned over the counter. "A news flash, Mr. Ackerman. It's not 1850 anymore, and we're not in antebellum Alabama."

Being six-three and weighing two-thirty, I like it when what I say leaves a person silent, with mouth gaping. Tobe and I found our motel room, with a queen-sized bed—the advertisement online had promised king-sized, along with Wi-Fi—and a view overlooking the I-90 freeway.

"Feelo?" I said.

"It takes so little to piss people off—like when someone calls you MEE-lan, or pronounces the *J* in your last name like *J* instead of *Y.*"

"Now I feel bad for poor Feelo." I pulled aside the curtains and looked out at the busy freeway. Cars and trucks rumbled noisily by. "Should we ask for a quieter room?"

She hung her bag in the closet and tossed her suitcase on the bed. "If you want to stay in some five-star hotel, hook up with the ambassador to Spain and not a homicide cop."

"The ambassador to Spain isn't as sexy as you are."

"You don't know that. He might be." She checked her watch. "We should head for the police department. The chief expects us."

"A chief," I observed, "with not enough Indians."

"If he had more Indians, we wouldn't be here. And while we're at it, Milan, Indians are from India. You mean Native Americans."

"If you say 'a chief without enough Native Americans,' the joke isn't funny."

"It wasn't funny to begin with." She opened her suitcase and removed her holstered gun, strapping it to her waist.

"Think you'll have to shoot somebody today?"

"You never know. But take away my weapon and I'm just a middle-aged black woman with a lousy attitude."

We went out to the gray Ford Taurus the Cleveland P.D. had assigned to her. When we began our trip from Cleveland, Tobe had said, "It's a cop car. I'm the cop, so I drive. That's the rules." She'd slid behind the wheel and patted the passenger seat beside her. "Hop in, Milan. Pretend I'm Morgan Freeman and you're Miss Daisy."

A six-minute trip from Conneaut to Queenstown took us through lush spring greenery, with the lake stretched before us on one side, looking bigger, cleaner, and more tranquil than it looks from Cleveland. Then again, the summertime view from downtown, with all those white sails bobbing in the distance, takes your breath away. But we were on a more peaceful road—although two recent local murders didn't make its citizens feel peaceful.

There wasn't much of Queenstown that was nonresidential, and virtually no retail. They didn't even have a movie theater, although I noticed a sign outside their library announcing a relatively new film showing every Friday evening. The police department in the "town center" was different from all other structures in the village, which are nearly a century old, and well cared for. The building also housed a small meeting room, and the offices of those who kept Queenstown running. Made of yellowish brick, it had been erected during the sixties—that crazy decade when everyone tried to decide whether they were a hawk or a dove, a hippie or the Establishment, a drunkard or a doper.

The P.D. itself boasted only two rooms—the large reception room, and the other room, the chief's office. He sat with his broad girth spread out behind an executive desk that was too big for the room. Pinned to a tropical sports shirt, the chief's gold badge looked silly. His head was shaved and very round, as were his face and body; he looked like a snowman. His name was on a plaque: Chief of Police Eino Koskinen. I wondered whether everyone in this county had a desk plaque.

Koskinen appeared as surprised as the motel clerk when he saw Tobe Blaine, armed and wearing her own badge. "Your mayor said you were coming," he said pleasantly, "but he didn't mention you were a—female detective."

"That's because," Tobe said, "the mayor and I never shower together."

Pursing his lips, he chose to ignore that. "And you, sir?"

I handed him my card and pronounced my name for him. "I'm accompanying Detective Sergeant Blaine."

"Accompanying," he said softly, reading my card. "Does this mean you're entitled to all the same perks and privileges?"

Tobe answered for me. "You'd be surprised at his perks and privileges, Chief. He asks good questions, too."

He nodded. "So where you-all staying at?"

I tried not to smile as I told him the name of the motel. "Yeah—just off the freeway. Well, listen now—I'm wondering," Koskinen said, stroking his chin, "if we're looking for a serial killer."

Tobe leaned her elbow on a filing cabinet against the wall. "May we get info on the victims?"

He sighed. "You're calling the shots." He took two thick files and led us back out into the outer office, which doubled as his "conference room," with a dinette-sized table seating six and mismatched chairs. He opened the first file and spread out the contents in front of me; Tobe had to crane her neck to get a good look.

"This was Number One," the chief said.

The photograph was of a middle-aged white male wearing a gray suit, dark blue tie, glasses, and one of those comb-over haircuts ineffectively hiding a bald spot, smiling into the camera while sitting at a table in a restaurant. "Paul J. Fontaine. He has a ranch, right on the Queenstown-Conneaut border. Raised and sold horses—not good horses, but he unloaded lots of them to the Amish. Also sold scrub veggies. He made a good living, but no millionaire." Koskinen puffed up his chest, or was he sticking out his gut? "I liked him."

"You knew him?" I said.

"It's a small town. Everybody knows everybody."

"Married or single?" Tobe asked.

"Me or him?"

Tobe sighed and pointed to Paul J. Fontaine's photograph. "Married to Maude Fontaine for twenty-one years," the chief explained. "Two teen kids, a boy and a girl. Paul was born in Queenstown; Maude went to Conneaut High School, down the road."

Tobe looked at me. "Locals. How did he die?"

Chief Koskinen moved the top photograph aside. The second had been taken at the crime scene—Fontaine at the wheel of his pickup truck, wearing a lightweight windbreaker over a white shirt, lying back against the seat, head back and mouth wide open. The left side of his chest was soaked with blood.

"Bullet wounds?"

"Knife wound—right through the heart."

"Where's the knife?"

Koskinen shrugged.

I asked, "Who did the autopsy?"

He looked annoyed. "The coroner. Who you think did it?"

"Where was the car?" Tobe wanted to know.

"In Sunset Park." He extracted another photograph—taken about ten feet away from the car with Fontaine's body still in it, in a small parking area next to a stretch of grass and trees on a ridge overlooking Lake Erie and an ancient beach that had been traveled by seventeenth-century Native Americans so often that it formed a natural road. "My officer Joe Platko found him. He was on his usual shift, just driving around, when he—uh—found Paul Fontaine."

"Was this near Mr. Fontaine's ranch?"

"About four or five miles away—between here and Conneaut."

"Why did Officer Platko investigate a car in a parking lot?"

Koskinen fussily neatened the report pages on the table. "Sunset Park is—the kind of place people visit in order to—uh, meet other people, if you know what I mean."

"I'm not sure I do know what you mean," Tobe said.

He sighed. "Aw, hell. You go up there if you're horny—hoping you'll meet somebody else as horny as you are."

"You mean prostitutes hang out in Sunset Park?"

Now the chief looked shocked and offended. "We have no prostitutes around here, Detective. This is a straitlaced town."

She nodded. "So townies go up to Sunset Park when they want to get un-laced. Is that it?"

"Mostly kids, doggone it. Teenagers deal with raging hormones."

Tobe's eyes locked with mine and she silently mouthed "Doggone it" and tried not to smile. "Doggone it" isn't an expression heard often in Cleveland.

I said, "How long had he been dead?"

"You'll have to ask the coroner that."

Tobe put in, "What kind of knife was it?"

"Ask the coroner that, too."

Scribbling *Coroner* in my notebook, I said, "Was the second victim knifed, too?"

"Nope." He opened another file. "Cordis Poole. Forty-nine years old—an insurance salesman for State Farm in Conneaut. Wife's Gwen—teenage son's Cordis Junior. Everybody calls him Junior, but I'm not sure he likes that."

I said, "He probably hates being called Cordis, too. It's a redneck name."

Atop the file was a candid photograph of Cordis Poole the elder, a high school jock grown chunky with middle age, grinning at the camera, holding a football and wearing a Steelers jersey. The second photo was of Poole lying facedown in some sort of creek or river in the darkness, the back of his skull crushed. "Looks like some sort of hammer or iron pipe, but we haven't found a weapon for either killing." Koskinen sadly shook his head. "I've been a cop twenty-six years—but murder isn't in my wheelhouse."

"Where was this photo taken?" I asked.

"Tinker's Hollow—at one end of the bridge." Rising heavily, he pointed to an Ashtabula County map hanging on one wall, his finger almost caressing the thin blue line that was Conneaut Creek. "Who knows if he was pushed off the bridge? You can't drive across it—it's been closed for years. They say Tinker's Hollow is haunted. *I've* never seen a ghost, but the rumor is that one of the Tinker brothers—from the nineteenth century—floats around there and says 'boo' and screws up your car. It's a spooky place in the daytime—and at night, it'll scare the piss out of you." He blushed and said to Tobe, "Oh, sorry, Ma'am—pardon my French."

Tobe waved it off. "I'm a cop, not a nun. What do these victims have in common?"

Koskinen said, "Similar incomes—Fontaine's a little more than Poole's. Decent homes, good marriages, no criminal records. Part of this community, like everyone else."

"They were friends?" I said.

"They lived about a mile apart, attended the same church."

"What church is that?"

Koskinen frowned. "The Baptist church. What difference does that make?"

"What else did they have in common?" Tobe wanted to know.

"They both came to town hall meetings, they were in Rotary—a big organization here—and far as I know, they never disagreed with one another."

"BFFs?"

"BFFs? What's that?"

"Internet shorthand for 'Best friends forever,'" Tobe said. "So— no feud between them?"

"The only feud in Queenstown is two next-door neighbors. One has two cats crossing over into the other one's yard and killing birds she feeds every day—and they both bitch about it all the time."

"Where was Cordis Poole's car?" I asked.

"In the lot of the Baptist church."

Tobe said, "Is Tinker's Hollow in walking distance from the church?"

"Not hardly. They're a couple miles apart."

She nodded. "Can we have a copy of these files, Chief?"

He glanced over at the copy machine in one corner. "These here are copies; I made them up for you. Addresses, phone numbers, job numbers, and everything else we could think of."

"We?"

"Well—Officer Platko discovered these murder victims, so we included everything we could for you."

"Officer Platko found both bodies?" Tobe asked.

"Teenage kids found Cordis Poole—they called Joe Platko."

"What time was this?" I said.

"Nine thirty at night, when he's on duty."

"What were kids doing in Tinker's Hollow at night?"

"What did *you* do when you were a kid? Either drinking beer, smoking weed, or making out." Koskinen rubbed his face as if it were dusty. "When Joe found the bodies, he called Highway Patrol; they're no better at these murders than me."

"Did Platko take these photos?" Tobe said.

"Joe doesn't carry a camera. He called me—I called the *Messenger*."

Tobe said, "Is the *Messenger* the Queenstown newspaper?"

"We're too small to have a paper of our own. It's the county's—located in Ashtabula. And both times Amy Klein drove over and took the pictures. She's their photographer, reporter, co-editor, and she probably sells ads, too."

"And who's on police patrol late at night, like midnight?"

"Nobody!" Koskinen snapped. "There's no gangs here. This isn't Newark or Vegas. It's a small town; nobody does crime. We don't need an on-duty cop in the middle of the night."

"Well," I said, "maybe now you do."

CHAPTER TWO

MILAN

"It's almost one p.m.," Tobe said as we left the police station, each carrying a murder file. "I'm hungry. Right now, if you put a decent sauce on it, I'd eat your shoe." Although Chief Koskinen had generously offered us his spare police cruiser so we could separate and hopefully clear up his double murder case quickly, we were still in Tobe's car looking for a restaurant. This part of Ashtabula County wasn't much of a dining-out neighborhood.

After ten minutes, we found a place. An old covered bridge had been moved piece by piece to its current location and turned into the Covered Bridge Restaurant, which sells promotional jackets and T-shirts about itself as well as comestibles. Ashtabula, geographically the largest Ohio county, boasts eighteen covered bridges, including the longest and the shortest ones in the United States.

I selected what they call a Sizzling N'Awlins Skillet, featuring chicken, shrimp, pork, andouille sausage, and more dress-up; I hadn't expected anything New Orleans-y in this northeast corner of Ohio. Tobe remarked that much meat could last me a week, and ordered a spicy chopped chicken salad. It arrived with a garnish of shredded white cheddar atop it as big as a tennis ball. The Covered Bridge wasn't exactly a health food restaurant.

Tobe pushed half her cheese off to the side. "I think the bereaved widows of the victims would do better talking to a female this afternoon."

"Be delicate," I said.

"I'm always delicate. The chief blushed saying 'piss' in front of me—how much more delicate can I get? Meantime, you can check the county coroner for autopsy results. And run down that *Messenger* reporter; she was on the scene both times."

I checked my notes. "Amy Klein," I said, booting up my iPhone. As a technophobe—which is another way of saying "too old"—I used to hate the idea of lugging around an iPhone on which you can look up everything in the world that ever existed. Now I never go anywhere without one. "I'll Google the address of the paper."

She scoped out the atmosphere of the Covered Bridge, which looked very much like pizza joints did in the 1950s. "Is there Wi-Fi in here?" "Only outhouses on Amish farms are without Wi-Fi."

"I'll remember that if I want to check e-mails in an Amish outhouse."

I tapped keys for a while with one hand while drinking Pepsi with the other. I found Amy Comunale Klein at the *Messenger* and wrote down the street address. Then I Googled the website for the county coroner's office. The home page suggested that website visitors "Write a Review."

"Who writes reviews for coroners?" I said. "The dearly departed?"

She pointed at my plate. "Chicken, shrimp and pig, all at once. If you eat all of that, you'll be the next coroner's reviewer. All those poor animals—*you're* the mass murderer."

I dropped Tobe off at police headquarters. By the time I reached the offices of the *Messenger,* the sun had taken refuge behind a bank of clouds. Amy Comunale Klein was expecting me. In her mid-fifties, with red hair cut short and many clanking rings and bracelets, she wore a frilly printed blouse and lime-green slacks, and tennis shoes encased her stockingless feet. I sat across from her in a too-small cubbyhole that was festooned with photographs of local celebrities I didn't know, and she asked most of the questions.

"What makes you think I know anything about killings?" she said. "I just take pictures."

"You write the stories that go with them."

"I did write up both victims. Want to see my clips?"

"I'm more interested in your feelings."

She thoughtfully tapped her long fingernails on the surface of her cluttered desk. "Seeing two corpses so close together—just a few weeks apart—is scary." She drew her index finger across her neck and made a horrible sound. "Paul Fontaine. That was a heck of a way to go. As for Cordis Poole . . ." She shuddered.

"Did you know them personally?"

She shook her head. "I don't get up to Queenstown often, unless someone up there makes news." She waved airily at the pictures on her cubicle walls. "I don't think Poole and Fontaine will make it to my Hall of Fame gallery, either."

"They were discovered late in the evening, so it didn't make the morning paper."

She laughed. "We're a weekly."

"You think there's a serial killer running loose?"

"You want me to guess? Journalists don't guess—even small-town journalists on weekly newspapers."

"The murder weapons were different."

"A knife and—probably—a hammer."

"But no gun," I said. "Even nutcases and ex-cons can pay cash for any kind of weapon without being asked a single question."

"This isn't Cleveland. It's a remote corner of Nowhere. We don't worry about government rules; we make our own."

"Murder no-no is a rule everywhere—or used to be, anyway. Why was Paul Fontaine in Sunset Park at night?"

"You think he called and told me about it?"

"You answer my questions with other questions, Ms. Klein."

"Amy," she corrected. "I make my living asking questions."

"If you help me out, I share it with the Queenstown cops, and the killer gets nailed. That'll help you, too."

Eager, she leaned forward. "Are you promising an exclusive?"

"If they arrest the murderer on Monday and your paper isn't published until Friday, that won't be much of an exclusive."

"Then why should I help you?"

"To stop the killings in your own backyard."

"I'm just a reporter."

"You're also a human being," I said, "as far as I can tell."

She chewed on that for a time. "Was I just insulted?"

"I wasn't sure you noticed."

She bestowed on me a reluctant nod. "You got me with that one. All right, Mr. Jacovich . . ."

"Milan. Tit for tat."

"Milan, then. Well, here's a thought to ponder. When Fontaine's body was found in his car—his barn door was open."

Puzzled, I said, "At his ranch?"

"You city guys!" Klein scoffed. "Never heard that expression? 'His barn door was open' means his zipper was down." Her scoff became a snicker. "Maybe he was jerking off when he got killed."

"Everyone masturbates," I mused.

Klein's snicker then turned into hearty laughter. "Maybe he *was* whacking off—unless someone stabbed Fontaine in the heart just because he had to pee."

The Ashtabula County assistant coroner looked weary. If I'd spent my life slicing open dead people and poking around inside them all day long, I'd be tired, too. Dr. Clarence York, who'd autopsied Cordis Poole and Paul Fontaine, seemed barely able to rise from his desk for a dead-fish handshake, and then melted back into his chair, his body clinging to every part of it like a cotton throw.

"We have occasional shootings up here," he said, pushing two skinny folders around on his desk as if trying to solve a jigsaw puzzle, "mostly in the city. But there's never been anything like this—not in Queenstown. A serial killer!"

"Why are you sure it's one killer, Dr. York?"

That jostled him. "Well, *because* . . ."

Brilliant answer. "What kind of knife was used?"

"A sharp one," he said.

"Thanks. And here I was thinking it was a butter knife. What about the weapon that killed Cordis Poole?"

"It must've been some kind of hammer," York said, "the kind you get in a hardware store."

"You didn't test the wounds to see what kind of hammer? What kind of knife?"

"I'm not a homicide cop like you are," he protested.

I didn't have the heart to tell him I'm not a cop. "The killer must've been strong to do that much damage to Poole."

"Here's the other thing, though, about Fontaine. You know that when the body was found, his fly was open."

"How do you know I know that?"

"Amy Klein called to say she told you. His zipper was down— but his junk wasn't hanging out or anything."

He was the first doctor I ever heard refer to a penis as "junk." I wondered, though, about that zipper. Two people meeting at a pickup beach—or Paul Fontaine having his own private moment?

Not that shocking; as I had said to Amy, *everyone* masturbates sometimes, although the only one mentioned in the Bible who actually played with himself was a guy named Onan. Hard to believe, but perhaps he takes the sole rap because no one wants to consider Moses or Jesus or Abraham sneaking into the bathroom with *Playboy*.

"Did he have sexual intercourse shortly before his death?" I asked the coroner.

"I'd say no."

"You'd *say* no?"

"I didn't test for that."

I never scream with frustration—but York was getting me close. "A man, sitting in his truck, stabbed through the heart and his fly open, and you didn't test for sexual intercourse? Doesn't a forensic pathologist work with you on autopsies?"

"Why would I ask one?" York said "Waste of good money. It's obvious in both cases what the cause of death was." He pointed a finger at me. "I did test for alcoholic consumption. Negative—they were both teetotalers."

"Both?"

"There's plenty of boozers in Ashtabula and Geneva—but not in Queenstown."

"Were either of them recreational drug users?"

"Not as far as I know," York said.

I was beginning to think Clarence York didn't know much of anything. "You didn't test for drugs?"

He was looking more exhausted by the minute. "One man's heart was stabbed; the other man's skull was caved in. Now why would I test for drugs? I don't solve murders—that's way above my pay grade. I do postmortems to report the cause of death—and after twenty-nine years with no promotion, I don't care if Fontaine was overdosed on illegal drugs or had his horn tooted by some bimbo." He rubbed the back of his neck. "I can't wait for retirement."

"When will that be?"

He swiveled around in his chair and looked at a wall calendar, gifted to his office by a hardware company in Ashtabula whose name was highly visible on the page. "Ten months and twenty-one days—and I'm counting every minute.'"

"Let's go back to Fontaine. He's found dead in a beachside park known for its pickups. True?"

York cleared the frog from his throat, suddenly uncomfortable. "I've never been to Sunset Park, but that's what I hear."

"Is it possible," I said, "that some man might cruise Sunset Park looking for another man?"

"You mean fag sex?" I never heard a doctor say "fag" before, either. His negative headshake was outraged. "That stuff never happens in Queenstown."

"No gays in Queenstown?"

"It's a religious community, sir. They frown on that."

"People who go to church don't like homosexuals?"

"You know what they say—hate the sin but not the sinner."

"Is that what 'they' say?"

"I'd venture a guess," York said, "that they've never even met one personally."

I put my notebook back into my pocket. "I appreciate your taking the time to speak with me."

He frowned with just one eyebrow—a difficult trick at best. "Well, it's always nice to chat with visitors from out of town."

I stood. "Call me if you have any more murders to chat about."

I drove back to Conneaut via a rural road along the lakeshore, tacky with cottages thrown up rapidly, followed by properties with very elegant homes.

When I approached Sunset Park, I pulled off the road and drove up to the parking lot where Fontaine had breathed his last. I strolled around, studying the ground, the lake view, the trees.

Most of the parking lot was invisible from the road—and vice versa.

Had Fontaine come to this make-out spot with a woman? Another man? There were no buses or shuttles in Queenstown; did they come in separate cars? Did they meet by appointment or by accident?

Had someone interrupted what might have been going on in Fontaine's car—a jealous husband or Fontaine's wife, or maybe even a gay lover—and stab him in a fit of rage? There'd been just one stab wound; a furious lover would have struck many times rather than just once. There might have been other marks on Fontaine's body. A struggle—flesh under the fingernails, strands of someone else's hair in the car.

Other than his open fly, he might have gone there for a number of reasons. Business after the sun goes down? Maybe he sold horses to farmers. A drug buy gone wrong? I found myself irritated with the local coroner and cops. Their "investigation" was useless, like a TV meteorologist checking the weather by looking out the window.

When I returned to the motel, keenly aware of Philo Ackerman's stare eviscerating me through the glass door to the lobby, I went to our room and made more notes to share with Tobe later. Then I Googled Conneaut and Queenstown, and learned all sorts of things I hadn't known before.

Conneaut had been settled early in the nineteenth century by immigrants from, of all places, Finland. The community center was once called the Finnish Community Hall, and third- and fourth-generation Finns still live in Conneaut, many of them with saunas and hot tubs they built in their backyard sheds or in their cellars. In the winter, Finland is even colder than Northeast Ohio. It's in their DNA.

This explained Chief Eino Koskinen's name, which had to be Finnish as well. I wondered if he flogged himself in the sauna with birch branches on a frosty Christmas day.

I was stretched out on the bed watching a Showtime movie when Tobe arrived, kicked off her shoes, and flopped into the only comfortable chair in the room. "Long day," she said. "I earned every penny of my salary—and you aren't even getting paid."

I clicked off the TV set. "I'm taking it out in trade, then."

She put a forbidding hand up like a traffic cop. "Not yet, pal. Tired and hungry."

"Which is more important?"

"Not sex. Busy day, huh? What have we learned?"

"Eino Koskinen is part of a large Finnish community here."

"Sorry, I don't know a damn thing about Finland, so I can't make a sarcastic comment. Tell me something else."

"Not much from Amy Comunale Klein at the *Messenger*, other than background I could look up on the Internet—and even less than that from the assistant county coroner."

"Assistant? Why didn't you talk to the boss himself?"

"The assistant, Dr. York, performed both PMs. He's bummed that he's still the number two guy after all these years—so he didn't give the autopsies more than a lick and a promise."

"*Lick* and *autopsy* in the same sentence? Nice, Milan."

"There hasn't even been a halfway . . . investigation. Koskinen is floundering, which is why we're here in the first place. As far as the PM goes, Clarence York is marking time for a year until he retires—and he said bringing in a forensic pathologist cost too much."

"Bargain basement coroner—a prize in every package. What else?" Tobe said.

I told her Dr. York's story—Tinker's Hollow is a spooky place to have found Cordis Poole in the middle of the night, and despite Paul Fontaine's half-staff zipper, he probably hadn't enjoyed recent sexual activity before someone tried to cut his heart out.

"What kind of knife?"

"A sharp one," I said. "Dr. York's direct quote. He also thinks an ordinary household hammer killed Poole, but he can't be sure."

"Because . . . ?"

"Because he just checks for cause of death and signs his name on the autopsy report." I sat up and swung my legs over the bed. "Well, if we're not going to tear up this whole room having wild sex right now, tell me about your day."

"I'll tell you while we're driving."

"Where are we going?"

"To dinner, silly. Where else?"

"I haven't seen anyplace to eat all day," I said. "Oh, well—we can always pick up a bag of potato chips and a Slurpee at the nearest Stop-and-Rob."

"Milan—there are other restaurants in the neighborhood besides McDonald's and the Covered Bridge." She jerked her thumb at her own chest. "And I found out where they are."

CHAPTER THREE

MILAN

We headed back to Ashtabula. Tobe had discovered the Bascule Bridge Grille on the Internet, very close to the bridge for which it is named that crosses the Ashtabula River. I pondered why restaurants in this county bear the same names as bridges.

We also passed a smaller park with an elaborate fountain, complete with carvings and monuments sculpted in very unusual-looking stone and overpowered by a large statue of Jesus. I'd later learn the entire structure had been commissioned by a local family in memory of other family members and was officially called the "Three Cousins Fountain." "Who makes statues in dark brown stone," Tobe wondered, "that looks like a Mounds candy bar?" She practically giggled. "I think we ought to call that statue 'Chocolate Jesus.'"

"That'll look great in your report," I said.

That sobered her. "Speaking of my report . . ." She fished her iPhone out of her jacket. "I spoke to Maude Fontaine. Whatever perfume she wears smells like the hand soap they put in public restrooms."

I shook my head, as I often do when Tobe catches a whiff of something. Her unusual condition is called hyperosmia, an acute sense of smell that often gives her a blinding headache, especially when there's some sort of strong-smelling perfume in the air.

"Maude Fontaine is quiet. Learning anything from her was like getting blood out of a turnip. She's bitter—but what brand-new widow wouldn't be? She didn't want to discuss her husband being in that pickup park with his fly open. I tried asking discreetly whether he was a womanizer, but it was awkward; Fontaine was supposed to have been at church that evening. Some sort of meeting. Apparently, Fontaine was very religious. He was a deacon in the Baptist church."

"Right," I said sarcastically, "and no churchgoer ever cheats. Any other fairy tales?"

"I didn't think women today still smiled bravely at hubby's adultery and never talked about it, because it's just not proper. I guess Maude Fontaine is still living in the 1930s." She snapped her fingers. "Wait—she wasn't even born in the 1930s."

"What about the kids? It's okay to talk about your own children, isn't it?"

She did something to the screen of the iPhone with her fingers. "Okay, here we are," she said. "Jennifer Fontaine is nineteen, in her second year at Michigan State. She came for the funeral and went back to school a few days after that. Koskinen told me that the son, Jason, is a problem high school senior who runs with a rough crowd."

"Queenstown *has* a rough crowd?"

"A teen gang in Cleveland or Detroit would make these kidlets look like Sugar Plum Fairies," Tobe said. "They're just full of piss and vinegar—but here they have nowhere to burn it off. So they stalk around talking tough—smoke weed, drink when they can, fight, drive too fast, wear their pants so low that most of their underwear hangs out. They don't get into anything serious, or Koskinen would hear of it. Jason Fontaine was in school today, so I didn't talk with him."

I nodded. "How about the Poole family?"

"Different angle. Cordis Poole, who'd never been in the military, was one of those super-strict, humorless daddies, demanding his son call him 'sir.' His wife, Gwen, was a little afraid of him."

Recalling the photo of Cordis in a football jersey—a husky, lantern-jawed, ex–high school athlete—made me uncomfortable. Bullying his own wife? Not a pleasant thought. "He was abusive?"

"Gwen didn't say so; neither she nor Maude Fontaine said much of anything between sobs. But Cordis was clearly a religious fanatic. Gwen is broken, and she'd die before admitting it, but I think she's secretly relieved he can't bully her anymore."

"Did he bully his son, too?"

"What I got from Junior is that he rebelled as soon as he reached puberty. He's pissed off at his father, pissed off at the world. He smokes, drinks, does weed, and apparently isn't upset that he's now a half orphan—except there won't be any more income after the insurance, and he'll have to figure out a way to get out of Queenstown and into the real world." Her next sentence was preceded by a sigh. "He asked me if it's tough training to be a cop. If there really is a tough crowd, my guess is he's the alpha male."

I cranked down my window halfway and let the breeze blow what's left of my hair above my rising hairline. "You think he might've killed his own father? That's a pretty chilling thought!"

"For me, fifteen chilling thoughts per day is par for the course. What do you think?"

"I think we ought to start talking to all these kids."

Tobe cleared her throat. "That's a problem. I've only met Cordis Junior, but I don't think he wants much to do with me. I got the feeling—nothing definite, just a gut rumble—that he's not too crazy about my race, either."

"Don't let it bother you."

"You mean racism? If it's subtle, I ignore it because—well, what can you do when someone doesn't really say anything directly offensive to you? But it's there and I live with it. City people are used to different races and different cultures—and if someone calls me the *n* word when I arrest them in Cleveland, I just laugh. Handcuffed criminals have called me worse than that. If people turn snooty and look down their nose at me, so what? I could beat the crap out of them with my bare hands. I just choose not to." Tobe waved absently at the passing scenery. "Up here, though, where the nearest WalMart is twenty miles away, it's a different ballgame. In the past eight hours I've gotten bad racial vibes from just about everyone, including the widow of a brand new murder victim." There was no mirth in her chuckle. "Damn Flo McHargue anyway; she did this on purpose!" She lightly punched the steering wheel with the side of her fist. "She's probably laughing her ass off. She doesn't exactly approve of our relationship, Milan."

"She's never approved of me—race had nothing to do with it."

"Ask me if I care." Tobe beat out a tattoo with her fingers on the wheel. "Talking to these teens will be difficult—by definition."

"Let Chief Koskinen do the honors."

"Chief Koskinen," Tobe said, "couldn't hit water if he fell out of a boat. He's friends with everyone in town—all the parents of these teens. You think he'll get anywhere with his questions—or *wants* to?"

"No." I closed my window and tried to smooth down my runaway hair. "But I know somebody who can talk to teens."

Her eyebrows lifted, and she cocked her head to one side, thinking about it. Finally she grinned and said, "Me, too."

CHAPTER FOUR

K.O.

Like when a kindergartner is working on a coloring book with crayons, sometimes life jumps out from between the lines and goes out of control.

Instead of being in the shower with Carli Wysocki—a morning ritual that often morphed into more than just getting clean—Kevin O'Bannion was packing a small suitcase with three days' worth of clothing, so he could investigate two murders. That he didn't own a suitcase and was borrowing one of Carli's that was a distressing shade of lavender wasn't helping his mood one bit.

When he'd moved into her apartment shortly before Christmas, he'd brought his cat and best friend, Rodney, to share their lives. Fine and good—Carli was an animal lover, too, although she'd never really lived with a pet before. And when Milan left for Ashtabula County, K.O. had taken on Milan's recently acquired dog, Herbie, to stay for a few days. Now that he was leaving to join his employer, the care of both animals had descended upon Carli alone. She wasn't thrilled with the idea of having to walk Herbie three times a day, rain or shine. The tension, while unspoken, had definitely thrown their sex life into a cocked hat the evening before.

So K.O. slammed his shirts and underwear into the case as Rodney perched on the bed's headboard, fascinated with the whole idea of packing. K.O. was convinced Rodney's look was saying, "Where the hell are you running off to *now?*"

Herbie wandered around his feet, too, and while K.O. had not yet learned to love the dog, he was grateful Milan had managed to cut down on, but not completely eliminate, his frequent farting.

Carli came into their bedroom, wearing her white terrycloth bathrobe and toweling her hair dry. When their eyes met she smiled at him, but he could tell even from across the room it wasn't the most sincere smile he'd ever seen.

"In case you haven't figured this out yet," K.O. said, "I don't want to go. But when my boss says jump . . ."

"I know," Carli said.

"Now you'll have to walk Herbie."

"He was staying with us anyway while Milan's gone. It's okay; don't worry about it."

He stopped packing and moved close to her. "I worry about us being apart for a few days."

"That I'll meet some hot-looking guy while I'm picking up dog poop in a plastic bag and he'll go crazy about me?" She flicked the damp towel at him and walked into the living room.

He had to laugh. Cleaning up after a dog would never be romantic, even with Carli. He took two Dockers pants from the closet, one khaki and one black, and packed them. He didn't know if he'd be anywhere too fancy to wear his jeans, but he'd learned from Milan to be prepared for almost anything.

She came back in with four CDs and handed them to him. "You might enjoy these in the car."

He took them from her—Foster The People, Bruno Mars, Alabama Shakes, and Justin Timberlake. He'd heard of none of them except Timberlake—and that was only after seeing him in a sexy movie costarring Mila Kunis, who'd been the star in one of his most powerful erotic fantasies before he had ever met Carli. He'd never bothered developing a taste for music, and Carli didn't listen at home either, but he knew she always played music in her car. "Thanks," he said, "I'll get to these when I can."

She touched his cheek. "When you do, think of me. Okay?"

"Okay," he managed to say—as though thinking of her didn't happen every minute of the day! He'd assumed his obsession with Carli would dissipate after they had begun cohabiting; it hadn't.

By the time he had finished packing, Carli was dressed too, in tight designer jeans and a black jersey. K.O. picked Rodney up and nuzzled him, enjoying the purr right next to his face. He leaned down and scratched Herbie behind the ears, admonishing him to be a good boy. Then he kissed Carli good-bye, a sensuous kiss that left the taste of her Colgate in his mouth.

Listening to Alabama Shakes's "Hold On" as he drove I-90 toward the furthest corner of Northeast Ohio, he ran over in his mind what Milan had e-mailed him and restated on the phone about the Queenstown murders. K.O. was supposed to hang out with these rustic teenyboppers and find out whatever he could about the killings from a more personal point of view.

He registered at the same motel as Tobe and Milan. The clerk, a distant Philo Ackerman, handed K.O. a message along with his room key card. It was unmistakably in his employer's familiar and almost unreadable handwriting: "Meet us here for lunch at 12:30 p.m."

After he had hung up his travel clothes in his room and glanced out the window at the traffic on I-90, he strolled out to the office.

"What's the best way to get to Tinker's Hollow?" he asked.

Philo Ackerman looked shocked, as if he'd never been asked for directions to anywhere before. "Why would you go to Tinker's Hollow?" he sputtered. "You can't go there. It's—private property."

"Oh? Who owns this private property? You? Then you must be Mr. Tinker. I thought from the plaque here on the counter that your name was Feelo Ackerman."

Ackerman's lips almost completely disappeared. He crossed his arms defensively across his chest and said, "My name is Mr. *Philo* Ackerman." His eyes narrowed. "Are you connected with that colored woman from Cleveland, too?"

"A colored woman? What color *is* she, anyway?"

Ackerman backed away from the counter as far as he could, perhaps expecting a slap across the mouth. He might have been correct. "I'm sorry—I'm not the Chamber of Commerce, you know. Tinker's Hollow is very hard to find. It's not even marked with a sign or anything."

"Fine," K.O. said. "And just so you know, I *am* connected with 'that colored woman.'" He left the office, not turning around to see Ackerman's face; that would have ruined the dramatic moment.

A filling station across the highway from the motel was attached to a McDonald's and to a Love's travel store catering to drivers who spent much of their life on the road. He ordered a McDonald's coffee from a tall, off-beat attractive young woman behind the counter who didn't smile and would barely meet his eyes, and carried it into the Love's store to look around. Almost all the T-shirts, jackets, and hoodies on sale bore sayings or commercial plugs.

Sipping coffee, he selected a bag of pretzel sticks, and approached the cashier. She was pretty, younger than him, long blond hair in a ponytail, wearing a Love's smock over her white blouse and black slacks. Her smile was bigger and warmer than necessary. "Hi," she said, and told him he owed her a dollar ninety-nine.

"I'm looking for more than coffee," K.O. said, putting two bills on the counter.

"Ooh," the cashier giggled.

"Can you tell me how to find Tinker's Hollow?"

Her blue eyes became large and wide, and she giggled some more. "Tinker's Hollow? You don't want to go there—it's scary."

"At eleven o'clock in the morning?"

"It's creepy all the time—but much worse at night." She lowered her voice to a near whisper. "It's haunted."

"Ever seen those ghosts?"

She shook her head. "Nobody sees ghosts—but they cause all sorts of trouble for you. Just being around there in the dark makes your skin crawl, and you don't even know why."

"Have you been there at night?"

"Every kid around here has been there at night."

"A make-out place?"

"Sometimes," she said, blushing prettily, "but mostly a thrill. And some people go looking for gold."

"Gold?" K.O. ripped open the bag of pretzels and offered her some. She shook her head. "Now I really want to go there."

"The legend says that more than a hundred years ago, one of the Tinker brothers buried a chest of gold and treasure out there somewhere—but no one's ever found it."

"I guess I'll have to look doubly hard, then. If you give me a general idea where it is, I'll find it."

Her face and eyes grew even more perky. "Too much trouble,"

she said. "My lunch hour starts about twenty minutes from now. If you hang around, I can take you there. I'm Kathy, by the way."

He shook her outstretched hand. "Hi. I'm K.O."

"K.O.? What kind of name is that?"

"One that I like," he said. "See you in twenty minutes."

He drove across the highway to the motel office. Philo Ackerman looked nervous when he saw him—but then, Philo Ackerman was always wound too tight, blinked too often. He apparently dealt with his nerves the way most people handle their excessive sweating—he made no effort to hide it.

"Have a piece of paper?" K.O. said. "I need to leave a note."

Ackerman waited a beat too long. Finally he found one and watched as K.O. penned: "Forget lunch. Already investigating. C U later." Then he folded the note in two, scrawled Tobe's name on the reverse side, and returned it to Ackerman. "Make sure the *colored woman* gets this, will you?"

He went outside and sat in his car for a while, eating what was left of his pretzel sticks, which would suffice as his lunch, wondering why Kathy, who'd known him less than three minutes, had volunteered to spend her lunch hour with him—and at a crime scene, too. He adjusted his rearview mirror so he could look at himself, and ran his fingers through his hair. No movie star looks, he admitted, but he wasn't all that bad—for an Irishman.

It didn't matter; he was totally smitten with Carli Wysocki—completely new for him, as he'd never been in a committed relationship before.

When enough time had passed, he drove back to the Love's store. Within minutes Kathy came out, sans apron, and jumped into the car.

"I wondered if you'd really come back," she said.

"I always keep my promises."

She laughed. "I've heard *that* before. Why Tinker's Hollow?"

He dug one of his business cards from his pocket. She read it and her eyes opened wide. "Wow, a private investigator—like in some of those old movies!"

"It pays the rent," he said.

"Kevin O'Bannion—oh, now I get the K.O. part. They're your initials."

"Right."

"Well, I'm Kathy Pape," she said. "Pape, not Pope—I'm not even Catholic. Are you going to Tinker's Hollow because Mr. Poole got killed there?"

"Something like that."

"Eeeww, now it's really creepy. Y'know, they say one of the Tinker brothers who owned all that land fell out of his carriage on the bridge and broke his neck. Now his ghost just hates strangers hanging out there, so he tries to scare them away."

"Clanking his chains?"

"I don't think ghosts have chains," she said seriously. "Only that guy in the Scrooge movies."

"Would you go into a haunted house, Kathy?"

"No way."

"So why Tinker's Hollow?"

"Why not? Mostly it's high school kids, hoping like crazy we'll see old Silas Tinker floating around with his bright green eyes."

"Are you a high school kid?"

She shook her head. "Graduated last spring. I want to go to Ohio State so I can teach—got a part-scholarship waiting for me—but I have to earn money for a place to live, and for a meal every so often. So here I am at Love's, selling pretzels to cute guys like you who happen to drive by."

"Thanks for the compliment," K.O. said, "but I'm in a very committed relationship with someone."

Kathy sighed. "My luck, as usual."

"You're pretty hot yourself. Do all the guys fight over you?"

She waggled her head as if to bounce her bangs out of her eyes—except she wasn't wearing bangs. "Yeah, when I was in school. But they're all boring jerks. They don't interest me anymore."

K.O. nodded, paused. Then: "Did you know Mr. Poole well?"

"Sure. I even went out with Junior a few times—his son." Kathy Pape shook her head and held up her fist, closed tight. "This was him—the old man. Stuffiest tight-ass I ever saw."

"Was there anyone in town who didn't like him?"

"Just about everybody—except the people at his church, who are just as tight-assed as him."

"What are they uptight about, Kathy?"

"You name it," Kathy said, "and it just cheeses them off. Religion, jobs, the Bible, politics, sex, black people, gays—if they wake up and it's cloudy outside, they're bent out of shape because the sun isn't shining on them. Kids here get squished down by parents with no sense of humor who won't give anybody an inch, so when they get to be sixteen or so, they get rebellious and do stuff most people have the smarts not to do."

"Like?"

"Drinking," Kathy said, "mostly beer, but they drink anything. Drugs, too—weed, mostly—and fighting and cussing and stealing."

K.O. had learned early about rebellion. It was hard rebelling against guards and teachers in juvenile detention. But the bullies who were locked up with him and tried to intimidate him had keened K.O.'s quiet defiance to the sharpest of blades.

After a time Kathy Pape poked him in the arm. "Slow down— turn in here."

"That's not even a road!" K.O. said, looking at a clear, wide gravel path heading down a relatively steep hill. "Loose gravel will knock hell out of anybody's car."

"That's why no one ever goes down here," Kathy laughed, "unless they have an old, crappy car like yours. So—drive on!"

CHAPTER FIVE

MILAN

It's difficult for strangers in Ashtabula County to find a place like Starbucks, which are all over Greater Cleveland. Where else *would* one sit at four in the afternoon—too late for lunch, too early for dinner, and hardly the setting for British high tea—and discuss the events of the day? That's why Tobe, K.O., and I wound up in the Mickey D's just across the road from our motel. No matter what one might think about McDonald's food—and I try not to think about it at all—their coffee is always good. Hot, too.

"Is this really the big deal restaurant around here?" K.O. wondered sadly. "Chicken McNuggets? Yummy! I should've packed a lunch. Okay—fill me in. What've we got?"

"Tobe, you start first."

"I talked with Joe Platko," Tobe said, explaining to K.O. who he was—the police officer who had found both victims. "He didn't admit it, but his 'investigation' was practically nil. He'd never seen a dead body before, and had no idea what to do about it. And the second corpse really freaked him out."

"I thought the Highway Patrol came in on it," K.O. said.

"By the time they got to Tinker's Hollow, it was the next morning after a heavy rain that washed away any evidence." Tobe rolled her eyes. "Remind me not to order steelhead trout from that particular creek."

"Steelhead trout is an Ashtabula County legend," I said, "but how would I know? I hate fish. Tobe, what else about Platko?"

"I met with him first thing this morning. Youngish guy, not

quite thirty, and I think I scared the crap out of him. He and his boss can't suggest any suspects. He thinks maybe it's different killers but can't imagine why two people from Queenstown got killed two weeks apart. Different M.O. for each."

K.O. had ordered a cappuccino—unusual for him, I thought— and he delicately sipped at it, licking the foam off his upper lip. "M.O.'s were both violent."

She nodded. "True—but someone in a rage would've slashed Fontaine to pieces, yet he took just one to the heart. As for Cordis Poole—a maniac would've mashed his head flat; but just one hit at the back of the skull, behind the ear, was all it took. So I'm thinking, Milan, these murders were carefully planned and expertly carried out."

"By who?" K.O. said.

"Whom," Tobe corrected him. "If I knew by whom, we'd all be heading back to Cleveland right now, and Police Chief Koskinen would have a crowded little jail—if he even *has* a little jail."

"Hook up with some of those teenage guys, K.O.," I suggested. "Get a feeling about them, find out their likes and dislikes. They're a truculent group."

"Truculent? Define, please."

"The dictionary," Tobe said, "calls it a shitty attitude—or maybe it's just in Ashta-BOO-la. Any of those kids had a hard-on for Fontaine or Poole they might actually admit to, Milan?"

"Kids won't admit that the sun is shining, especially not to anyone older than them."

"I'm shaking in my boots," K.O. said, his tone as dry as an artfully constructed martini.

Tobe wondered, "And if one decides to get tough with you?"

K.O. popped his knuckles loud enough to make two truck drivers eating dinner at the next table look up from their Big Macs and supersized fries. "I wouldn't worry about it."

"K.O.," I said, "this Kathy took you to Tinker's Hollow today, right? You didn't have a fishing pole, so you didn't fish—and I assume you didn't go there to neck."

Tobe laughed out loud and smacked the tabletop with the palm of her hand. "Neck? Where've you been for the last fifty years, Milan? *Neck?* Seriously?"

K.O. saved me from making a further fool of myself. "It rained the night of the murder, before anyone found Cordis—no blood, no footprints, nothing. But there's scrub brush and weeds on the bank of Conneaut Creek, right near the condemned bridge. They were broken and bent all the way down to the water—about as wide a path as if someone had been rolled down the hill."

Tobe almost beamed. "Nice, K.O. So Poole was killed somewhere else and then driven there and dumped."

"How I figured, too. Thanks." K.O. turned to me. "Do I get a bonus for that, boss?"

"We're not getting paid."

"*You're* not getting paid. I'm on salary, remember?"

"How could I forget?" I said. "Why not get your—little friend to introduce you to some of those teens she knows personally?"

"Kathy Pape." He looked at his watch. "Her shift was over and she went home an hour ago."

Tobe said, "Is she in the phone book? Call her, tell her you want to hang out with her and meet her buddies . . ."

"I'll give it my best shot," K.O. said, taking another sip of cappuccino. "Milan, what have *you* been doing all day?"

"I've been on my smartphone," I said, taking out my notebook and squinting at my lousy handwriting. "Paul J. Fontaine; everyone in Queenstown knows him, but no one's exactly in love with him. He's been in court, fighting three different lawsuits—two Amish families in Conneaut and another farmer down around Geneva were out for his hide. Fontaine sold each of them horses, all with major health problems. One horse started vomiting massive amounts of blood and died of a stomach disease. Another one was so sick, he got sent to the slaughterhouse for about one-tenth of what the Amish man paid. The one in Geneva has major difficulty breathing. These problems emerged within a week of Fontaine selling them, even though he swore they were perfectly healthy."

"Damn his soul to hell!" K.O. muttered. "Let me talk to these guys Fontaine cheated. Maybe one of them gets as pissed off as I do when animals get mistreated."

"Suppose," Tobe said, "some guy owes you three grand—and you need the money he won't repay you. The last thing you'd do is kill him—because then you'd never get your money back."

K.O. slumped back, irritated.

"You'll be better off getting closer to these kids," I said.

"K.O." Tobe sounded stern. "No 'maiming.' If you rip off some-one's nose, or make him limp for the rest of his life, it's my ass, not yours."

"Stay cool," I added.

"I'm always cool," K.O. said. "So, are we going out for dinner, or are we ordering Big Macs?"

After some discussion, we sent K.O. off to make a date with Kathy Pape. Tobe and I decided it would be helpful to touch base with the buyers of Fontaine's unhealthy horses.

We met with the farmer in Geneva first, calling ahead to make an appointment. Driving to Geneva, we had our own dinner in a little restaurant in the so-called business district. The waitress told us it was a historic place everybody goes to. But that night, apparently everybody stayed home.

About halfway through our meal, another middle-aged man and woman entered with a preteen daughter in tow and took a table on the far side of the room. Naturally all three did a double take when they saw us, and the woman leaned forward and covered her mouth with her hand as she whispered something to her family while she looked at us with great disapproval.

Tobe smiled. "I guess they left their white sheets and hoods at home." It was loud enough that the family might have heard it, but they didn't react—or chose not to.

We stopped paying attention to them until the waitress arrived with their dinner. Then, they all held hands while Daddy said grace, including his thanking the Lord for protecting them from "those people who might be dangerous and wish to do us harm."

"Those people?" I said.

Tobe shook her head in amused disgust. "Is that what he calls 'saying grace'? I wonder if the Lord will protect him if I march over there and shoot him in the kneecap."

"No, the Lord would be pissed. If you shot off that kneecap, Daddy wouldn't be able to kneel down and pray before bedtime."

Tobe shook her head in frustration. "It was Florence McHargue's idea coming here—and her fault."

I realized I hadn't given Lieutenant McHargue much thought

at all recently. That was a good thing. Sometimes when I think about our ten-year discomfort with each other, it brings on a severe headache and a few beers too many.

After finishing dinner and leaving the restaurant without a single glance from our grace-saying buddies, who pretended we didn't exist, we had some time to kill. We decided to check out nearby Geneva-on-the-Lake.

It's a little town, geared for lower-middle-class tourists, but much of it appeared startling to the eye, even in the glow of the setting sun. Perched on the edge of Lake Erie, the entire main street looked as if someone had handed a set of tempera paints to eight-year-olds and told them to paint the city whatever color they chose; neon red and blue and yellow pastels were all over the place like a Hollywood wet dream of Alice's Wonderland. There were several bed-and-breakfasts in houses smaller than my apartment, restaurants that fried or barbecued everything, a good number of pizza stands and burger joints, and even more saloons. There was no dearth of motorcycles in the lots of most establishments, either, as leather-clad bikers make Geneva-on-the-Lake their unofficial home away from home.

"Fifty years ago," I told Tobe, "there was a stabbing here one night that turned into the Riot of 1965. It made the national news."

"Why?"

"Nobody was able to figure that out," I said. "A bunch of young guys got liquored up one weekend night, got hold of a bunch of Confederate flags, and waved them in the faces of people who don't like Confederate flags."

"Shit! I didn't move north to have to see one of those obscene flags again. And this ghastly paint gives me the creeps."

"Do you suppose our killer's hiding out in this town?"

"Could be—although my guess is the town is too small, too compact to hide here for long." Tobe rolled up her car window and rubbed her nose. "Sorry—my hyperosmia again. The odor of fried foods bothers me. So does the smell of beer. But I dig the lake breeze, don't you?"

"There's no lake breeze in Cleveland Heights," I said.

"I haven't hunted a killer in Cleveland Heights yet, but there's a first time for everything." Tobe tapped the dashboard clock. "Let's get hustling, Milan."

Richard Nowicki's farm seemed to be deep in rural America but was only a two-minute drive from Geneva-on-the-Lake's main drag, on a road also boasting four different vineyards; other than the lake itself, local wine was the county's main attraction.

Starting from his ancient barn, Nowicki's vegetables were planted nearly as far as the eye could see. I'd learned that he didn't work for any of the giant farming corporations that control an alarming amount of how much we Americans eat and what's *in* it. In fact, he was an independent farmer—one of the last of a dying breed.

Richard Nowicki was a tall, white-haired man with a flowing white beard, too big and macho for anyone to mistake him for an out-of-work Santa Claus. The crow's-feet about his eyes and the year-round sunburn that stopped about an inch below his hairline marked him as a farmer who spent most of his time outdoors. He welcomed us and led us into the barn.

Despite the warm evening, Chocklit, the dark brown horse with his name scrawled on the wall beside his stall, was draped with a blanket, and although neither Tobe nor I knew anything about horses, his difficulty breathing was evident.

"This is the horse I bought from Fontaine," Nowicki said, lovingly stroking the horse's neck. Chocklit wasn't too ill to come to the gate of his stall for a carrot and a hug. "Twenty-five hundred bucks—and he got sick like this about three days after I brought him back with me."

"Did you have a vet check him out?" I asked.

Nowicki shook his head. "Not until he got sick. The vet said it's an asthmatic condition. I should've noticed it before I bought him." He hit his forehead with the heel of his hand. "Dumb ass."

Tobe said, "Did you try canceling the sale?"

"Sure I tried! Fontaine wouldn't budge, so I was going to take him to court. The hearing would've been next month." He shrugged. "My fault—I shoulda known better. Fontaine had a lousy reputation."

"Why buy from him in the first place?"

"I wasn't looking for a workhorse," he said. "I have all the modern farm equipment I need, and I hire people to do the picking. I bought him for my kid to ride—she's fourteen." He stroked Chocklit's neck gently again, and the horse leaned into his hand. "Damn, she loves Chocklit, she thinks he's so beautiful." He scuffed his boot at some hay on the floor of the barn. "I don't know if we can save him. If we do, it'll cost me a fortune. But Fontaine? Look, I know what you're here for. I hated Fontaine's guts—so does my daughter—but not enough to kill him." He tried not to grin. "Not for twenty-five hundred bucks, anyway."

"Somebody did," Tobe said. "He cheated two Amish families with sick horses as well."

Nowicki nodded. "The Amish don't kill people; they don't fight. It's against their religion."

"What about your religion?"

He frowned. "I'm not sure what you mean."

"I mean does your religion say it's all right to murder people if they happen to deserve it?"

Puzzled, Nowicki said, "What's religion got to do with it?"

"You tell me," she said. "Fontaine went to church regularly. So did Poole. Maybe somebody at church was mad at both of them."

"I wouldn't know that. I don't go to church." He looked from Tobe to me and back again. "Which one of you is the lead cop here anyway?"

"That'd be me," Tobe said. "Detective Sergeant, Cleveland Homicide. Mr. Jacovich here is my—assistant. He asks questions, too—but he's not a police officer." She took a deep breath. "There seems to be a bit of a race problem around here."

"It might seem that way, from your perspective. No harm meant," Richard Nowicki said. "Most people who work my farm are African American. I work right beside them in the field, joke with them, eat lunch with them, listen if they need to talk. And when I throw parties around here on the Fourth of July and at Christmastime, they're all invited with their families, as my guests. I got no problems with them, or anyone else."

"I didn't know about a black community up here," I said.

"Didn't used to be, really." Nowicki glanced at Tobe. "Some

moved here to be close to family members who're in the prison—
in Conneaut—that opened about thirteen years ago. It was a state
prison then, brand new and clean, and they had some good programs, educational programs. Some of the cons were training dogs
to be companions for disabled people who need them. They had it
pretty good, as prisons go. But about three years ago, Ohio sold it
to a private company—the first prison in America to go 'private.'
Since then, even though there are regular inspections, there's
inmate abuse, horrible conditions, lousy sanitation, really awful
food, as I understand—and no more dog training. Now they put
three cons in a cell built for one—just terrible stuff. It's turned into
a damn chain-gang prison like in Louisiana sixty years ago." He
took off his straw hat and ran a hand through his white hair. "So
I hire relatives who moved up here to bring those poor bastards
a shred of hope or pleasure on visiting days." His hands turned
palms upward. "Least I can do."

I looked at Tobe, who shook her head and said, "I won't open
that can of whoop-ass unless I have to." She turned back to Richard
Nowicki. "You seem open-minded about race. Is that true in Fontaine's church?"

"Far as I know, those church folk are all white." He shrugged.
"But there's a big drug problem here—and the junkies are mostly
white, too."

Junkies, I thought; that expression disappeared sometime in
the 1970s. "Did Fontaine do drugs?"

"I wouldn't know about that. We weren't friends or anything—I
just bought his horse." He rubbed his hand up and down against
Chocklit's nose, and the horse tossed his head, his breathing
growing more laborious. "The vet's coming by tomorrow for
another look at him, but tonight, I gotta boil some water and try
getting him to breathe in the steam, open his lungs a little."

"We might come back and talk to you some more, if that's okay,"
Tobe said. "And I sure hope Chocklit feels better."

"Aw, that's real nice of you to say, ma'am."

"Thanks for making time for us, Mr. Nowicki."

"My pleasure—uh—Officer."

Tobe flicked her eyes at me; she wanted to correct him to say
"detective sergeant." But she chose not to.

It was a hike from Richard Nowicki's barn to our car. Tobe said, "Nice guy. Talkative, kind, likes horses, loves his daughter—pretty good-looking, if you're into curly white hair and a beard."

"I'm not. So he's off the suspect list?"

"He's not *that* nice."

Her cell phone buzzed in her pocket, and she answered it. "Blaine here . . . Yes . . . You're kidding! Okay, we'll be there in a few minutes. Thanks." She replaced the phone in her pocket. "That was Chief Koskinen. Shit!" she said, sighing deeply. "We've got another dead body."

CHAPTER SIX

K.O.

When K.O. called Kathy Pape to see if she could introduce him the next day to some of the guys in the so-called "rough crowd," she suggested it would be a better idea if they went out that evening instead, because the boys hung out together at the small park in the middle of Ashtabula.

They decided to meet at eight o'clock at a different McDonald's, this one at the I-90 exit ramp to Geneva, hard by some gas stations, a few restaurants, several signs advertising nearby wineries, and various shops surrounding the off-ramp. Parts of the county were more sophisticated than K.O. had thought.

Kathy had arrived early and was sipping a Coke. Her Love's store smock was gone; this evening she was poured into cut-off camel toe denim shorts and a snug T-shirt, and her loose blond hair flowed past her shoulders. Her makeup, while not overdone, was more glamorous than what she'd worn as a cashier that morning.

"Hey," she said, extending her Coke. "Want a sip?"

"No, I'm trying to quit."

"That's funny." She sucked on the bent straw until the pop was gone and the straw gurgled in the ice. "Let's go. I warn you—these boys won't like your being with me."

"I'm not *with* you, Kathy. I'm hooked up elsewhere."

"Well—they might not like you because they don't know you."

"Me?" K.O. said. "I'm a pussycat."

In Kathy Pape's ancient Chevy, with the windows cranked down to let fresh air circulate, they drove to Ashtabula along Lake Erie, and K.O. couldn't help noticing small cottages built with a great view of the lake. Many of them looked beaten up, in need of a paint job or a mowing, as if the residents didn't give a damn how they looked.

When he mentioned it, Kathy said, "Those cottages were built after the Second World War, usually for summer homes or weekly rentals. But now people live in them all year long. We keep waiting for Lake Road—the highway we're on now—to crumble and fall into the lake again, and take these cottages with it."

"Again?"

Her laugh was one short, mirthless burst. "It's happened before—twenty or thirty years ago."

Their car crossed over the Bascule Bridge into the harbor area. In the distance were industrial piers; (sixty) foot-plus ore boats came and went frequently, one of the few industries that kept the city of Ashtabula going.

As they approached the park, K.O. said, "This is a long drive from Queenstown just to hang out. Do your pals smoke?"

"Weed. They all spit, too—like nobody ever learned to swallow. Gross! They're still in school, anyway."

"They're all younger than you?"

"Not all," she said. "Some got held back a grade or two."

He laughed. "Why? Everybody's got a calculator now."

"Guys rebel—starting with not doing their schoolwork."

K.O. said, "Isn't eighteen years old a little late to be rebelling?"

Kathy's blue eyes sparkled. "Like I said—it's Queenstown."

They left the car about a block away and walked toward the park in the twilight, not far from what used to be a vibrant downtown. At the end of the Bush years, many retail establishments had folded their tents and quietly stolen away from an economy Congress hadn't bothered to fix. The city leaders had turned the main street into a pedestrian-only mall, and since there were no longer any places for cars to park, they had built a sprawling public garage. It took several years for the mavens to discover that the idea was a disaster, so they redid the street once more so people could drive on it. Most storefronts were now vacant, and ponder-ous bank buildings and old burlesque theaters had been remodeled into restaurants, senior centers, and in one case, a church in which everyone spoke Spanish.

"There they are," Kathy said, pointing with a red-tipped finger toward a cluster of nine male and four female teens waving pop cans and puffing on joints K.O. recognized by smell. A few waved or called out Kathy's name as they approached, but most openly studied K.O.

When Kathy introduced him, no one offered K.O. a handshake. The tallest of the young men came toward them, standing close to K.O. The smell of marijuana from the butt he held was also in his hair and clothes, and on his breath.

"Aren't you kind of an old fart to be hanging out with Kathy?" he demanded.

K.O. said, "Aren't you kind of *young* to give a damn?"

"Hey, Cordis—cool it!" Kathy pouted. "He's my friend."

"From Cleveland," K.O. added. "I was hoping to talk to you guys. You're Junior Poole?"

"*Cord* Poole. I'm no junior anymore."

K.O. tried looking sympathetic. "Sorry for your loss."

Cord Poole tossed his head, possibly to take his hair out of his eyes, but more likely to let the world know his father's death wasn't much of a loss at all.

K.O. gave him a business card; Cord looked at it and then flipped it away. It caught in the breeze, did a few somersaults in midair, and then tumbled off to join the other discarded rubbish in the street. "I already told that Cleveland spook cop—nobody had it in for my father. Me? I didn't say two words to him in the last five years."

"And he didn't say two words to you?"

Cord snickered. "He said a million goddamn words, but I never paid attention to any of them. Nobody gets along with a Jesus freak."

"Your friends didn't like him either?"

Cord Poole tried to stick his chest out farther than his belligerent chin. "My friends," he said, "like who I like. They don't like who I don't like."

One of the other teens had wandered over; short, muscular already running to fat, wearing a pair of mid-calf shorts with

ankle socks and training shoes, a gray T-shirt, and a red railroad
bandana wrapped around his neck. His build said he was probably
an offensive tackle on the high school football team. His head was
shaved bald except for a crewcut strip down the middle, dyed a
bright red. He said, "Nobody liked Cordis Senior much. But we
didn't hit him on the skull, if that's why you're here."

"Who are you?" K.O. said.

"They call me Cannon."

"Because," Kathy Pape giggled, "he's built like a cannonball."

"Hey, shut your pie hole, Kathy! Nobody asked you."

"Why didn't anybody like Mr. Poole?" K.O. said.

"Religious nutcase," Cannon answered. "Couldn't say two sentences in a row without mentioning Jesus."

Cordis Poole Junior snarled, "I say whatever I want about my
father, Cannon—but nobody else can!"

"I'm trying to help," K.O. said. "Just asking questions."

Junior's head whipped around angrily, and he glared at K.O.
"Nobody needs your help—or you hangin' with Kathy, either. Pick
on somebody your own age."

"Quit it, Cord," Kathy said. "Don't get all jealous; you and I
haven't dated for over a year. And he hasn't even hit on me."

"No?" Cordis crinkled his nose. "How come? Is he queer?"

Cannon giggled stupidly. "Maybe he is. We fuckin' hate queers,
don't we?"

Cordis shifted his body a little bit, now looming over K.O. "Is
that right? Are you queer?"

"How bad," K.O. said quietly, "do you want to find out?"

Cordis joyfully popped his knuckles. "Hot diggety damn, I think
he *is* a fag."

K.O. sighed. "I'll make you a proposition, Junior." That made
the muscles at the corners of Cordis's jaws jump. "Drop trou, turn
around, and bend over, okay? You'll figure out I'm gay if you get
fucked. But you'll know I'm straight if I put my foot so far up your
ass they'll be picking my socks out of your nose for a month."

Cordis's ears turned purple. He sputtered, doubled up both
fists, ready to swing. K.O. said, "Don't even think about it, Junior.
I don't fight fair."

"Yeah? How many guys you whipped?"

"Better question," K.O. said, "is how many guys I've *killed*."

A new voice cut through the evening air and stopped the two young men in their tracks. "All right, both of you, knock it off!" Another teen, this one wearing gray Dockers and sunglasses he didn't need this late in the evening, came forward and stepped between the two men. K.O. recalled that the only person he'd seen wearing sunglasses at night was Arnold Schwarzenegger in *The Terminator*.

Cordis growled, "I can take him. I'm way bigger than he is." But his eyelids batted like a frightened first grader's. Perhaps Cordis was one of those bullies who loudly threaten, while silently hoping someone steps in and breaks up the fight before it starts—before he gets hurt.

"Back off, Cord," the new teenager said—a good-looking clean-cut kid. When he talked, no matter what he said, he curled his upper lip over his teeth as though he were sneering. Maybe that was his Dick Cheney impression.

The recently arrived young man turned his attention to K.O. "Why'd you kill all these men you say you did?"

"Because the government gave me a paycheck to do it, and a rifle. Are you Jason Fontaine?"

Jason Fontaine nodded. "You looking for me?"

"I'm a private investigator, assisting the police department in Queenstown." K.O. glared down the others in the group, especially angry Cordis and his chubby backup, Cannon. "Can we talk?"

"I guess."

Kathy Pape came over to them. "Can I come, too?"

"It'd be better if you didn't," K.O. said.

"You mean you're gonna leave me with Cord? That's no fair."

Jason said, "I've got no secrets."

K.O. said, "The more the merrier, then." The three of them strolled away from the group. Cordis and Cannon glowered after them—two hunting wolves who had let their prey escape.

At the sidewalk, Jason said, "What do you need?"

"Queenstown is a dot on the map," K.O. said, "but two men are murdered two weeks apart—so something bad is going on. Your dad's death must be hard on you, but if there's anything you can tell me . . ."

"Like?"

"Like if he had enemies."

"I never paid attention to his business," Jason said. "He cheated customers. That's a fact he bragged about—but I can't think of who might've stabbed him."

"He didn't have a beef with any of his friends?"

Cordis Poole hollered over, "He didn't *have* any friends!"

"Stuff it, Cord!" Jason shouted back at him.

"Hey, my old man didn't have friends, either," Cordis said, approaching them. "Holy rollers don't make friends—they *preach*. Who gives a shit?"

K.O. felt awkward, but the next question had to be asked. "Sorry—but were either of your fathers seeing other women?"

Jason said, "He was very moral! Very religious! He never even looked at another woman."

As far as *you* know, K.O. thought but didn't say. Apparently the open zipper wasn't information flashed around by Chief Koskinen or Officer Joe Platko or the *Messenger*—at least not yet. "He went to church a lot?"

"If he wasn't selling horses, he sold religious bullshit," Kathy Pape said. "He thought every word in the Bible was true and came straight from God, but he cherry-picked what he wanted to believe—which is being a hypocrite. They're all hypocrites at that church."

"The Baptist church?"

Kathy Pape nodded agreement. "They're all against abortion, gays, gun control—and they get all that from the preacher."

"Reverend Thomas Nelson Urban," Jason said. "*Junior.*"

"Another junior in Queenstown," K.O. said. "Do you go to church, Kathy?"

"No! I quit when I was fourteen. My parents punished me, grounded me, took away my phone, but there was no way I'd go back to that church. Or *any* church. And I stay away from that preacher."

K.O. said, "Pastor Urban is narrow-minded?"

"Pastor Thomas Nelson Urban, Junior—" Jason Fontaine's voice was rumbling, rough, and he sounded more like an elderly politician than a high school senior. "—is a miserable sack of shit."

CHAPTER SEVEN

MILAN

Her name had been Annikki Jokela, but everyone in Queenstown called her Annie. Her late husband, Paavlo, also of Finnish descent, had died of prostate cancer four years earlier, bequeathing her a pleasant, unassuming little house with a one-car garage, a modest stock portfolio, and a life insurance policy worth $150,000, most of which she'd invested in corporations like Exxon and AT&T. Like many other homes in the area, hers had a shed in the backyard containing a hot tub and sauna. The Jokelas had no children.

Annie, a churchgoer, had worked as an administrator at Queenstown High School and volunteered at the food bank in Ashtabula. She was three weeks short of her fifty-eighth birthday.

When Tobe and I arrived at her house, Chief Koskinen's car was already there, in addition to that of Officer Joe Platko. Tobe looked through the window of the house and identified Platko to me. He was talking to a frantic-looking woman of about sixty, who twisted a large handkerchief in her hand, alternatively crying and screaming.

Koskinen came around the side of the house, walking slowly. His skin was ashen, his eyes red. He almost staggered when he saw us, and raised his arm halfheartedly. "Back here, Detectives."

"Detectives, plural," I whispered to Tobe as we followed him behind the house. "I just got promoted."

Koskinen, head sunk between his shoulders, ushered us into the outbuilding. Annikki Jokela, dressed in a short-sleeved blouse and dark skirt, was hanging over the side of the merrily bubbling hot tub, her head and upper body submerged, her mouth and eyes wide with terror, her feet not touching the floor. The smell of chlorine was strong enough to make Tobe rub her sensitive nose in discomfort. Steam rose from the water, hanging in wet streaks on the walls as if this were the seventh circle of hell.

"I've known her practically my whole life," Koskinen said softly, fingers massaging his eyes, trying not to look at the dead body.

"Who found her?" I asked.

"The woman who's in the house now, DeeDee Kadison. I guess she's Annie's best friend—she lives about three houses down."

"She called you right away?" Tobe asked.

"She called 911; they called my office. Then I called you."

"You were in your office?"

He nodded. "When I'm not busy during the evening, I usually stay in the office. Paperwork, research, or just being there when somebody needs a cop." The corners of his mouth curved downwards.

"Did DeeDee go back home to call, or use her cell phone?"

The chief frowned. "She used the phone in Annie's house, Detective. If you were going practically next door to see your best friend, would you carry a cell phone?"

I asked, "Did she have a key to Annikki Jokela's house?"

"Lots of folks here don't lock their doors, at least until they go to bed." His inhale was quivery. "We can't move her until the coroner's office gets here."

Tobe pulled rubber gloves from her pocket and put them on. "Has anyone touched the body?"

Koskinen shook his head. "Not till the coroner gets here. Do *you* have to touch her?"

"I don't solve homicides with my hands in my pockets."

Koskinen's jawbones jumped beneath his skin.

"Can we shut off the hot tub heat, and the bubbles?" Tobe said. "Bad enough she's dead, Chief—let's not *cook* her, too."

That upset him even further; his head bobbed like a palsy victim's. Shielding his eyes with his hand and mumbling an obscenity, he disappeared into another room. Moments later the bubbles stopped.

Tobe approached the body, studied it from all angles, especially the face, as the submerged head was turned to one side. Then, squatting next to her, she carefully lifted Annikki's skirt partway, then dropped it again. "She wet herself, maybe at the moment she died, but there's no apparent rape or sexual imposition—so this is probably not a sex crime. Her panties weren't disturbed." She sighed. "Plain white granny panties. Do people wear those anymore?"

"Don't ask me. I only know about *your* underwear." I sighed. "Three murders in less than two weeks. That's a hat trick."

"What?"

"Not a hockey fan, huh? In the 1940s there was a gentlemen's hat shop in Toronto. A pretty elegant shop, too—everybody who was anybody would go there to buy a hat. All the Toronto Maple Leafs—the hockey team—bought their hats in there, too. And one day, before a big game, the hatmaker told one of the players that if he scored three goals all by himself in that game, he'd give him a free hat."

"You're losing me, Milan," Tobe said. She was still studying Annikki Jokela's body.

"That very night," I went on, "the player scored three goals and got his hat—and people started calling it the hat trick. And ever since then, when anybody does something three times, they still refer to it as a hat trick. Three murders in Ashtabula County, back to back. Ergo . . ."

"The Ashtabula Hat Trick. Christ, Milan, does everything with you have something to do with sports?"

"No, but we're in the homicide racket, Tobe. If you've got the name, play the game."

"I still don't get it. Three killings—two men and a woman. Different methods and M.O.'s. One killer? Two killers? A group of killers?" Tobe rubbed the back of her neck, then her eyes. The smell of chlorine was kicking off one of her headaches. "If these killings have some basis in sex, forget it. Bubbling hot water would wash away any semen from her open mouth. Only the PM could tell us if she swallowed."

Chief Koskinen walked in as Tobe was talking. Now his white face was taut with fury, and he shook a wrathful finger under Tobe's nose. "Annie was not that kind of woman! How *dare* you talk smut about somebody you never met!"

Tobe spoke gently. "Chief, I do *not* think this a sex crime, though that's not much of a relief. I'm sorry."

Koskinen growled like an angry grizzly, then left again, hands deep in his pockets, his head down, studying where he stepped.

"Wow," I said.

"Well, we learned one juicy tidbit without asking a question."

"Which is?"

"Annikki Jokela and Eino Koskinen were knocking boots. Did you see the way he took off into the atmosphere when I mentioned that the water might have washed away the semen in her mouth?"

"This must be especially rough for him, then."

"Was this relationship serious—or just friends with benefits?" Tobe wondered. "He's never around to find the bodies—but he *is* the top Queenstown cop."

"He personally knew all three victims."

"Everyone in this town knows everyone else. It's not Tokyo."

"If it *were* Tokyo, they'd have a decent sushi bar. Not much ties the victims together—but one thing all three had in common."

Before I could continue, Dr. Clarence York blasted through the doorway, followed by two ambulance attendants who looked as if they worked part-time as bouncers in a shadowy bar. Trailing them was Amy Comunale Klein of the *Messenger*, pocket recorder in one hand and digital camera in the other.

"Here you are again, Ms. Klein," I said. "This must be tough on you, taking gruesome pictures."

She shook her head almost angrily. "Tougher than usual." She waved me off, shrugging, and began snapping photographs like a tourist.

Clarence York was unhappy to see me again, and evidently in no mood to talk. His ambulance guys looked bored and uninterested, as if they'd showed up at a hot dog stand or the library.

As the coroner's crew took photographs, with Amy Klein getting in their way and they in hers, Tobe and I realized we were uncomfortable sharing a space with all of them, the nose-stinging odor from the hot tub, and a drowned corpse with wide, terrified, staring eyes. We took our leave and moved across the yard to the main house.

Joe Platko was now sitting on a straight chair opposite DeeDee Kadison, who'd stopped sobbing but was still red-faced and red-nosed, with eyes bloodshot from weeping. Close up, Platko didn't look like a cop; he looked like the neighbor's kid who comes over every Saturday and mows your lawn.

I gave the living room a speedy examination. Photos of Annie Jokela and a rugged-looking guy in his sixties—the late Paavlo Jokela. A photo of Annie and other people at the Food Bank, smiling at Christmastime as they stood behind a serving line. A large painting of a saintly Jesus loomed over the mantel. On one wall was a bookcase full of tomes dealing with religion, Christianity, and Jesus himself, and a few large and dusty volumes on the bottom shelf about Finland and those Finns who had relocated to America.

As soon as she learned who we were, DeeDee Kadison started sobbing again. Finally I went into the kitchen to get her a drink of water. When I came back, Platko had gone somewhere else, and Tobe was on the sofa next to her, speaking in soothing tones, covering Ms. Kadison's hand with her own and patting her gently. "DeeDee," she was saying, her voice soothing, "I know how close you were to Annie, how much you loved her. So I'm hoping you can help us."

"I'll—try," she said, gulping air to catch her breath.

"That's fine, DeeDee." Tobe let go of her hand and leaned forward, elbows on knees. "I know Annie was a wonderful person . . ."

"Oh, God, *yes!*"

"Was there anyone she didn't get along with? Anyone who might not have liked her?"

"Everybody loved her!" DeeDee Kadison wailed. Tobe and I exchanged quick, knowing glances. Each time a friend or family member of a murder victim is questioned, they insist that the departed was beloved by all and sundry. *Nobody* is universally loved, and our job, if we are to identify the killer, is to find who *didn't*.

"She worked at the high school. Did the kids love her?" I said.

That slowed DeeDee down. "I don't know. High school kids only love themselves. Nobody hated her, though." She mopped at her running nose and tried pulling herself together, sitting up straighter on the sofa. Her voice quavered again. "She was *such* a good person!"

"Did she play cards?" Tobe asked. "Bridge, canasta, rummy?"

DeeDee shook her head. "No. She liked board games like Clue and Yahtzee. And she always watched *The Bachelor* and *The Bachelorette*." She thought about it some more. "And *Wheel of Fortune*. Not *Jeopardy*, though; she thought it was too high-hat. Now me, I like *Jeopardy*, even if I can't answer those questions."

Fearful she'd lapse into a further discussion of her television habits, I said, "Did Annie have a boyfriend?"

She gulped loudly. "She was a widow."

"Widows sometimes fall in love again."

She shook her head vehemently. "Not Annie. She loved her husband so much—when he died, that was it."

DeeDee Kadison was either lying, or not paying attention—but Tobe let it slide. "DeeDee, did you and she go to the same church?"

"Oh my, no! I'm Lutheran."

"Did her other friends go to the Baptist church?"

She puffed out her cheeks and then blew the air noisily through her lips. "Why do you want to know that?"

"We want to know everything," I said.

"Religion is personal, sir. Most people don't talk about it."

Here in the twenty-first century, people think religion is too personal? Ah, well . . .

We stayed with DeeDee Kadison for another ten minutes, asking if she'd seen anyone around Annie's house earlier that evening—or a strange car. She said she hadn't. Still teetering on the quivering edge of hysteria, she barely remembered her own name. We excused her and suggested she go home.

Moments later, Coroner York and his crew solemnly filed from the outbuilding carrying Annikki Jokela on a stretcher, encased in a body bag, and loaded her into the back of the ambulance under the watchful eye of Chief Eino Koskinen. When they drove away he stood in Annie's driveway until the red taillights disappeared into the night, then moved to his car as if twenty-pound weights were strapped to each ankle.

Joe Platko had strung yellow crime-scene tape all over the outbuilding and padlocked it tight. Now he stood near us as Koskinen's car quietly pulled away. I turned to him. "Your boss is having a bad time."

"Officer Platko," Tobe said, "did you like her?"

He took off his cap to run a hand through his hair. "I didn't dislike her, exactly. She's one of those small-thinking people who wanted everyone else to think like she does. She wanted to make it illegal to buy any birth-control products in town; no pills, condoms, diaphragms—nothing. And naturally, no abortion."

"No birth control," Tobe said, "makes more illegitimate babies. And she didn't even have a child."

"It's the principle of the thing," Platko said.

"Are people in Queenstown getting killed because of their religion?" I said.

"I wouldn't think that. I'm a religious guy, too; I go to church whenever I can."

"The Baptist church?" Tobe wanted to know.

He nodded, putting his cap back on. "It makes me uncomfortable sometimes, though. I don't always agree with everything the parson says."

"I don't agree with everything *anyone* says," I told him. "Life'd be better if we thought for ourselves once in a while."

Platko considered for a bit whether or not to be offended, and eventually decided it would be too much trouble.

As we drove back to our motel, Tobe said, "I hope he gets out of here. He seems to be a decent cop—but he'll never learn anything else by staying in Queenstown."

CHAPTER EIGHT

K.O.

"I miss you," K.O. whispered into the phone.

"I miss you too, Kevin," Carli said. "But you haven't been gone very long." He pictured her perched on the arm of the sofa in their own apartment, dressed and ready to go to work. He was lying on the bed in his motel room in Conneaut, Ohio, wearing the underwear he'd slept in. The conversation was in no way sexual, but it was intimate.

"Are Rodney and Herbie okay?"

"They're fine," Carli told him. "I walk Herbie three times a day, and I came home during my lunch hour yesterday to make sure they both were all right. And Rodney's been very loving. He slept between my legs all night."

"Now I'm jealous of Rodney," K.O. said.

"How long will you be up there in—what's the name of the place again? Kingsbury?"

"Kingsbury's a neighborhood in Cleveland, where people got murdered eighty years ago. This is Queenstown. I don't know how long we'll stay."

Carli said, "I hate sleeping alone anymore. It's your fault."

"Guilty as charged. Hang on until you can fall asleep with my arms around you."

Her pause was momentary. Then: "Don't get killed, all right?"

He tried not to laugh. "I haven't gotten killed yet."

"Yes, but—three murders already!"

"That only happens," he said, "in Queenstown."

They talked for a few minutes more; then K.O. showered, put on clean underwear, Dockers, and another shirt. It was seven forty-five. He was set to meet Milan and Tobe for breakfast at nine, but he needed coffee now to kick-start his working day—real coffee, not the stuff regurgitated by the motel coffeemaker on the bathroom counter.

In no hurry, he walked across the road to McDonald's. The traffic was slightly heavier than usual, Ashtabula County's version of rush hour. The sun hid behind a morning cloud, only hinting it might appear and warm up the day this close to Lake Erie.

Sipping by the window, he saw Kathy Pape's car drive up and park near the end of the lot. He waited five minutes, then ordered another coffee from the pretty but unsmiling young woman, this time with cream and sugar, and went through the archway from McDonald's to Love's.

"A morning present," he said, extending the new coffee to Kathy. "I hope I didn't keep you out too late last night."

She laughed. "There was a near fistfight every two minutes. Congratulations for keeping my attention." She pried the lid from her cup. "I thought those kids were tough—but you're something else."

"Nobody's born 'tough.' You need an education just to survive."

She rolled her eyes. "I sure need that education. As soon as I save up enough money . . ."

"Your family can't help, even a little bit? What do your parents do for a living?"

"My mom works at a dry cleaner's. My dad's a real estate guy—and nobody seems to be buying houses these days." She rubbed her upper arms, but the air-conditioning wasn't making her shiver. "He always brings his work home and complains about it. I want to get out of here as soon as I can."

"Does your father have any thoughts about these killings?"

"If he does," Kathy said, "he doesn't share them with me. He doesn't share anything unless somebody buys a house. And he's not crazy about the nig—uh—people who moved here to be close to their families in prison."

"Some of the inmates' families must be pretty angry," K.O. said, and Kathy nodded. "Maybe mad enough to kill somebody."

"Wow! I don't know about that, K.O."

"When can I talk to those high school guys again?"

"You mean like Cord and Jason?"

He hesitated. "I don't *think* they killed their fathers. I'd rather talk to some others. Like Cannon, maybe."

She giggled nervously. "They don't like you. They think you're a fag—they even said so. They don't like fags much."

"I've been called names they never even *heard* before. Shall we hang out at the park again tonight?"

"If you want to buy those guys a coke or a burger, we could meet right next door at McDonald's for a while," and here Kathy grinned, "just about dinnertime."

K.O. knew he was on an expense account, so he eagerly agreed. "What time tonight?"

"I don't know—I can't reach them until school's over with."

"Terrific. Just call the motel and leave a message. I'll be there."

"Oh?" Kathy's eyes twinkled. "What room are you in?"

The young woman in the McDonald's outfit who'd just poured his coffee approached Kathy's counter to say hello to her. She wore flat shoes—as anyone in their right mind would while working at McDonald's—and her gait was that of a female athlete. Kathy introduced her to K.O.

Mia Aylesworth's beauty might stop traffic if she bothered with it at all. She had a slim but strong-looking body beneath her blue and yellow Mickey D blouse, and wore tight black pants with strange, randomly placed white stripes. Her cap was tilted far back on her head, revealing a dark brunette Marine boot camp buzz hairdo topped with a modified Mohawk crest that made her look even more interesting, and a rigid, uncompromising jaw. K.O. wondered if she'd forgotten how to smile.

"Mia graduated a year before me," Kathy explained. "She was *some* athlete—gymnastics, volleyball, swimming, even karate— and she's smart as a whip, too. All A's on her record."

"Impressive," K.O. said.

"And she can also take out her dad's car engine, replace worn-out belts, change the oil, and even change a tire by herself."

Mia shrugged it off. "That was a million years ago. And I didn't get A's in everything. Don't build me up, Kathy."

"K.O. is a private eye," Kathy gushed. "He's asking questions about the killings."

Mia Aylesworth looked away, muscles on each side of her jaw jumping, and she seemed to grow smaller. "I don't know anything about that. I gotta go back to work. See you, Kathy."

She made her way across the store and through the archway to McDonald's. K.O. said, "Is she always in a bad mood?"

"She's had a lousy time. Her mother's dead, and her older brother—Tate was his name—hung himself in their garage. Mia found him that way when she came home from school, and had to cut him down—not easy for her because he probably weighed fifty pounds more than she did. How gruesome was *that?*" Kathy shook her head sadly. "She hasn't been the same since. She stopped dating, quit all athletics in her senior year, ignored three college scholarships—and she just works for McDonald's."

"Why did the brother commit suicide?"

"Who knows?" She giggled inappropriately. "You can't ever figure out us teenagers, can you?"

K.O. checked his watch. "I should meet my boss and find out what I'm supposed to do today. Just leave a message at the motel for me about tonight—Room 114; I'll meet you and whoever you come up with later today for an early dinner."

"Gee," she said, "I'd get pretty tonight if you're taking me out for dinner. But at *McDonald's?*" She giggled some more.

K.O., in a chair by the desk in Milan and Tobe's motel room, watched as Milan brooded. Tobe, in the bathroom, was carefully applying her makeup.

"You think the prison is involved with these killings, K.O.?" she said, working shadow into her eyelid with her little finger.

"Inmates' families might be ticked off—for good reason. Connected with the murders? Who knows?"

Milan said, "We can't track down everyone in town with a relative in the slammer."

Tobe added, "We should follow what leads we have, first."

"Leads?" K.O. asked.

"Just one. They were all members of the Baptist church."

"We'll visit that church today," Milan said. "K.O., you'll talk to those high school guys again tonight?"

"I'm buying them all dinner at McDonald's. On your tab, Milan."

"The Cleveland police is buying dinner," Tobe said, coming out of the bathroom. "But no supersize fries; we're not *that* rich."

"So," Milan said, "head over to City Hall in Conneaut, poke around, see if any locals have arrest records. Find somebody who's been violent."

"Someone who's been violent?" K.O. paused. "That'd be me."

"Damn!" Tobe said, snapping her fingers in frustration. "I can't even arrest you, K.O. You're not in my jurisdiction."

After Milan and Tobe left, K.O. repaired to his own room. There was a sharp rap on the door, and then someone opened it without being asked to.

"Housekeeping!" The fiftyish black woman barged right in, announcing herself. Surprised when she saw him, she stopped in the doorway, and the look on her face wasn't pleasant. "Still here, huh?" She seemed to not approve. "I'll come back later."

"Do whatever you need to do. I won't be in your way." He closed his suitcase and stowed it in a corner.

The woman sighed. Her mouth was perennially pursed as if she'd just bitten into a lemon.

He moved to the window and sat down, watching her. She bustled around, doing things in the bathroom, emptying the trash, dusting the tops of the table and dresser, making the bed. No eye contact.

K.O. tried being friendly. "Have you worked here long?"

"Almost two years."

"Like your job?"

Finally she looked at him, then closed her eyes. "It's a job."

"Right. Have you lived in Conneaut for a long time?"

She stopped fluffing up the pillows. "Why you care?"

"Just making pleasant conversation."

She glared at him as intensely as a cat who'd just stalked an unsuspecting sparrow nibbling on the grass. "You a cop, right?"

"Not exactly."

"Don't give me no 'not exactly' business. You either a cop—or you're *with* cops. That's what the manager said."

"You mean Mr. Ackerman?"

The sound she made fell somewhere between a scoff and a snort. "Ackerman! Redneck!"

"He said something racist to you?"

"He don't have to." Now she was putting the pillows back into place on the bed, actually slamming them. Her exasperated exhale pushed a few stray hairs off her forehead.

"Why don't you quit, then?"

"Can't find no other job around here."

"Leave," K.O. suggested. "Move someplace else."

"Can't. I got family here. He can't move, so I can't."

K.O. guessed that some family member was a prison inmate, which was why she wasn't fond of cops. Her eyes teared up, and she dabbed at them with her wrist. Her lips, which might have forgotten how to smile long ago, almost disappeared.

"I'm sorry if you're stuck here, Ms.—uh . . .'"

Suspicious, alert: "What you want to know my name for?"

K.O. said gently, "I'm not a police officer, but if there's anything I can do . . .'"

"Nothin' you *can* do," she said. "'Cept maybe counting four years, seven months, an' twenty-three days before I get outta this damn town!"

"Can you spare some time to talk to me, ma'am?"

"I got to put clean towels in the bathroom," she protested.

"Just for a few minutes. I'm here because of these murders. I imagine you've heard about them, Ms. . . . ?"

She sighed. "You gotta know my name, it's Pauline Pinkard, for all the good it'll do you."

"Thank you, Ms. Pinkard. Did you personally know these people who got killed?"

She laughed with her throat and not her eyes. "They didn' hang around with people like me. I know a little *about* 'em, though. Don't like 'em—or *didn't* like 'em."

"Why?"

"Different reasons. The woman with the funny name—Miz Jokela that got killed last night?" She considered. "Is that a Jew name?"

"I don't think so."

"Well—she went after the school board about six months ago; wanted 'em to ban playing football."

"Are you a football fan?"

"Who cares? She got up an' say, 'Why the town gotta pay all this money to watch a bunch a Negroes dress all up in them fancy uniforms and knock each other's brains out?'"

"Negroes," K.O. repeated softly, reaching for the notepad next to his bed. "Did she really say that?"

Ms. Pinkard nodded. "Her pastor say that first."

"The Baptist preacher?"

"That's him."

"Do you attend that church too, Ms. Pinkard?"

"Are you funnin' me?" she demanded. "You think black folks go to *that* church?"

"The preacher doesn't like black folks?"

"He won't come right out an' *say* so. But we get it, all right. We ain't stupid!"

"Cordis Poole who got killed? Was he the same way?"

"Anybody who listen to the preacher feel that way."

"And the first one to die? Paul Fontaine?"

"Lordy, lordy!" Ms. Pinkard said, looking ceilingward for the God who was probably elsewhere, "he be worse'n all the rest of 'em."

"Why's that?"

She made sure no one was listening, then leaned in toward K.O. "Couple times a year he sell food to the prison. Did you know that?

K.O. shook his head.

"You know what he do for a living? He raises horses. Now what that mean to you? He sell that prison *horsemeat!*"

"You're kidding!"

"The warden swears on a stack of Bibles that it's beef—like he believe in God in the first place! But the ones locked up in there, they ain't all stupid. *They* know what they eat and what they don't! Make you sick to your stomach!"

"The cons—uh, prisoners—must be ticked off about having to eat horsemeat. Did everyone know Fontaine was doing that?"

"These days, he gotta do *something* with 'em to make his money,

because farmers don't even *use* horses anymore—just the Amish."
She pronounced it wrong: "AIM-ish" instead of "AH-mish."

K.O. carefully considered his next question. "Ms. Pinkard, do
you think someone from the prison might have killed these three
people for the things they've done?"

"How somebody in jail gonna stab Fontaine in the heart?"

K.O. smiled at her, closed his notepad, and slipped it into his
shirt pocket. "I never thought of that."

"Listen, Mister," she said, "forget what I told you. I just come
in here with clean towels. I don't know nothin'. And I don't *say*
nothin', neither."

K.O. reached for his wallet. "I appreciate the conversation. I'd
like to pay you for your time . . ."

"Just forget about it, okay?"

"Well—like I said, if I can help in any way . . ."

"Pinkard!" The voice from the door was harsh, angry. Poised in
the archway was Philo Ackerman. Anger creased his forehead and
red spots mottled his cheeks. "Let's get crackin', girl," he barked,
waving his hand at her as though she were a spider crawling up
the wall. "We don't pay you to sit around chatting with the guests."

"I don't notice Ms. Pinkard *sitting around,* Mr. Ackerman,"
K.O. said, standing up. His tone could have flash-frozen a pizza.

"I'm not talking to you," Ackerman sniffed.

"Yes, you are. And you don't talk to someone older than you and
call her 'girl,' or use her last name without a Ms. or Mrs."

The woman gathered up all her cleaning materials and scurried
past Ackerman, not daring to look back and meet his glare.

Then Ackerman said, "Don't be an idiot, young man. How do
you *expect* me to talk to her? She's only a servant."

K.O. breathed deeply. "Give me a moment. Calling her a
'servant' is bad enough—but I'm still working on 'only.'"

Ackerman looked down his nose. "You're obnoxious."

"You've got no idea how obnoxious I am." K.O. moved quickly
across the room, startling Ackerman, who didn't have enough
sense to get out of his way, and got right into Ackerman's face,
smelling coffee with sugar and flavored Coffee-Mate on his breath.
"If you do *anything* to Ms. Pinkard—fire her, or dock her wages,
or get abusive or insulting to her, you'll *have* to talk to me. And

then I'll hurt you. Bad. Call the cops afterwards and have me arrested, but I guarantee the hurting you'll remember the rest of your life won't nearly be worth it." Gently, he placed his hand flat on Ackerman's chest and pushed him slowly across the hallway. "I have an anger problem. I work on it every day—but you piss me off, Feelo. Go away."

Ackerman stumbled backwards, his shoulders hitting the opposite wall in the corridor. Gathering whatever dignity he had left, he said, "I don't mean disrespect to her. It's just the way some people up here talk. But don't threaten me, young man. I'll not put up with it." He turned on his heel and stalked off toward the front office.

K.O. went back into his room, shut the door, and leaned against it. What the hell kind of place, he wondered, *is* this?

He waited about five minutes and then went out to his car and pointed it toward the Conneaut City Hall. Wishing he'd hit Philo Ackerman. Wishing he'd got into it the previous evening with Cordis Poole or with his buddy, Cannon. That would have been exciting, at least. Sitting in a City Hall records room for the rest of the day, shuffling through papers about people he didn't know—he could almost taste the boredom.

CHAPTER NINE

MILAN

First thing in the morning, I put in a call to an old friend. Ed Stahl won a Pulitzer Prize for journalism but takes less care of the medal than he does the recurring ulcer he bathes with Jim Beam every night. He writes a regular column for the *Plain Dealer,* which recently presented pink slips to many of its writers and support staff as they cut down home delivery from seven days to three.

Is print journalism dead? Not yet—but it's choking like hell.

Ed, who wasn't imbibing at nine o'clock in the morning, is a relentless pipe puffer—and pipe smoking went out of date twenty years ago. He's the only person powerful enough to break a law and smoke all day at the newspaper in his little cubicle, while tap-tapping on a computer he hasn't really figured out how to operate. Not even the editors have the guts to stop him. What he knows but hasn't written about Cleveland, its secrets and its wens, would fill several volumes.

I asked Ed if he could share information with me on the Conneaut state prison.

"Why call me about prisons?" he snarled at me; I was used to him snarling. "Ask me about what I *know*—Bulgaria, or pre-Columbian art, or the sex life of Brazilian goatblowers."

"I'm desperate to learn about Brazilian goatblowers. Not right this minute, though."

"This'll cost you a minimum of three drinks at Nighttown."

Nighttown is the restaurant at the top of Cedar Hill in Cleveland Heights that its owner, Brendan Ring, has made into one of the best jazz clubs in America and one of its friendliest bars. It's just a short stroll from my apartment, and I used to drink there before it became a jazz icon. If I had a dollar for every Jim Beam I've bought Ed Stahl in Nighttown, I could retire. I said, "More abuse to your ulcer? I'd be an enabler."

"Enabling is what you do best, Milan." I heard Ed strike a match and then puff on his pipe until it was burning happily. "As I recall, the Conneaut Correctional Institution went from state owned to privately owned some years back—and that's when everything turned to crap. Talk about prison being *punishment* . . ."

"It's that bad?"

"The last I read, it's overpopulated worse than Mexico City, and all the cons are living up each other's asses twenty-four/seven. As for the food—I'm not sure, but I hear they feed them what McDonald's throws away every night. It's all about profits, Milan. That's the way businesses run this country these days: profits. Five cents is much better than three cents.

"The *real* hell of it is that they ship out the inmates to work at all sorts of jobs for other companies. The prison is like a temp employment agency, except *they* take the profits and make the cons work for peanuts, or sometimes for *no* peanuts. It's private business, just like any corporation in the country—so the owners make money from the way they feed and house the cons, and make *more* money putting them to work for nothing."

"That's slavery."

"Lincoln freed the slaves. At least he thought he did."

"Do you suppose," I said, "the relative of one of those cons could've gotten pissed off enough to kill someone?"

"If it were me," Ed said, "*I'd* kill somebody, too. Those greedy shitbirds are as bad as Wall Street. They'd sell their grandmother for a buck and a quarter!"

"Are you getting mellow in your old age?"

He brought the mouthpiece closer to his lips and almost whispered, "I'm not getting *too* mellow. But what I see at *any* privately owned prison turns my stomach."

"A lot of minorities behind bars there?"

Ed sighed. "Like every other Graybar Hotel in the country. From what I hear, though, none of the murder victims up there had anything to do with the prison. All your crap is happening three counties away from me. Why don't you bend the ear of some reporter in Ashtabula?"

"I did," I told him, thinking of Amy Comunale Klein. "She's meaner than you are."

Tobe and I were glad to get out of our room that morning. Not that there was anything particularly wrong with it. It was relatively neat, the shower had been washed down more or less recently, we could see ourselves in a sparkling mirror in the bathroom, and the towels and washcloths were clean. The low-paid housekeepers worked hard and did a good job.

However . . .

Have you ever wondered, even when staying in an expensive five-star hotel, how often the bedspread is laundered? The answer is: rarely. Think about that next time you go to bed in a hotel or motel, and wonder how many different people had sex on the bedspread in the last four months, or even sat on it bare-assed while they put on their socks—and you're *sleeping* beneath it.

After downing a quick breakfast at some nameless coffee shop in Conneaut with the imaginative COFFEE SHOP sign in the window, we headed to Queenstown and the Baptist church for a morning chat with Pastor Thomas Nelson Urban Junior. I'm no more inclined to automatically trust a clergyman than I am to automatically *distrust* a contract killer. There are good and bad in every profession.

The church was freshly painted and immaculate Western Reserve white, its steeple shimmering in innocent contrast against the soft blue sky. The white-painted parsonage was right next door. When we saw the man in garden overalls on his knees at the edge of a gladiola patch, we assumed he was a hired landscaper and asked him where we could find Pastor Urban.

"I'm the pastor at this church," he said, standing up with some difficulty and trying not to grunt. He wasn't old, but not young, either, and it was clear that his knees gave him trouble. The garden was overgrown with what I recognized as lavender, chrysanthemums, petunias, and even a few pinkish roses adding glorious bursts of color. Obviously Pastor Urban tended the flowers with loving care.

We introduced ourselves as police officers from Cleveland, come to help Chief Koskinen solve a triple murder. The first thing out of his mouth was "I'm so glad you're here. God bless you." He didn't offer to shake hands, but he dusted off his knees and removed his gardening gloves. "It's warm out here, isn't it? Shall we go inside to the parlor for a nice glass of iced tea?"

I hadn't heard the word *parlor* since I was a child. He led us up the front steps to his living room and made a sweeping gesture at the sofa, beckoning us to sit.

"Mother!" he called. "We have visitors. Some iced tea, please— for three?"

A woman murmured from somewhere else inside the house. Urban moved to an easy chair facing us, but didn't sit down right away. He stood, shifting his weight from one foot to the other. "The people who've died," he intoned, "were my friends. I take these deaths very personally."

"They all attended this church?" Tobe asked.

"They were members, yes."

"Loved by their fellow members?"

Urban smiled beatifically. "Christians love each other. The Lord says to love thy neighbor."

"Maybe somebody *didn't* love them," I said, "because they were brutally killed."

His smile disappeared like steam from a teakettle, and he groped behind him for a chair to sit on. "That's—terrible. But no one here would ever do anything like that."

"You'd be surprised what some people will do," Tobe said.

Urban looked grave, and tried to sound important. "I'm not surprised by very much, Officer."

Tobe said through her teeth, "It's *Detective*, Pastor. Detective Sergeant, if you want to get technical."

A woman came in with a tray: a pitcher of iced tea and three glasses. In her mid- to late thirties, with shoulder-length hair that might have been styled in the 1950s and not touched since, she wore an apron over a casual dress with long sleeves—on a warm day in late spring.

"Thank you, Mother," the pastor said. "These are our guests from Cleveland. My wife, Mrs. Urban."

He referred to his wife as "mother" despite her being at least fifteen years younger than him? And he hadn't mentioned her first name, nor had he told her our names. I cocked my head, listening for the singing of the slaves as they picked cotton out on the plantation.

"Thank you for coming," she said quietly. She put the tray down on a coffee table that was faux antique, and almost curtsied as she backed out of the room.

"Allow me," he said when she'd gone. He poured out three glasses of tea, handing one to me first before passing another to Tobe. She and I didn't dare look at each other so as not to laugh. Then he raised his glass in a kind of toast and said, "God bless you both."

"You have a say as to the subject of your sermons, don't you, Pastor?" I said.

Urban's smile was a teensy bit smug. "I'm sort of the big boss around here. The decider—I think one of our presidents said that. My flock is socially conservative. It wouldn't shock us if whoever killed these wonderful, kindly people is a—liberal. Or a . . ." He could barely bring himself to say the words. ". . . a homosexual pervert. Or a ne—."

He forgot for a moment to whom he was talking; looking at Tobe now, his face went as white as chalk. He stumbled and stuttered, then hoped the word he'd started would come out differently. "Or a *knee*-jerk—uh—radical."

Knee-jerk. Nice save—but it didn't work.

Tobe didn't say anything and she didn't *do* anything. For almost a minute she just *looked* at Pastor Thomas Nelson Urban *Junior,* making him even more discomfited. One of Tobe's looks can mess you up worse than a punch in the nose.

Finally she said, "*Knee*-jerk, is it?"

"Well . . ."

"So no *liberals* belong to your church?"

He squirmed on the bench. "I don't ask people their politics. But this is a pretty conservative . . ."

"Homosexuals?" Tobe interrupted. "Any gay churchgoers?"

"I—I wouldn't think so. We don't encourage homosexuals to attend our church—although there are others, somewhere, who welcome them." He put his fingertips over his lips. "We don't hate homosexuals—or hate *anyone*. You know what they say: Hate the sin but love the sinner."

"Really?"

"I wouldn't think gay people would *want* to join this church. We only have about two hundred seventy-five actual members. But lots of non-members come every Sunday, too."

"You've said from your pulpit how sinful gays are."

"That's what the Lord says in the Bible."

Tobe leaned forward, elbows on her knees; her glare might have ripped out Urban's lung. "What about *knee*-GROS, Pastor? Any Negroes attend your church?"

He kept his eyes on me, fearing even to meet Tobe's eyes. "They're welcomed. Everyone is welcome in the House of God. But they're probably more—comfortable in their own church."

"Comfortable? You welcome *any* Christians, don't you?"

"Of course. But people feel easy around their own. That's why there are Catholic churches, Spanish churches, Jewish churches . . ."

"Never miss going to a Jewish church on Yom Kippur," Tobe said.

Pastor Urban had just about enough, and rose from the bench, shaken. But Tobe had one more question. "Do you know anyone who disliked all three victims?"

"This church is all about love, Detective—not dislike. Love. Love of one another, the love of Jesus—because He loves *us*, too."

Interesting; Jesus loves *us*, Urban said. Did he include everybody in the word *us*, or just the members of his church—and not liberals or homosexuals or *knee*-groes?

He coughed to clear his throat. "I don't want to rush you, but I must arrange Annikki Jokela's funeral. I want to make it respectful—full of grace." He stood up and waited until we did, too, then guided us toward the front door. "We appreciate your being here," he told us as we headed down the front steps, and then, as if he'd forgotten to say it in the first place: "God bless you."

Tobe and I drove away in silence for a few minutes. At length I said, "Well, *he's* a barrel of laughs."

"I'd bet he's really funny on Sundays."

"Is he our murderer?"

She considered that. "He might be the next victim."

"How so?"

"He's—vocal. He doesn't like liberals or gays or blacks. He's the preacher, and sheep pay attention—they trust him."

"So," I said, "if we find a gay black liberal somewhere in Queenstown, can we just slap the cuffs on him?"

She smiled with one corner of her mouth; I loved that smile. "You don't have cuffs to slap, Milan—and you can't arrest anybody. Check your P.I. license."

We reached the police station in a few minutes; in Queenstown, everything is close to everything else. Chief Koskinen was scrunched over behind his desk, his bald head bent low and showing traces of hair his razor hadn't gotten to yet. He wore the same clothes he'd worn the night before. His red-rimmed eyes and the luggage bags beneath them looked as if he hadn't slept, either.

"Are you okay, Chief?" I said.

He barely shrugged his shoulders, as if even the slightest movement was agonizing for him. "No. I'm just—here."

The coffee pot was empty save for yesterday's dregs on the bottom. Tobe said, "How about I brew a pot for us?"

Koskinen just shook his head.

"Chief, we're here for you," I said. "With a little help from you, we might get things figured out quicker."

He attempted to sigh, but the elephant sitting on his chest made that difficult. "I don't feel much like a cop," Koskinen said, pausing to breathe deeply between sentences. "I feel like staying in bed with my head under the covers." He rubbed at his eyes. "I suppose you figured Annie and I were—seeing each other."

"Our sincere sympathies," I said.

He looked from one of us to the other. "You're a couple, too. That's—good. Good luck to you."

"Chief," Tobe said, "now we're *really* motivated to find the killer so you can arrest him personally."

"I hope you do, Detective, because I'm just about played out."

Tobe pressed on. "The victims are of both genders. But except for Paul Fontaine's open zipper, there's no hint of sex crimes. Fontaine cheated people in business, but Cordis Poole and Annikki

Jokela didn't. The men were married, she was a widow. The men had children, Annikki had none."

"They all have two things in common," I said. "All middle-aged, and all members of the Baptist church. I wonder if any of them had stock in the company owning the prison?"

"Did Fontaine *hire* relatives of cons?" Tobe asked. "That might have made him vulnerable to some people."

Koskinen sighed. "You might be looking for trouble in the wrong place."

"If we knew the *right* place to look, we'd have been out of here yesterday." Tobe hooked one leg over the corner of the chief's desk and got comfortable. "Do *you* regularly attend the Baptist church?"

It was apparent Koskinen wasn't really running on all cylinders, because he answered slowly: "No. I'm not—religious."

"You didn't go to services with Annikki?"

"I wouldn't go to *that* church to see the birth of Christ with the original cast!" he said angrily, but the emotion drained from him immediately. "Annie went every Sunday, and some evenings, too. I just went with her on Easter and Christmas Eve. Those days were important to her."

"How many church members are friends of yours?" I asked.

"Not close friends—none of them. Cops don't really get close to non-cops. I guess you know that, Detective Blaine. The pastor irritates me, and I guess some of his flock believe just like he does."

Tobe said quietly, "Did Annie believe like he does?"

Eino Koskinen's lips became a straight, thin line slashed across his face. "Sometimes."

"About what?"

He propped his elbow on the desk and supported his chin with his hand. "Unions, for one. Pastor Urban hates unions, wants to turn Ohio into a right-to-work state, and Annie agreed with him, even though she doesn't know anything about unions. Me? Most police officers belong to a union. So do I. So that's one problem."

"Just one?" I asked.

"She—had no use for homos, either."

"Why's that?"

"She said what Urban says, that they're sinners. He tells parents that if they have a girly-type son, or a masculine daughter, they should punch the crap out of them until they get over it."

I said, "Doesn't sound very Christian to me."

"Urban wants to make gays feel so uncomfortable and unwanted that they'll go away—to some fag island somewhere."

"Fag island, eh?" Tobe said wearily. "Are there many gays in Queenstown?"

Koskinen said, "Probably a few, but they keep quiet about it." He put his chin on his chest and stared at the desktop for too long. "I don't know if anyone's gay or not."

Tobe nodded. "What else about Urban?"

"Well, lots of Queenstown people—and not just Baptists, mind you—hate the president's guts."

"The president of the United States?"

"I didn't vote for him either, but I hardly hate him." Pale as he was, Koskinen's face flushed, and he turned away for a moment. "I don't want to insult *you*, Detective. Or shock you."

Tobe smiled with everything but her eyes. She always smiles when she knows what's coming. "Go ahead, surprise me."

"Well, some of Pastor Urban's people are kind of—racist."

"*Kind of* racist," I said. "Like being *kind of pregnant*."

"I have no problems with anyone," Koskinen hurried on, "whatever color they are. But in that Conneaut prison, lots of inmates are minorities."

"So," Tobe said, "minority families live in the area, and that's the trouble?"

"Don't get me wrong," Koskinen protested. "I don't like when people put down minorities—and I hate the *n* word. I'm just telling you what you wanted to know about churchgoers."

"Including all three victims who were Baptist church members?" I said.

He struggled with that, trying to create some way to convince us that Annie Jokela, his late, lamented lover, wasn't a bigot. Finally he gave up. "Including all three victims."

We left Koskinen in his grief and walked back out to our car. Tobe said, "It's Friday."

"Yep."

"I figured we'd be out of Queenstown by today."

"Are we hanging around? There's not much to do in Ashtabula County on the weekends."

"Not necessarily," she said. "I've heard about one place that really rocks. Everyone managing to get into trouble shows up there. Probably a place we should visit, and ask around."

"Where'd you hear about this place?"

"Platko mentioned it to me last night. He says if there's any trouble around here, some boozer in this joint is probably behind it."

"Do they lose tempers and have fistfights?"

"No more than once an hour except on Saturdays. Damn near every one of their customers has a criminal record for violence. Besides that, on Sunday we're going to church."

I turned my body sideways to face her. "You're kidding! I haven't been inside a church since I got back from Vietnam."

"It's not a Catholic church," Tobe said. "You won't have to kneel or cross yourself or spritz yourself with holy water. Besides, it'll be fun—a sleazy bar tonight and church Sunday morning."

"And where exactly *is* this sleazy bar?"

"Neatly tucked away on the main street of the Conneaut harbor. It's a pool hall, too: the Corner Pocket."

"I wonder," I said, "if we'll meet the same people in the Corner Pocket tonight, and again on Sunday morning at the Baptist church."

CHAPTER TEN

K.O.

This time they were waiting for K.O. at the more spacious Mc-Donald's just off the I-90 Geneva exit—all except Jason Fontaine and Cordis Poole Junior. Five high school boys, two girls, none of them welcoming, none even smiling. They sat with Kathy Pape at two large tables in the corner against a broad window, but no one ordered anything until K.O. arrived to buy it.

Kathy was dressed like a Barbie doll, wearing a short flared skirt, three-inch red heels, breasts threatening to burst through the jersey top. She might have arrived there in a Mattel box.

Cannon, it turns out, was born Aiden Royle. His father, K.O. discovered later, owned several dry-cleaning establishment franchises in Ashtabula and Conneaut, and was also a deacon in Pastor Urban's church. The other boys, Jake, Jay, Art, and Rudy, presented sullen faces to make themselves look much tougher than they really were. Both the *J*'s—K.O. began thinking of them as a team—wore baseball hats with the bills off to one side, and jeans low enough on their hips to display too much of their loud print boxer shorts.

The two girls, Patty and Sandy, were faux Gothic, dressed in Dracula black and sporting kohl eye shadow, and black lipstick and fingernails. Sandy had a large sketch pad in front of her on the table, reminding K.O. of a police sketch artist in hell.

After they ordered and collected their meals, K.O. tucked a receipt for nearly a hundred dollars into his wallet; when kids are offered a "free" dinner, they order everything on a Mickey D menu, supersize it, and top it with more fattening desserts. Sandy opened her sketch pad and began drawing, the tip of her tongue protruding from one corner of her mouth in concentration.

K.O. waited until they'd all finished eating, even paused for the deliberate farts and belches that followed, before he asked if they all got along with their parents.

"Check my hair, for crysakes," Cannon grinned, patting his bright red strip. "You think my parents *like* the way I look?"

Sandy snickered. "The way we dress, the way we act—we all try to piss off our families, just for the fun of it. That's what kids do."

Rudy said, "Didn't *you* get in trouble with your parents when you were our age?"

"I'll bet," Cannon said, puffing his chest out in a swagger he'd obviously worked hard to perfect, "his parents are bent outta shape 'cause he's a fag."

Some senior citizens looked over angrily because the group was chortling and talking too loudly; their glare reinforced their patent resentment.

"I let it go last night, porky-ass," K.O. said quietly. "Don't push your luck."

Cannon's swagger fled his face and posture. He remembered K.O. mentioning he'd killed people, and he didn't want to find out if that was the truth.

K.O. said, "You all seem to have a problem with gays."

Rudy said, "Well, they're sinners."

Jake's nose wrinkled as if he'd just smelled something bad. "What they *do* is a sin. That's fucking *gross*. Just thinking about it makes me throw up in my mouth!"

Patty added, "It's an abomination. The Bible says so."

"Where do you hear all this?" K.O. said. "In church?"

"We don't go to church anymore," Cannon said.

"So you get all this stuff about gays from your parents?"

The kids looked discomfited. Jay said, "*They* hear it from Pastor Urban—and then talk about it at home."

"Why do they care what others do in their own bedrooms?"

"Cuz," Jay reiterated, "it's gross!"

"Your parents put down black people, too?"

A moment of silence; then Patty said, "The niggers are all criminals. That's why they're all in jail."

"The people who work in stores," Cannon offered, "watch them every fuckin' minute so they don't steal anything."

"Interesting. What else about your parents?" K.O. said. "Do they all have guns, too?"

The group murmured in the affirmative, nodding their heads, Jake and Jay playfully elbowing each other in the ribs. K.O. said, "Do you all know how to shoot?"

That sobered everyone. Finally Rudy said, "My old man always keeps his gun locked up so I won't play with it and accidentally shoot myself."

"Or shoot *him*," Cannon added. Nobody laughed.

"You and your father aren't on the same page, are you, Rudy?"

Rudy took a moment before answering. "You either turn into a God-fearing freak-o like him, or you stay the hell away from him and count the minutes before you can leave for good."

Jay said, "My father, too." Then he worriedly added, "It's not like I ever wanted to shoot him or anything . . ."

K.O. sipped his now-cold coffee. Sandy held up her sketch pad so he could see what she'd done.

"It's the way I see you, anyway," she said. The sketch was more of a caricature of K.O., except this figure snarled angrily, muscles bursting from his shirt. In each hand was a smoking pistol.

K.O. said, "It looks more like Clint Eastwood, back when tough guys didn't talk to empty chairs."

"*You* have two guns," Sandy said. "My dad only has one."

"My picture has two guns. I don't even have one."

Through the Gothic makeup, Sandy blushed. Splashes of color on her cheek made her almost pretty—the way teenagers used to be.

"I'm not teasing you," K.O. said. "You have real talent, Sandy. Going to major in art in college?"

"Nuh-uh. My dad says I have to major in nursing or in business, or he won't pay a cent for my college tuition. Especially art. He says nobody can make a buck doing art."

Jay and Jake nodded. Rudy said, "I always wanted to be an actor, but my father would kill me."

"Funny choice of words," K.O. said. "Is there anyone in town who could get so mad that they'd actually kill somebody?"

Everyone got quiet, not even looking at each other. Finally Patty said, "Nobody liked Mr. Poole or Mr. Fontaine. I mean, they were jerks. So was Annie Jokela—*sort* of, anyhow. But we don't know anyone who'd actually murder those people."

K.O. sighed and shrugged. "Maybe not," he said. "But all your parents own guns."

Someone sucked at their straw and made a too-noisy gurgling sound. Kathy Pape cleared her throat and pointed out what K.O. hadn't yet thought about.

"The funny thing, though," she said, "is that none of those people who got killed were shot."

"Food for thought," Milan Jacovich said when K.O. related his early evening at McDonald's. He, Tobe, and K.O. were conferring in K.O.'s room; outside it was just getting dark. "These high school kids are really interesting. They think the killer is just using bare hands."

Tobe said, "Stabbing people to death isn't exactly bare hands, nor is an iron pipe, or whatever brought Cordis Poole down. As for Jokela, I assume no weapon was involved. But we'll have to wait for the assistant coroner to come down from his retirement daydream."

Milan said, "*I* own a gun. If I went cuckoo all of a sudden and wanted to kill a bunch of people, I'd shoot them, wouldn't I?"

"So," Tobe said, "we're looking for somebody with strong hands and a strong stomach who prays the loudest."

"Praying?" K.O. said. "What's that all about?"

"We're all going to church Sunday morning," Tobe said. "So don't wear jeans."

"I never go to church! I barely know where there *is* a church."

"You'll find out Sunday morning."

"Sunday? *Man!*"

Milan said, "You thought we'd be out of here in two days?"

"It's almost Saturday! I was gonna be with Carli."

A Milan sigh. "You spend your *life* with Carli."

"Well, *you* two spend your life together, too."

"True," Tobe said, "but unlike you, we haven't moved in together.

Why don't you just invite her up here? It should be a fun weekend. It's nice in Ashtabula County, what with the lake and all . . ."

"Carli's taking care of the animals."

"Have her bring them up, too."

K.O. shook his head. "You can't take a cat on a vacation."

"I thought," Milan said, "your neighbor feeds Rodney when you two are off somewhere. Have Carli bring Herbie with her."

Tobe said, "Milan will walk him. Won't you, lover boy?"

K.O. looked out the window at I-90, the traffic humming along on a Friday evening. "The manager, or whoever the hell he is—Mr. Ackerman—won't like that. He probably hates dogs, too."

Tobe moved to the dresser and checked her hair in the mirror. "Philo Ackerman can kiss my well-worn butt! We're here in an official capacity, and he can like it or lump it."

Laughing, K.O. said, "He *won't* like it, Tobe. He already refers to you as 'that colored woman.'"

"He won't like my badge rammed up his ass, either." She gave her hair a final pat, then moved away from the mirror. "Call Carli, kiddo, and invite her. Tonight we're going to a really elegant lounge in Conneaut for a cocktail or two. You should come with us."

"An elegant lounge?" K.O. said. "What's that?"

"Top of the heap," Tobe said. "It's the Corner Pocket."

CHAPTER ELEVEN

MILAN

The so-called business district of the Conneaut Harbor area was almost half a mile from the water, but you could see it from the front door of the Corner Pocket saloon as you gazed past a sprawling parking lot that almost no one ever used. The number of boats berthed in the harbor had shrunk alarmingly in recent years, and the business area had evolved into a hard-ass neighborhood of boilermaker taverns, boat supply shops, and a tiny so-called deli stocking processed foods in plastic pouches along with beer, smokes, and chewing tobacco.

It was dark now. K.O., in the backseat, was still irritated about the coming weekend in Ashtabula County.

I halfway turned to talk to him. "Carli is okay with joining us tomorrow?"

He grunted. "She'll be here around noon. But she won't go to any church. We figured that out on our fourth date."

There were few parking places on the main street in front of the Corner Pocket, and we had to drive around the block to find one. It was cooler near the lake; Tobe's windbreaker hid the hardware she carried on her hip.

As we strolled toward the tavern, I asked her, "How much good will your piece do here?"

"A cop is a cop," Tobe replied. "Wherever I am. The only time I'm not carrying is when I'm in the shower—or in bed with you."

"I didn't hear that," K.O. said, putting his fingers in his ears and loudly singing "La-la-la." K.O. hates it when Tobe and I talk dirty.

The building, like many overlooking the harbor, was more than a century old and had housed a tavern for its entire existence. During the 1920s, when selling alcoholic beverages was illegal, it fashioned itself as a billiards hall, but it served alcohol anyway, usually in teacups. The teacup industry thrived during Prohibition, as did the booze industry, run mostly by organized mobsters. But few did a roaring business selling meth back then; methamphetamine arrived much later. When handing out this assignment, Flo McHargue told Tobe the profusion of meth labs operating in small houses in mostly rural Ashtabula County was surprising, and that meth cookers and murderers were not entirely strangers.

We weren't visiting the infamous Corner Pocket about meth labs, though, nor even to enjoy a relaxing end-of-the-week drink. In such a small neighborhood, some saloon regular must have known at least one of the victims and could shed some light for us.

My alcoholic consumption in the old days wasn't excessive. Ten drinks per week was about all I could handle; now that had petered down to three drinks per month. My boozing days took me to some of Cleveland's sleaziest taverns, mostly for work. Tough spots, ethnic bars in which I was the only one who didn't belong there. Hippie hangouts in which just the scent of weed in the air could get you stoned. Strip joints. Truck driver joints. Mafia taverns. And my home-away-from-home beer joint, Vuk's Tavern on East 55th and St. Clair, where I had my first legal drink and where the owner/bartender Vuk keeps a Reggie Jackson baseball bat behind the counter in case anyone gets out of line. I've been to all of them.

But I bow to the Corner Pocket.

We could hear the juke box playing when we were still half a block away. I didn't recognize the song, or even if it was a song at all; my pop music knowledge stopped somewhere between the retirement of Rosemary Clooney and the death of Frank Sinatra. When we opened the door, the sound almost knocked us over— blaring rap, unusual music in an all-white tavern. Everyone was shouting, trying to be heard. The Ohio laws against smoking in a public place were ignored, too; cigarette smoke hung over everything like impenetrable London fog, saturated with the stench of stale beer. It was Friday-night crowded, and all were puffing away, including the smattering of women present. Serious players used the two pool tables in the rear. Most wore baseball caps with bills turned toward the back. Many men hadn't shaved for at least a week. I'm not sure about the bathing.

When we entered, everything went silent except the juke box. They all stared at us, or more precisely, at Tobe—as if she'd just landed in Conneaut Harbor from the planet Klingon. This might have been the first-ever interracial visit to the Corner Pocket. She rubbed her nose and said to me out of the corner of her mouth: "Boy, this place stinks! Migraine headache ahead."

We approached the bar; the boozers cleared a wide place for us to stand, as if we were lepers. The bartender, his body broad as a three-story building and his cheek stuffed with Mail Pouch chewing tobacco, regarded us as if looks could kill, and deliberately paused before he finally grunted, "Yeah?"

K.O. and I chose Bud, one of only two brands available. Besides a martini, only consumed in more upscale lounges, men hardly ever publicly order a cocktail with a name—no Grasshopper, no Sex on the Beach, no Suffering Bastard, not even, God help us, a Brandy Alexander—especially in a place like the Corner Pocket.

Tobe ordered a beer she had no intention of drinking since she was on duty, openly checking out the place by looking in the dirt-streaked mirror behind the bar. We didn't like what we saw. Many customers dozed on chairs tucked in corners. Most still awake had that unmistakably stoned look—slack mouths, vacant eyes, yellow skin, and slumped shoulders.

When our drinks were placed before us, the barkeep said, "That's twenty," and waited.

"Twenty dollars?"

"Beer's five bucks apiece. The extra five bucks is my tip—all included." He smiled a Dracula smile at us. "This is a high-class joint."

I put a twenty on the bar. He snatched and pocketed it rather than put it in the cash register, then strutted to the other end of the bar, to the cheers and applause of some customers.

I asked Tobe, "Does that twenty bucks buy us information?"

Tobe's eyes flicked from one face to another in the mirror.

"Be patient. Someone in here has to be suffering from a too-big mouth." She lifted her glass, said, "Slainte," and knocked it back. Then she turned and faced the crowd.

"Excuse me. *Excuse me!*" she said. Her voice, louder than I'd ever heard it, could have reached people two towns away. Everyone got very quiet, though the music still blared. She took out her badge and showed it around so all could see. "I'm Detective Sergeant Blaine—*police*. I don't want to screw up your Friday-night fun, but there's been some killings around here. Did anybody here know Paul J. Fontaine personally?"

No one moved.

"No? How about Cordis Poole? You all knew Cordis, right? Good old boy, football hero back in his school days?"

Everyone stayed quiet, tense, as if watching an open-heart surgery on cable TV. Tobe said, "I don't give a damn what you snort, smoke, or shoot into your veins. That's not why we're here."

No response except a quiet murmur. She continued, "Maybe I should question each of you personally, huh?"

One of the men stepped forward, a cigarette in his mouth, another tucked behind his ear, and the rest of the pack rolled up in the sleeve of his brown T-shirt, which proclaimed in vivid yellow letters: SAVE A TREE. EAT A BEAVER. He brandished a pool cue like a Watusi spear, just in case a marauding lion wandered by. His eyes weren't focused; one went off in an entirely different direction from the other.

"We don't talk bad about dead people," he said.

"Talk *good* about them, then," Tobe said.

"Not to you, bitch."

Standing next to me, K.O. stirred, but I put a hand on his shoulder. "Let's go, Tobe," I said. "This isn't our kind of place."

"*That's* for goddamn sure," a woman at the pool table murmured.

"Tobe?" the T-shirt man said to me. "You and her are on first names? I'm impressed. You like your pussy the way I like my coffee, huh? Hot and black."

"I'm just wondering," I said quietly, "how far up your ass I can jam that pool cue before it'll have to be removed surgically."

He didn't seem worried. I outweighed him by about forty

pounds, but he was twenty years younger than I am—and he had an entire support army at his back. Then again, I was accompanied by the toughest fighter I've ever known—a policeman with a gun.

"They say," he continued, "if you fuck a black bitch it changes your luck. Izzat true?"

"It's *your* luck that's changing," K.O. threatened, but the T-shirt guy ignored him.

"Or," he said, "do you get lucky just by touching that nigger hair?" And he reached out and rumpled Tobe's hair with his free hand.

Or tried to. She moved fast, and within a millisecond he was face down atop the bar, his arm twisted so far behind his back that he could scratch the top of his head. Tobe's other hand was at the back of his neck, grinding his nose into the beer-soaked wood. His pool cue hit the floor and skittered several feet away. A gasp arose from the startled crowd as though they were watching a high trapeze act without a net.

Tobe held T-shirt motionless as he groaned for half a minute, looking into the mirror to see what went on behind her. "Anyone else want to rub my nigger hair for luck? Don't be shy, now."

Apparently not.

I said, "Since no one here has the balls to talk to us in front of your buddies, contact the Queenstown police department; ask for Detective Sergeant Blaine. I'd tell you to write it down, but I'll bet every one of you will remember."

Tobe waited for anyone else to step forward. When they didn't, she drove her knee up hard between T-shirt's legs. His moan was at least two octaves higher than his normal speaking voice, and twice as loud, too. Tobe said, "Well, at least *he'll* remember."

She finally released him, and T-shirt sank to his knees, whimpering. I'm not sure which hurt more, his testicles, or the arm and shoulder she might have permanently dislocated. Then the three of us turned, side by side, like the Wild Bunch, facing a group of drunk and stoned Friday nighters who hated our guts. "Let's be heading out," she suggested.

We moved slowly toward the exit, and while dagger looks whizzed through the smoky air, no one seemed anxious to stop us. However, just as we got to the door, the bartender called out, "Hey, lady!"

All three of us turned around. The beers K.O. and I had ordered were untouched on the bar, but he was holding Tobe's glass above his head. "Now y'all come back and see us again real soon, okay?" Then, pouring her beer out, he smashed the glass on the edge of the bar with disdain and swept the broken shards into the sink. Tobe's beautiful yellow-brown eyes narrowed, becoming snake eyes.

She didn't speak.

Back in the car, K.O. said, "I bet some of them were packing guns."

"I shoot better and faster than they can. And I have." She flicked on her bright headlights with a bit too much enthusiasm to light up the dark road on which we traveled. "None of them ever shot anything more threatening than a rat in a junkyard."

K.O. nodded. "What was breaking the glass all about?"

It took Tobe fifteen seconds to answer. "Nothing."

"And where'd he get the southern accent all of a sudden?"

I said, "Watching *Hee Haw*." My look told him to Let It Go. He cocked his head in puzzlement, then shrugged and stared out the window at the dark.

After a few silent minutes, Tobe said, "Not the best evening ever. But one of those pencil-dicked knuckle-draggers will show up in Koskinen's office tomorrow to spill his guts about one of the victims and be a 'good citizen.' Then he can get drunk, go home, slap his wife around, and feel like a patriotic American."

At the motel, K.O. said good night and disappeared into his room three doors down from ours. When we went inside our room, Tobe quietly unhooked her holster and put it and her gun into the top dresser drawer. Then she kicked off her shoes and sat down on the edge of the bed, looking into space.

"Sorry," I said.

She stood up, taking the weight of the world with her, and shucked her windbreaker. "When the Civil Rights Act first passed, Southern bartenders would openly break the glass a black person drank from, right in front of them, so no Caucasian could put his lips near it again." She tossed the jacket onto a chair. "Never thought I'd see *that* in the twenty-first century, though." She moved her shoes to the side of the bed with her foot.

"Let's go home tomorrow," I said. "Flo McHargue can pick somebody else."

"Replace me? Not on your life." Grimly, she said, "When we nail the killer, I want to be the one to slam shut the cell door." Then she grinned, and the tension bled out of the room.

"Good cop," I said.

"Good broad all around." She came over to me, put her arm around my neck and pulled my head down to her, and tongue-kissed me hard. "So now let's boff our brains out so I can forget the Corner Pocket and remember I sometimes actually like white guys."

"*Some* white guys." I lovingly cupped her left ass cheek.

"We don't have champagne—but there's a drink machine down at the end of the building. If you get us two bottles of Mountain Dew and a bucket of ice, when you come back, I'll be naked. But don't rush or you'll hurt yourself."

I inhaled cool night air as I stepped outside with our ice bucket. The lights on the soda pop machine glared red and green. I purchased a Mountain Dew as the slot sucked up a dollar bill, and a bottled ice tea for myself, also costing a dollar. Then I walked out of the alcove, just in time to see Kathy Pape get out of her car, fluff up her hair, adjust her bra straps, and knock on K.O.'s motel room door.

CHAPTER TWELVE

K.O.

Kathy Pape sported the same outfit she had worn at the McDonald's meeting earlier that evening, but what K.O. noticed the moment he opened the door was that she'd redone her makeup and hair to make herself even more sexy-looking. To say he was surprised at her nearly-midnight visit would hardly cover it.

"I wasn't expecting *you*, Kathy," he stammered. "It's late."

"That's okay. I have Saturday off."

"You should be in bed."

Her eyebrows wiggled lasciviously. "That's why I'm here." She marched past him into the room, then turned. "Are you gonna shut the door, baby, or are we putting on a show for the neighbors?"

"Uh—my girlfriend will be here in the morning."

"It's not morning yet."

"Kathy, this is a bad idea . . ."

"Oh, come on! You're cute, and I know you think *I'm* hot. It's a beautiful night, I don't have to work in the morning, and what the hell, right?" She put her arms around his neck. "I mean, who in their right mind turns down a good time?" She pulled up her shirt and bra to reveal one voluptuous breast as she put her tongue in his left ear.

He pulled his head away and tried to disengage her arms. "Kathy, I'm committed, okay?"

"She won't know."

"*I'll* know."

That stopped her cold for half a minute. Then, stunned, she

stepped back. Her arms fell to her sides and she sank onto the edge of the bed, looking pole-axed. "Nobody ever turned me down before."

"If it helps, I would've hit on you the day I met you if I weren't—involved."

"Small consolation."

"I'm hooked on somebody—*seriously*. So I have to say no."

"No," she almost whispered. After a few moments she pulled her shirt down, hauled herself to her feet, and headed for the door. "You got a problem, K.O. You're not like all the other guys. You're different. And I'm missing out because of it." She crossed her arms across her chest. "You know what *my* problem is? Lousy timing."

He walked with her to the door. "I guess I should say thanks for dropping by."

"Don't bother," she said. "Will you at least hug me good-bye?"

"Sure." K.O. hugged her—what he thought was an avuncular hug until she ground her crotch into his, her hands on his ass pulling him closer to her, and almost swallowed his face with her open mouth.

He tried to gently disengage himself. "Kathy—no."

She let go, stepped back, and sighed. "Well, you can't say I didn't try."

"My job here is important," K.O. said. "You helped me a lot."

"Well, I'm finished helping; you're on your own." She moved to the door, opened it, then turned back for one more parting shot. "Your girlfriend's gonna be here in the morning, but what am *I* supposed to do?" Her pretty face morphed into that of a demon from a bad horror flick. "I *hate* it when I don't get what I want, K.O. Think about *that* for the next few days."

She didn't slam the door, exactly. She didn't close it quietly and gently, either.

K.O. shook his head, glad she'd gone, but he was worried anyway. Kathy's exit line sounded like a threat. Carli would arrive late the next morning. What if Kathy wanted revenge? Not violence—at least he didn't think so. Causing trouble? A distinct possibility.

Brushing his teeth before going to bed, he noticed Kathy's

smudged lipstick all over his mouth, which made him worry all over again. Had he inadvertently left lipstick stains on any of the towels that Carli might see? How could he explain that? In their relationship, the longest of K.O.'s life, Carli hadn't displayed the slightest jealousy. However, he doubted she'd ignore lipstick traces in his motel room.

Kathy Pape was certainly attractive, but only eighteen—too young for him. Even though he was still in his mid-twenties, his experiences had matured him at a young age. And she was buddies with all those creepy teenagers who hung around in the Ashtabula city park, and who'd only agreed to meet with him earlier because he had paid for their dinners. Who knows what violence they were capable of? They were tough hooligans, or *thought* they were. They hated their parents, gays, blacks, their preacher, and his church. They probably hated K.O., too.

When he stripped to his underwear and slipped between the bedsheets, K.O. wondered if he'd actually watched a killer scarf down the dinner *he* had bought at McDonald's? How old must one get before murder was no longer a big deal? He couldn't remember any convicted killers in juvie, stuck in there cheek by jowl with purse snatchers, shoplifters, and weed smokers, but there were lots of armed robbers, rapists, and violent offenders, guys who savagely beat elderly neighbors for the few bucks they'd hidden away in coffee cans.

K.O. had grown up knowing how to fight hard and mean, and had perfected it in the juvenile justice correctional system. He'd had a moment in the parking lot the previous evening when he had wondered if he'd have to take on all of them at once.

Sleep eluded him as he tossed. He'd been in a tacky tavern or two in his lifetime, but the Corner Pocket was a highlight. The "Eat a Beaver" shirt guy had known Tobe was a cop from the beginning, but chose to insult her and try to rumple her hair anyway. He had had no idea she was nobody to mess with.

As he thought about it, K.O. decided it was not *just* a racial thing. The three of them were strangers to this bar and neighborhood, and it was obvious they weren't at the Corner Pocket for a festive Friday evening. Some of the customers were probably drug peddlers; most were drug users. A few might even have a meth lab in their home kitchen and wouldn't want a trio of cops asking questions.

It had been a good idea to leave when they did. Still, they should have talked one-on-one with somebody. Maybe he'd go back there tomorrow, he thought, and get deeper into conversation with some drug freaks to find a new avenue for Milan and Tobe to follow.

But Carli was arriving in the morning, and he wouldn't take her into such a sleazy joint with him. What a terrible idea *that* would be!

It took him too long to fall asleep.

K.O. stopped at McDonald's for coffee the next morning without going into the neighboring Love's store. He figured Kathy Pape was still angry with him.

Most men would set themselves on fire before refusing wild, passionate sex with an attractive young woman. So why, for the first time ever, had he said "no"? It would have been so easy.

Except he was really in love. He'd never encountered love before—LOVE in capital letters. But now he *knew* no other woman would interest him the way Carli did.

This McDonald's, smaller than the one where K.O. had hosted the teen meeting, was relatively empty, although a long line of cars and trucks waited for their coffee in the drive-by line. Behind the counter, as usual, was Mia Aylesworth, the young woman Kathy Pape had introduced him to, still looking bored and unhappy.

"Hi," he said when he reached the counter. "Mia, isn't it? I'm K.O. We met through Kathy?"

She nodded without enthusiasm. "Can I help you?"

"A large black coffee, please, and don't leave room for cream."

She busied herself at the coffee pot. When she came back with his coffee he said, "So how you doing today?"

Sigh. "Same as yesterday. Same as tomorrow."

"Kathy introduced me to some of her high school buddies last night." He sipped at the coffee; it was too hot. "You probably know them, too. Tough guys."

"Weenies!" she snapped, eyes suddenly flashing fire. "Gutless, cowardly weenies."

"You mean Jason Fontaine? Cordis Poole Junior, and Cannon, and the rest of them?"

"They don't have one brain between them. They wouldn't have an idea of their own if it walked in and bit them." Nervous, Mia rubbed her hands together. "They play war games on their iPads, but that doesn't take brains. They learn hatred from their parents—or from other people with authority."

"Teachers?"

"Maybe," said. "Or from that—that—Preacher Urban." She pronounced the clergyman's name as though it were an obscenity.

"The kids said they hate church, and never go."

"Their parents go, though, and listen, and then come home and feed that shit to their kids at the dinner table."

"Do your parents go to church?"

"My mother's dead. Cancer. My father stopped going to that church a long time ago. So did I."

"Why did you stop?"

"Because they're supposed to preach love in that church, but they preach just the opposite." She took a quick glance at the drive-through window, but none of her coworkers were eavesdropping.

"Are those kids willing and able to have killed three people?"

Her lips almost disappeared and her chest heaved. Her fingers crept up near her throat. "How would I know that?"

"You wouldn't. I'm just asking if you think they could have."

"They don't have the balls to kill anybody—or to think for themselves. They're bullies. Bone-deep, mean-spirited bullies, picking on people who can't defend themselves."

Troubled, K.O. said, "Do they pick on you?"

Mia's jaw jutted out a bit as she spoke through gritted teeth. "Not anymore they don't."

"Why not?"

"Because I don't talk to them or even see them. If they come in here, I won't serve them. And about a year ago, I kneed Cannon right in the—umm—right in his groin."

"Why?"

Deep sigh as she walked toward the kitchen. "I can't even remember."

K.O. sat at a table by the window to finish his coffee, trying not to stare at Mia. The more he looked at her, the more interesting she became to him. Not Barbie-doll gorgeous like Kathy Pape, but truly beautiful in a different, unique way. He recalled her last name and jotted it down in his pocket notebook. He might want to speak with her father, too, perhaps to get an adult perspective on the teen boys that rubbed Mia the wrong way. Kathy Pape had told him Mia's father worked at the prison.

When she finally noticed K.O. watching her, Mia looked away from him quickly, a flush coloring her cheeks.

Becoming painfully aware he was drinking too much coffee, K.O. drove to the Queenstown police headquarters. Tobe's car was parked right next to an Ohio state police cruiser. Inside, there was no one manning the front desk, but Milan and Tobe were sitting at the table, along with a uniformed state trooper, Brian Hollinger. Tobe introduced the two of them.

"Chief Koskinen didn't come in today," Hollinger explained, "and the other two local officers are patrolling, so I'm filling in for him. If that's okay . . ."

"It's okay with me," K.O. said.

Tobe's look at him was not warm. "Lots of things are okay with you, aren't they, K.O.?"

"Excuse me?"

Milan said, "I saw Kathy go into your room late last night. I'm surprised about that, K.O.—considering."

K.O. felt his throat beginning to close. "It wasn't like that," he stuttered. Then, to Tobe: "It wasn't like that."

Tobe waved him away and flipped open her notebook. "Forget it. It's not my business."

K.O. frowned, about to ask her *what* wasn't her business, when Milan pushed a file folder across the table to him. "Autopsy report for Annikki Jokela."

"That was fast, Milan."

"They don't have many murder victims in Ashtabula County, and I'm guessing Coroner York wanted to just get it out of the way. Koskinen couldn't deal with it. I wouldn't either, if she'd been my . . . Well, just take a look."

Several photographs of Annie Jokela had been included in the report; shots of the body half in and half out of the hot tub, shots taken at various times during the postmortem examination. K.O. didn't freak out, faint, or vomit while looking at the photos of the woman, naked, with her chest cut open and spread wide to show the lungs and heart, nor even the ones in which her face had been peeled back over her skull. After three years in the Middle East wars, few things surprised him. He was more interested in the photo of the back of Jokela's neck when the coroner had flipped up her hair. The finger marks were completely visible.

"Strangled?" he said.

Tobe shook her head. "Nope. It seems the killer gripped the back of her neck and forced her face into the hot tub; there was chlorinated water in her lungs."

"Knife in the chest," Milan said. "Smashed-in skull. Now drowning in a hot tub. This doesn't sound like a serial killer to me."

"With serial killers there's usually a pattern," Tobe said. "The same M.O., or maybe a signature. The same method of killing, or leaving a souvenir like a leaf or a flower, or a particular type of stone—some sort of mark made on the body." She pointed at the file. "Nothing like that shows up with these three."

"But as I see it," Milan added, "the victims aren't random. They knew each other, they were churchgoers, and they had authority."

"And," K.O. added, "none of them liked black people or gays. Something's going on in this town, and we're not getting it. Maybe we should talk to that girl Mia's father—she's the one who works at Mickey D's. I'll take that one. I'm getting to know her pretty well, now that I've got her talking."

"Forget it, K.O. We'll interview him. You just hang around and wait for Carli to arrive," Tobe said very quietly. "If you've got the balls."

K.O.'s eyes half closed in anger—the cute Irish look was no more. "All right, you two, what's the deal anyway? Did my syphilis test come back positive?"

Tobe and Milan exchanged glances, then both looked at Trooper Hollinger. After a tense moment, he got quickly to his feet. "I'll be in the other room if you need me."

Milan waited until the door was closed. "This is awkward. Last night I wasn't spying on you when I saw Kathy. I was out getting drinks and—it just happened."

K.O.'s jaws jumped as he ground his teeth together. "I wasn't expecting her," he said tightly. "It was a surprise visit."

"Hmm. Surprise!" Tobe said without mirth.

"I don't suppose you'll believe she wanted to have sex but I sent her home. Within two minutes."

"That *is* hard to believe," Tobe said.

"Would I lie to a cop? I couldn't help Kathy coming on to me, but I didn't take advantage of her. So believe it or not, Detective Sergeant Blaine."

"Lighten up, both of you," Milan said. "K.O. always tells the truth. If he said he tossed Kathy out before anything happened, we'd better believe him."

"Will Carli believe him?"

"We won't mention it to Carli because it's not our business. K.O. can tell her—or not."

Tobe couldn't miss Milan's emphasis. She pantomimed locking her mouth and throwing away the key.

Milan said, "Does Mia's father work on Saturdays?"

"How the hell would I know?" K.O. snapped.

"Well, isn't it lucky we're right here in the police station so we can find out." Milan got up and left the room in search of Hollinger. Finally Tobe said, "Sorry. I *do* believe you. Most guys your age wouldn't turn down a tumble with a sexy kid like Kathy."

"I'm not 'most guys.' Remember that."

"I'll try. Are you going to tell Carli?"

"I tell Carli everything."

"And does she tell you everything, too?"

He ruminated on that one. "She tells me everything that's important—everything that happened since we've been together. Before that? Well, it's probably better we don't talk about it."

"Unless they're younger than three and a half, everyone has baggage, K.O. You store it in the attic somewhere and move on."

"Do *you* move on, Tobe?"

Tobe thought before she answered. Racism was rampant in North Carolina, where she'd grown up—and here it was again in rural Ohio. Fighting to become the first black female homicide detective in Raleigh. Falling in love with a biracial cop and then that sorrowful middle-of-the-night visit from the precinct commander that every police officer's significant other dreads—learning that he'd been shot dead by a drug-addled driver. Moving north to Cincinnati and finding out Cincinnati was not really north *enough*. Relocating to the edge of the lake separating the U.S.A. from Canada, and trying again to fit in.

She took a deep breath. "Yeah, K.O. I try to move on. So do you. You moved from a shitty place in your life to a pretty good place now. I'm proud of you for that."

Milan came back clutching a piece of paper. "We lucked out," he said. "Trooper Hollinger knows John Aylesworth. He's not working today; he's coaching a kids' baseball team. So we know where to find him." He turned to K.O. "Tobe and I will go chat with him, K.O. You go on back to the motel and wait for your girl."

CHAPTER THIRTEEN

MILAN

"Do you really think K.O. will tell Carli about Kathy?" Tobe asked me as we headed for the baseball park where two Little League teams were slugging it out on the diamond. "If nothing really happened, why would he bother saying anything to Carli?"

"Yes—because he's the most honest human being I know. Carli will find out about it eventually, and he won't want to defend himself. He's silly in love."

"Then I tip my cap to him. People cheat when they're young—and when they're older, too."

"I'm older," I said. "Fifteen years older than you."

"Fourteen years! Don't make it worse." The morning sun was bright, and Tobe donned her sunglasses. They looked like two-hundred-dollar Ray-Bans, but she'd bought them at Discount Drug Mart for about twelve bucks. "You don't cheat?"

"On you? Never."

"You haven't had a chance yet."

"Not gonna happen," I said. "I don't cheat."

"Didn't cheat on your wife, either?"

"No. She cheated on me, and eventually dumped me for the guy she cheated with. But that taught me how lousy the betrayed party feels—about their spouse, about themselves, about life. I'd never want to do that to anyone else." I looked out the side window at Lake Erie as we glided along its shore, feeling the familiar pain inside my chest. My ex-wife Lila had left me for Joe Bradac twenty years before, and although I had stopped loving her even before she left, surprise hurt never goes away; it asserts itself at the most unsuspecting times.

"That's good," Tobe said, a wicked grin taking shape, "because I wouldn't cheat on you right back, just to get even. Instead, I'd rip out your lung."

"I'll have to remember that," I said, reaching over and gently squeezing her thigh.

A few minutes later we were at the ball field—actually two of them, built back to back, outfield to outfield. We'd been told by Trooper Hollinger that John Aylesworth ran a janitorial service that took care of plumbing and other repairs at the Conneaut prison. On Saturdays he coached a team called the Lakers. Lake Erie was three blocks away from the baseball diamonds, so I guess the team name fit—unlike that of the more famous Lakers who play basketball in Los Angeles, where there isn't any lake within miles.

The kids were on the field in sky-blue T-shirts with the team name displayed, wearing dark blue caps with a big red *L* sewed on, ready to defend any ball hit by the opposing team, the Angels. There were two black faces out there, both in the infield, and one gawky youngster playing right field who might or might not have been Latino; the rest of the Lakers kids looked Scandinavian.

John Aylesworth paced behind first base, where his team sat, snarling out orders to the fielders to move this way or that, to throw the ball to third base to hold the runner, or just to "Be ready!" As he shouted loudly with his hands to his face, forming a sort of megaphone, it was obvious that his right hand was misshapen in some way, the wrist permanently bent.

When the inning was finished and the teams were changing from their offensive to defensive positions, Tobe approached Aylesworth and explained who we were, showed him her badge, and said we'd like to speak to him for a few moments.

His answer was loud and memorable.

"I can't talk now! We're playing a fucking baseball game!"

Tobe returned to me. "They're 'playing a fucking baseball game'—with ten-year-olds. Let's sit and watch until it's over."

"What if it goes into extra innings?"

"Then our asses will ache like crazy."

We sidled into the hard bleachers behind first base, surrounded by Lakers parents—mostly males because it was Saturday—yelling and cheering for their offspring, but most of the noise came from the kids themselves, chanting, "Here we go, Bobby, here we go!" Or even worse, "Hey batter hey batter hey batter batter batter . . ."

We watched for a while. Tobe said, "Why haven't you taken me to an Indians game?"

"Because major league ballplayers never sing 'Here we go' in the dugout."

"You've forgotten our first kind-of date," she said.

"I have?"

"Breakfast at the Big Egg on Detroit Road. You might recall I wore a bright Cincinnati Reds jacket."

"I didn't notice," I said. "I was too busy looking at your eyes. So you're a baseball fan—the Cincinnati Reds and the National League. Whoopee! *More* good news. Want some peanuts while we wait?"

"I never eat salted peanuts in the shell while I'm on a murder case. The shells get into your teeth and make it harder to yell, 'Stop or I'll shoot!'" Tobe's elbow nudged me. "You shouldn't have turned in your badge, Milan."

"If I had," I said, "you and I would've never happened, because I'd never have risen as high as you in the department. And it's a rule you can't date someone with a higher rank than yours."

There were two more innings to sit through. Final score: Angels 12, Lakers 4. When we finally got to talk with him, John Aylesworth's disposition had grown even worse since his team had lost.

"I don't know why Koskinen called for reinforcements," he almost barked. He crossed his arms across his chest so that his misshapen right hand was tucked almost out of sight at his left elbow. "He's supposed to be chief of police! Talk to him about bad guys. Maybe he can get you into that prison, but I sure as hell can't. I don't know a goddamn thing about these killings, and don't want to. I got to put up with crap just doing my own job."

"Are there gangs inside the prison?" Tobe asked. "Does one con run the whole place? If so, I'd sure like to get in there and have a nice long chat with him."

He clamped his mouth closed, breathing loudly through his nose, his face reddening more from annoyance than the bright sun on the ball field. Then he flopped down onto the bench where his players had recently been sitting. Whatever toughness he'd displayed had drained out of him; now he was weary. Played out. Empty. "Whaddya want from me, anyway?"

"You knew the victims personally, did you?"

"The two guys, yeah, I knew 'em. The woman, not so much. I met her a few times when my daughter was in high school."

"Anybody *not* like them?" I asked.

"I don't know about the woman—Annie Whatsername. Poole was a jack-off, a Jesus freak—but nobody wanted him dead."

Silence. Then Tobe asked, "What about Paul Fontaine?"

Aylesworth rubbed his forehead as if massaging away a sick headache. "Everybody hated Fontaine with a passion."

"Why?"

"Because he breeds horses any old way he can, then slaughters them and sells the meat to the prison and tells 'em it's beef!" He leaned over and spit on the ground carefully so as not to hit his own shoe. "Cons are no rocket scientists, but they know the difference between beef and something else!" He made a face as though scant moments from throwing up. "It's none of my beeswax. They could be selling atomic bombs to the Chinese, for all I know."

"Who *is* the boss in the prison? The one all the other cons are afraid of?" I said.

He snickered. "Be easier trying to talk to the pope!"

Tobe's retort was crackling dry. "We have an appointment with the pope next week. So what's your guy's name?"

"I'll tell you," Aylesworth said, "but he's not a big talker to cops. You'll be pissing into the wind. He's Elijah. Elijah Jackson."

I wrote that down. Tobe said, "Elijah, huh?"

The coach hauled himself to his feet and began collecting the aluminum bats his team used. I'd never picked up an *aluminum* bat in my life. I guess everything changes, even kids' baseball in the park.

"Elijah, all right," Aylesworth said. "The big boss, the Big Kahuna. You know what name the other cons gave him?"

I could have guessed, but chose not to. Aylesworth tipped the six bats onto his left shoulder with his good hand. "They call him the Prophet."

I called Chief Eino Koskinen at his home. He spoke so softly I could barely understand him, but I finally convinced him to contact the prison warden and set up a visit for us that afternoon. We headed to the farthest corner of Conneaut, just before we would have stumbled over the state line into Pennsylvania. "The warden of a privately owned prison," I said, thinking out loud. "Doesn't that make him a hired gun?"

"*I'm* a hired gun, Milan," Tobe said.

"True. But you're hired by a city, and not by your Uncle Charlie who just happens to own a prison."

She still wore sunglasses, but nevertheless she squinted into the bright afternoon sun. "Who told you about my Uncle Charlie?"

As we turned onto the prison grounds, it didn't seem all that imposing, especially if you ignored the barbed wire surrounding the place, and the gun turrets manned by guards with long-range rifles. Compared to Alcatraz, San Quentin, Sing Sing, and Folsom, it looked almost pleasant. It disturbed me, though; the United States boasts 4 percent of the world's population, but 25 percent of the world's prisoners.

Even the nicest prisons in America are shitholes. They're "correctional institutions," not vacation resorts. Privately owned prisons for the purpose of profit are nowhere nearly as decent as the ones run by the state or federal government. Decent costs money.

Warden Melvin Glasser wasn't overjoyed at our visit; it was a Saturday afternoon, and he really wanted to go home early to watch a major golf tournament on television. Besides, we were from another county; we might just as well have come from another galaxy.

"Why you have to talk to Elijah Jackson?" he grumbled as he led us through several clanging gates that locked behind us. "He's been here for the past eight years, some of that in solitary. How could he know anything about these murders?"

"That's what we want to find out," I said. "We can't talk to every con in here, so we're settling for the boss man."

Glasser's walk slowed as he awarded me a glacial glare. "*I'm* the boss man, Mr. Jacobson."

"Jacovich," I corrected. When someone mispronounces my last name, I frequently let it go. "Jacobson" wasn't even close. "That's interesting, Warden. If you are the boss of a regular business, you can fire someone you don't like—but you can't fire anyone in a prison. You just put 'em in solitary."

Tobe said, "This *is* a regular business, just like Coca-Cola or Exxon oil. It's here to make money."

Glasser's face turned as stony as an Easter Island statue, and he said no more until we arrived at an interview room. One long table ran its entire length. Down the middle of it was a strip of thick steel welded into the wood, standing more than a foot high, to make sure nobody could slip anything illegal across the table to the con without being seen. Warden Glasser said, "Stay on your side of the table. Don't touch the prisoner and don't give him anything."

"We don't have anything to give him," I said. "We emptied our pockets at the door."

Glasser looked at his watch. "You got fifteen minutes."

Tobe said, "Is that all? When Chief Koskinen arranged this meeting with Jackson, he didn't mention a time limit."

"Fifteen minutes," Glasser repeated. "Where the hell you think you are? Club Med?" He pointed to two chairs, indicating we should sit in them; then he stalked out of the room.

"If this were Club Med, all our meals would be included," Tobe said, "along with room service and a mint on the pillow every night."

"Ever been to a Club Med, Tobe?" I said.

"No. Back in Raleigh, we called them Club *Dead*."

"Cute," I said.

A steel door on the other side of the room was unlocked, and two armed guards escorted Elijah Jackson in and led him to a chair on the other side of the table, plunking him into it none too gently, and then retreated. Through the small window in that door I saw them hanging around, just in case Elijah went insane and tried to eat us.

Not that it was likely he'd do anything violent. There was a wide, thick belt around his waist to which chains were attached, leading to cuffs on his hands, which were so tightly bound that he'd have to duck his head way down just to scratch his nose. The chain connecting both his feet was no more than twelve inches long, which made him move like a duck.

Yet the restraints didn't seem to bother "the Prophet." He had a confident air about him; his skin and his eyes were golden. His beard was full, his Rastafarian dreadlocks cascaded below his shoulders, and his posture, even weighed down by chains and buckles and clasps, was that of a man who knew exactly who he was and where he was going. If he were wearing a thousand-dollar Armani ensemble instead of an orange jumpsuit, he'd probably own a sizable chunk of the world.

We introduced ourselves, but from the get-go, he had no interest in me whatsoever. "Detective Sergeant?" he said, cocking his head as he studied Tobe. "Hot shit rank. You must be good at your job. I bet you'd be good at a lot of things, huh?"

"We're not here to talk about me, Mr. Jackson."

"Uh-uh," he said, shaking his head. "You're here just so's I can look at you. Can't even remember the last time I saw a hot black bitch like you."

"That's because they don't let you watch TV in your cell."

"There've been some murders in Queenstown," I told him, "and we hope maybe you can shed some light for us."

"Shed some light," he repeated. "Man, I love that! Shed some light."

"We left a carton of cigarettes and some magazines for you at the front desk."

The Prophet laughed. "So you brought me some smokes, an' magazines that probably don't have sexy pictures in them, and you expect me to tell you something important in return, huh? So why exactly am I s'posed to do that?"

"We're not accusing you of anything," Tobe said, "because you're in here. But maybe you know something that can help us out. You know a lot of things."

"About what? You-all are from Cleveland. I never even been to Cleveland, I don't know shit about Cleveland. Jim Brown, maybe. Hey, is he still alive?"

"Yeah, but he's bald now. Let's talk about the killings in Queenstown," Tobe said.

Elijah Jackson shrugged. "I don't know nothing about any three killings."

"You know everything that goes on everywhere. You know more than I do, Prophet. You're the boss man."

Jackson actually preened. "Nice of you to say, detective lady."

"I didn't mention the number three to you, so you're not only in an information loop about the three killings, but you know who got killed, and probably why. You *might* even know who did it."

I said, "Did you know the victims?"

"Sure, they'd come here on visiting day and bring oatmeal cookies." He twisted his mouth off to one side, almost as if he were disgusted with us. "Now, I don't know about the lady; she worked at the high school. Oh yeah—she was shagging the top cop in Queenstown, too."

"Is that prison gossip, Prophet?"

"Nope. It just is what it is."

"How about Cordis Poole?"

Jackson nodded. "They say he was a big guy." He looked at me. "Big like you. High school athlete who got fat."

I felt my cheeks glow red. I *am* a big guy, but I'm not fat, even though I should drop about fifteen pounds. I sucked my gut in. "Is that all you know about him?"

"Know he's a whackadoodle babbling about God all the time. He bullies his son, bullies his old lady. And if you don't go to his church and think like he thinks, in his book you're some kind of fuckwad." He shifted in his chair, and his chains clanked—Marley's ghost, except he was enjoying the hell out of this. Accustomed to attention and respect from his fellow inmates, he was loving it from outside people, especially a stunning black woman like Tobe.

"Any of your friends go to his church?" I said.

"They wouldn't get a big welcome there."

"Okay, then," Tobe said, "let's move along to Paul Fontaine."

"The horse butcher!" Elijah said.

"He butchers horses?"

"Probably doesn't do it hisself. But he sells horsemeat to this joint, and we gotta eat it! So he's nobody's friend in here."

"And you know that," Tobe said, "because . . . ?"

"Because I know stuff, detective lady. That's why you're talking to me in the first place."

I said, "Do all the inmates know they're eating horsemeat?"

"Yeah. And by the way, *inmates* is a real pussy word, like when you're talking to the Archbishop of Someplace. We're cons. Convicts. *Prisoners.*" He deliberately clanked his chains again.

"Does any con's family living outside know about this, too?"

"You think I sit around on visiting day and lissen on what everybody says to their families?"

"Maybe," I said, "someone *did* tell their family about Paul Fontaine, and they decided to do something about it."

"And then killed the other two just for the hell of it?" Tobe looked right at me as she said it, making me feel like an idiot.

"Listen up," Elijah said. "Them three people who got killed, they were religious nuts. The bully didn't sell horsemeat, and the lady wasn't a bully, but they babbled all the time about Jesus. Now, I can't tell you who killed them—but I betcha whoever he is, he's an atheist."

"Are *you* an atheist?" Tobe said.

"I don't even know exactly what atheist *is*. I made lotsa loot selling meth to white folks; I never had time for church or Jesus."

I asked, "Do you think all atheists sell meth?"

"Nope. But all meth sellers are atheists."

A guard rapped sharply on the window in the steel door and held up two fingers, indicating we didn't have much time left.

Tobe said, "Look, we know you control things in here, Elijah, and you run stuff on the outside, too. So why shouldn't I believe you got word to one of your mules outside to waste this Fontaine guy for selling you horsemeat to eat?"

"Good question, detective lady," the Prophet said. "Sure, I get messages from my outside homeboys. But there's this one guy in Ashtabula—and I'm giving you no name—ratted me out and got me shut up in here in the first place. There's another guy, and I damn well know who he is, who's fucking my woman when I can't get out and do anything about it. So if I tell my homeboys to kill somebody, it sure as hell won't be this Paul J. Fontaine who sells horsemeat. He wouldn't even be in the top ten."

I stood up. "I think we've run out of visiting time." Then I looked at the Prophet. "You're an interesting guy, Elijah."

Tobe rose, too, and we headed for the door. "Thanks for talking with us."

"Hey, detective lady. I helped you. You can help me. Just pull up your shirt there and flash your tits for me before you go? Just for a second? I never seen a lady cop's naked tits before."

"Ask me again," Tobe said, "when you get out of here in another fifteen years."

As we were walking back through the prison to pick up our belongings, Tobe said, "Thanks for coming, Milan. Without you there, he would've sung me a medley of every song ever written."

"Fascinating. At Mardi Gras in New Orleans, when you flash your boobs, all you get are beads tossed at you."

Tobe got quiet; I could tell her thoughts were of long ago. Eventually she said, "I never flashed my boobs at Mardi Gras," which told me she'd visited the Crescent City at carnival time, to party with the man she'd loved—the one who became a police casualty.

I didn't push it. Maybe she'd tell me more about it someday, or maybe not. In any case, we spoke little to each other until we were in her car, heading back to the motel.

I said, "Why do they call him the Prophet? He's not prophesying anything."

"Elijah was an Old Testament prophet, back in the Jezebel days."

"I haven't read the Bible since I was ten years old."

"Isn't there a Gideon Bible in our motel room?"

"There's a Gideon Bible in every hotel room in the country."

"Good—then brush up on it," Tobe said, "because in case you forgot, we're going to church in the morning."

CHAPTER FOURTEEN

K.O.

K.O.'s motel room looked as if it had been ransacked. Clothes—shoes, jackets, and underwear included—were scattered all over the floor, along with blankets and the bedspread. Carli's suitcase was still near the door, unopened. Herbie, Milan's ungainly but ultimately lovable dog, was busy examining a room he'd never visited before, sniffing everything that was new to him. He didn't even notice he was dragging his leash behind him, as neither K.O. nor Carli had made any effort to unclip it for him.

They were busy, all wrapped up in one another under the sheet. They'd barely had time to say hello when she arrived shortly after twelve. Within two minutes they were thrashing around, clothes flying, not caring whether anyone in the next motel room could hear them or not. At the home they shared, they often made love at night just before going to sleep, less occasionally in the morning when they were in a hurry to get somewhere. But a nooner in a dinky motel room was a new adventure for them both.

"Wow," Carli whispered.

"Was it that good?"

She laughed, snuggling into K.O.'s neck. "Sure—but the wow is that we've only been apart two days. We tore each other's clothes off like we hadn't seen each other in a year."

"It felt like a year," K.O. said.

"You didn't even say hello to Herbie when we came in."

"I had other things on my mind." He rolled over, his hand trailing almost to the floor. "Hey, guy, how ya doin'?" Herbie approached and licked his fingers. "Do I have to get out of bed now and walk him?"

"I took him for a walk before we came in. And I brought his food and water dishes, but they're still in the car."

K.O. grinned. "I hope he pooped right where Feelo Ackerman will step in it."

"Who's Feelo?"

"Philo—Philo Ackerman. He's the manager of this place." He tapped the bed between them. "He's a complete asshole."

"Is he the murderer you're looking for?" Carli asked.

"Probably not—but if he steps in dog shit, it'd make my day."

She pushed herself up so her back rested against the head-board, and pulled the sheet higher, tucking it under her arms, covering her breasts. Why do women hide their bodies after having sex, K.O. wondered. He'd seen every inch of Carli many times, including two minutes earlier.

He'd never understand women.

She said, "How's this case going?"

He put his hand out flat in front of him and tipped it back and forth. "So far nobody's confessed."

"Some killer is walking around free and you spent all this time in bed with me?"

"Priorities," K.O. said. "And I do have somebody to talk with later this afternoon."

"A suspect?"

"Everybody's a suspect."

"Even me?"

"Especially you." The top of Carli's head was against his cheek. He kissed her hair, inhaling the scent of her lavender shampoo, and she raised her chin so their lips brushed.

"Are we going to have any *fun* this weekend?" she asked. "Besides the fun we had already."

"I guess Milan and Tobe will suggest someplace to go."

"What're we going to do with Herbie?"

"He's Milan's dog, not mine."

"How'll he feel about that?" Carli said.

"Milan? Or Herbie?" K.O. took his arm out from under her, and shifted around in the bed to look at her. "We have to talk, Carli."

"Is this going to be bad?"

He paused. "Not—exactly."

"Okay—*what* exactly?"

"Well, first—tomorrow morning we're going to church."

"To get married?"

"That's not the only reason to go to a church."

"Oh, shit!" Carli said. "I hate going to churches. It bores me. We won't have to pray, will we?"

"No law says we have to. We'll get dirty looks, though."

"From the Prayer Police."

"Yeah." He ran a hand through his already-mussed hair and cleared his throat. "Uh—there's something else . . ."

He reached down, groping for Herbie without looking, but the dog had sighed and stretched out in a corner of the room, under the window. K.O. wished he had his own cat, Rodney, curled up on his lap; he'd feel more secure. "When you drove in about an hour ago, did you notice the McDonald's across the road from here?"

"I'm never looking for a McDonald's. Why?"

"It's right next to a Love's store."

She giggled. "Is that a store that sells dildos and edible underwear?"

"It's where truck drivers go to for snacks, T-shirts, and things like that." He stopped, floundering. How would he tell Carli about Kathy Pape the previous night? *Should* he tell her?

Finally he managed to get the words out: "Okay. So I met this girl who works there . . ."

Carli, who hadn't brought a robe with her for the weekend, had gotten out of bed shortly after K.O. began his so-called confession and slipped on a long T-shirt and her panties and sat in the chair by the desk. If she *had* to hear about the man she loved deep-throat-kissing another woman, she didn't want to be naked.

K.O. was still in bed, both pillows propped behind him. "I told her to go home. She was really cheesed off. She threatened she'd get even with me—but she *did* go home."

Carli said nothing.

K.O. would have sold his soul for one sip of water, but even though there was a half-finished bottle on the nightstand, he didn't touch it. He was miserable, even though he had done nothing to apologize for. "You *do* believe me, don't you?"

She considered that. "Was this Kathy a good kisser?"

He shook his head. "I didn't kiss back."

"Hmm. You're tougher than I thought you were."

"I am?"

She shrugged. "Why wouldn't I believe you?"

K.O. said, "Lots of guys cheat."

"Sure they do; it's easy. But I know you're not that kind of guy, and unless I miss my guess, you're not tired of *me*, yet."

"Yet? I'd never get tired of you," K.O. said earnestly. "You might get tired of me, though."

"I might. I might get hit by a bus next Thursday at three o'clock in the afternoon, too. But right now, you're my guy. So if that one kiss was innocent on your part, and it was all the fault of that horny, pushy bitch, then that's what it was. It was honest of you to tell me. It took guts. Now let's forget about it." She stood up and stretched; the flash of the flowered thong beneath the T-shirt discombobulated K.O. all over again. "Get your body out of bed; you have things to do this afternoon."

They dressed slowly, talking about other things, but there was still awkwardness between them. K.O. knew he'd done nothing wrong, and he chose to accept her belief in him. Still, he could tell by the set of Carli's jaw and the expression in her eyes that another element had entered into their relationship.

Seeds of jealousy are in everyone. K.O. felt it if any strange man struck up a conversation with Carli, even if only asking directions. He carried many insecurities with him; perhaps Carli had them, too.

But when they were ready to leave the room, Carli said, "You do what you have to. I'll be fine. I'll wander around the county, see the sights, maybe shop a little." She donned a lightweight jacket and then clipped the dog's leash onto his collar. "But we'll have to drop by and say hello to Milan and Tobe first."

"Why?"

"I'm returning Herbie to Milan. My dog-sitting days are finished."

*   *   *

John Aylesworth was in a saloon just a few steps from the
Ashtabula harbor. The bar was pleasant, more or less quiet at this
early hour of the afternoon. It was no "elegant cocktail lounge," but
it was nothing like the Corner Pocket. K.O. had asked around and
learned this saloon was where Aylesworth unwound after a long
shift cleaning up after prisoners who'd been *born* mean.

Aylesworth was drinking red wine—not the booze of choice
for most prison employees. But there were many wineries near
Geneva; wine was one of the unique amenities, other than the lake
itself, that brought tourists and visitors to the county.

Aylesworth slammed down wine as if it were boilermakers. He
wore a white shirt, top button open, with the sleeves probably
an inch or two longer than they should have been, to disguise
his bad hand. His daughter Mia very much resembled him, at
least around the eyes and in the stubborn chin. K.O. introduced
himself, extending his hand for a shake, which Aylesworth completely ignored. Finally, K.O. explained why he was in Ashtabula
in the first place.

Aylesworth's face became still, and he made a point of looking
into the back bar mirror rather than at the young man who'd sat
down next to him. "I don't know anything about any murders."

"Everybody in Queenstown knows about the murders, Mr.
Aylesworth, and the rest of the county, too. It's pretty big news
around here."

"Well, of course I know what happened . . ."

"I spoke to Mia today . . ."

"My daughter?" He angrily leveled a forefinger at K.O.'s face.
"You stay away from her, you hear me?"

Surprised, K.O. said, "She just pours my coffee."

The man fluttered his hand impotently in the air. "She doesn't
know anything about these killings, either. You don't need to be
hanging around her." He looked away, trying to ignore K.O.

"I didn't flirt with her. We just chatted, kind of aimlessly."
K.O. waved at the bartender and said he wanted whatever it was
Aylesworth was drinking. "Mia doesn't seem to like boys from her
high school much, does she?"

Now John Aylesworth's eyes half closed, and his face took on
a purplish hue. Anger turned to rage, and his voice, previously

loud, became a whispering hiss. "Those lousy little shits! Bastards! Scum of the earth! I hope they all *die!*"

That set K.O. back on his heels. "Why are you so angry with them?"

"I'm more angry with their parents, who've twisted and corrupted their minds from the shit they hear in their goddamn church—and Pastor Urban is the worst of them all. I hate every fucking one of 'em—and if I could . . ."

Aylesworth, probably talking louder than usual, began coughing and choking, accidentally swallowing air, struggling to get himself under control. Finally he stopped hacking and wiped his now teary eyes. "Forget it," he croaked, more to the bartender than to K.O. "I didn't mean that. I'm—just having a bad day, that's all." He cleared his throat, stood up straighter, and looked at his wristwatch, still not meeting K.O.'s eyes. "I'm sorry, I have lots to do tonight. I can't spend any more time with you. I'm—busy." He threw a fistful of cash on the bar, chugged down the last of his wine, and left hurriedly.

K.O. didn't know much about wine—or about *sipping*—but after his second taste, he decided not to waste his time with it. He had no way of knowing it was one of the cheaper Ashtabula County reds.

As he drove away, he decided to follow up again with the teens. John Aylesworth had one hell of a temper when he mentioned them.

As for the regular customers of the Corner Pocket, somebody was in on something, but wouldn't have cooperated with the police the previous evening in front of his buddies. If one of them didn't come forward, K.O. might return there and ask his own questions—and a Saturday night there would be even more rowdy than a Friday.

He stopped in the motel's front office to check for messages. He hadn't seen the woman behind the counter before. Her dyed-red hair was overpermed, her almost invisible brows had been filled in with a reddish-brown pencil, and she had one of those unremarkable flat faces one might forget within minutes. She had her own tacky name plaque on the desk in front of her: Mrs. Hiatt. No first name—unless, K.O. thought, her first name *was* Mrs.

"Where's Feelo today?" he asked.

"Who?"

"The man who's usually on duty."

"Oh—you mean Philo. Mr. Ackerman." Mrs. Hiatt wagged her head back and forth. "He generally takes Saturdays off. Saturdays and Mondays. And Sundays he doesn't come in until after lunch— he goes to church first."

Another churchgoer. Was "Feelo" in danger, too, without knowing it? For that matter, did Mrs. Hiatt attend a later service?

K.O. stopped at the drink machine for a Pepsi and took it back to his room. It was four thirty, now—Saturday business, and with it the work week, was slowing to a stop. He wondered where Carli was—and where Milan and Tobe were, too. That made him uneasy. In Greater Cleveland, he was loose, easy, confident in going off on his own. The more time he spent in Ashtabula County, the more he realized he was out of his element.

He crushed the now-empty can and tried to score a basket with it in the trash can on the other side of the room, but missed, and it clattered a few feet short of the mark. He went to fetch it and throw it away when a knock at the door startled him.

It was Carli.

"You never got me a key, Kevin," she said, brushing by him and into the room. "We got too busy too fast."

"You mean if I weren't here, you'd sit outside to wait for me?"

She peeled off her jacket and shook her head. "No way. I'd have just gone back to the McDonald's across the highway."

He didn't move, and he willed his face not to move, either. He didn't even dare take a breath. Finally he said, "Gone back?"

"I didn't have coffee. I wandered next door to Love's."

"Oh."

"Yep. Kathy's pretty hot," Carli said. "But you know that."

He had to swallow before he could speak. "She's—cute."

"I introduced myself. I think I surprised her."

"You talked to her?"

"Naturally."

"Carli, like I told you—"

"Oh, she told me, too," Carli said. "Told me all about it. How passionate it was. How the two of you fucked for hours."

"She's lying. She wasn't in this room for five minutes."

"Lying? Why would she lie? Is it just the fury of a woman scorned?" Then Carli laughed.

It took K.O. a few moments to react. Then he said, "Am I missing a joke?"

Carli flopped down on the bed. "I just asked her one question. After that, I wouldn't believe her answer, whatever she said."

"One question?"

"I just asked her whether you're circumcised."

"*What?*"

"The look on her face made me want to laugh."

Shaky, K.O. managed to sit down on the edge of the bed. "And what did she say?"

"Who cares? She had a fifty-fifty chance of being right, but it took her too long to answer."

"What did you say then?"

"Not much," Carli said. "Just that if she ever came near my man again, I'd rip every single dyed-blond hair out of her head and make her eat it. See? You're not the only big-shot alpha guy around here." She stretched luxuriously. "What time are we having dinner?"

He couldn't answer right away. He had to recalibrate his brain after hearing a conversation about his penis between two beautiful women. Life, he realized, has its complications. Finally he said, "Probably about six thirty or so. Why?"

"Why?" Carli said, and giggled. "*Why?* Kevin, are you just going to sit there on the edge of the bed, shocked right down to your toes—or shall we fill up the next hour in a more interesting way?"

CHAPTER FIFTEEN

MILAN

Thanks to our Internet search for a good restaurant, we discovered Biscotti's near the harbor, occupying a rehabbed building more than a century old. A pleasant meal with people I cared about; Tobe, K.O., Carli, and I hadn't shared a foursome dinner since the previous fall when we'd gone to the Northcoast Downs harness track with an ex-client who dropped dead on us between races.

Whatever had gone on the previous night with K.O. and Kathy Pape either hadn't been discussed, or he and Carli had toughed it out and moved on, because they mooned over each other now as if it were the third date between them rather than almost a year's anniversary of cohabiting.

K.O. said, "Do you suppose you guys can keep Carli company for a while this evening?"

"I don't even want to know why," Tobe said.

"I hope I can get one or two of those school guys talking one on one, when they aren't showing off for their buddies."

"Why can't *I* come with you?" Carli demanded.

"It could get unpleasant."

"I wouldn't let that happen," Tobe said. "I'm the only one around here with a badge and a gun—so I call the shots. Carli, you're not going anywhere near this investigation. You're our charming dinner partner, and I suppose you're K.O.'s love slave, too—or more likely vice versa—and that's it. So let's scout up a movie—or rent a DVD from one of those red boxes outside a supermarket."

"The trick in Ashtabula County," I said, "is *finding* a supermarket. Besides, Tobe, I have an errand of my own I'd prefer running all by myself."

"Are you driving back to Cleveland tonight?" she said.

"Not without you. But I plan on going back to the Corner Pocket in Conneaut—alone."

"Like hell you will! This is my case, Milan, not yours. You think I'll let you walk into that crap-hole by yourself—unarmed? They'll chew you up and spit you out before you finish your beer."

"It was you who got them going. This isn't Cleveland, Tobe, it's a shitty little bar in a small, struggling lake town that originally was 95 percent white before they built the prison, and if you go into the Corner Pocket again, with or without me, you'll wind up shooting somebody."

"So?"

I looked around in case any of the other diners were eavesdropping, but after their first startled gape at Tobe when we came in, they went about their business. "Someone in there knows about the victims, I'll bet you a million bucks on it. They're skeevy guys— but nobody wants to wake up dead in the morning, so they'll be hesitant to talk. At least one of them will—but they won't talk with you, Tobe. They'll just be thinking about new ways to piss you off."

"You're cutting me out of my own case?"

"Let's just say I'm going somewhere tonight without you."

Carli said, "You guys are dumping both of us!"

"Pretend," I said, "that we're both going to an all-male schvitz."

Tobe laughed, reaching over to squeeze Carli's hand. "Like there *is* a schvitz in Ashtabula County. It's just you and me now, Carli. Let's go back to the hotel, get some ice, all the pop we want, get into our jammies, and check to see if they have HBO."

"Jammies?" K.O. said.

"Did you have hot, crazy Saturday nights like this when you were twenty-five, Tobe?" Carli wanted to know.

"Let's wait until Milan and K.O. go away, and I'll tell you," Tobe half whispered. "Otherwise they'll both break down and cry."

At ten past eight, the Corner Pocket was already crowded and noisy. On a small-town Saturday night, if a bar wasn't bursting at the seams with people desperate to drink away their week and fall asleep to awaken the next morning with the mother of all hangovers, they might as well padlock the door and move somewhere else.

I had to shoulder my way in. It was lucky I was as big as I am, or they might not have let me in at all. The crowd didn't grow threateningly quiet as they had the night before when they first saw Tobe, but most recognized me, and buzzed about it amongst themselves, their muttering indistinguishable, like the yada-yada rumbling of a crowd of extras in the background of a movie. It was a longer walk than it looked from the door to the bar, because no one would step aside for me, and I had to walk around them. Their command of the English language apparently stopped before they got to the page that discussed the use of "Excuse me."

The same bartender saw me coming and planted himself right in front of me. Tonight he was wearing a sleeveless undershirt. From wrists up and neck down, he was thoroughly tattooed, and bushy black hair sprouted from his armpits like the wings of a raven.

Nevermore.

"Well, looky who's here. You didn't finish your beer," he said. "Tough shit, because I didn't save it for you—I figured you wouldn't be back."

"I wouldn't disappoint you, so here I am. I'll try another beer."

He shrugged. "That'll be twenty—up front."

"Twenty bucks for one beer? Your price has gone up since last night."

"It's like the stock market," he said. "Prices go up, and then they go down."

I was surprised he'd ever heard of the stock market. "When do they go down?"

"The minute you leave."

I fished a twenty from my pocket and slid it across the bar. "I guess I'm really thirsty, then." He tucked it into his pants and turned away to the cooler. I said, "Don't spit in my beer, okay?"

"Spitting in your beer costs extra," he said, bringing back a beer and opening it. I watched carefully that he didn't spit or do anything else in my beer bottle—no glasses this time. Then I turned my back on him, looked out at the room, and took a swig.

No one seemed ready to physically attack me. The T-shirt guy from the night before had returned. He wore the same jeans but had changed into a different shirt, this one reading ASS—THE OTHER VAGINA. He chose not to meet my eyes. *One* Corner Pocket coward, anyway.

Several of the others moved closer to me, though no one brandished a pool cue like a weapon. A young guy wearing a battered Pittsburgh Pirates cap came so close to my face that I worried he'd kiss me. His breath alone could have gotten me drunk. He wrinkled his nose, studying me, and then loudly announced, "Man, you're *old!*"

"When I wake up tomorrow," I said, "I'll still be old. But when *you* wake up, you'll just be the same dipshit you are right now."

"Wooh!" he said, swaggering, but he backed away from me, just in case.

The bartender said, "What's the big idea comin' in here and insulting my customers?"

Like any other bartender in the world, I was sure he had a club or a bat tucked away behind the bar with which to crush a misbehaving customer's skull. I chose not to face him, figuring he wouldn't hit me in the back of the head. "I just dropped in for this nice cold twenty-buck beer—and for somebody to talk to."

"The poor guy's lonesome," the bartender said. "Somebody tell him your life story."

A fiftyish, bearlike man came up behind me. With his wild, unkempt whiskers making him look like a stunt double who'd escaped from *Duck Dynasty*, he leaned over my shoulder, breathing into my ear. Beer and onions for supper. "How come you got nobody to talk to? You dump that nigger cunt you been fucking?"

I never count to three; it's far too obvious. *Everybody* counts to three. Instead I counted out two inside my head, and then ripped my elbow back as hard as I could, the point of it catching his neck, right under his chin. Wide-eyed, he slammed back against the bar as he tried holding on to the edge to keep himself upright. It didn't work; he slid to the floor in slow motion, his legs flat out in front of him as he clutched at his throat, gasping to breathe.

The soft buzzing turned ugly. Three men and one woman took a few steps closer to me, but that was as far as they got—for the moment. Nobody was afraid of me, despite my size, but they remembered from the previous night that Tobe was heeled. They might have thought I was a cop, too, with a weapon under my coat. I tried to ignore the pain in my elbow; my funny bone was tingling. When I was sure I hadn't killed him—I hate it when I kill people—I stepped away from the bar and into the center of the room.

"Three people were murdered in Queenstown," I said. "Some of you knew them. Maybe you liked them, maybe you didn't. The point is that somebody's on a killing spree. There's three down and who knows how many to go. They'll probably do it again, and one of you here tonight could be next. So if anyone's got anything to tell me—even the slightest piece of information might help. And check out your friend on the floor in case anyone decides to use the *n* word again."

Mumble mumble. Some exchanged glances, a few whispered, but nobody moved. One guy toward the back, holding a pool cue, said with contempt, "Fuck this guy! Come on, let's play!" He and his friend resumed their pool game. Nobody laughed, applauded, or stepped forward. I felt like an actor reciting Hamlet's soliloquy to an empty theater.

"It'd be a shame," I said, loud enough to cut through the jukebox noise, "for the state troopers to shut this bar down tight for—oh, let's see—health reasons? Serving drunks? Not breaking up fights before somebody gets hurt or killed? Allowing smoking in a public place in spite of the statewide ban? How many of you really *do* cook meth in your kitchen, probably just the other side of the wall from your kids' bedroom? The Highway Patrol will love that! *Oh*, and let's not forget twenty bucks for a bottle of Bud."

"Hey, man," the bartender whispered, not sounding threatening. I'm sure they all thought I was indeed a law officer, and I hoped nobody would ask to see my badge.

"Tell you what," I said, louder than before. "I'm going outside with my beer—which is illegal. I'll hang out by my car across the street for ten or fifteen minutes, if somebody wants to talk with me. Otherwise, cops will have arrest warrants and a padlock tomorrow morning, and bust up your meth labs by noon. Your call."

Of course, I was lying in the key of A-flat, hoping no one would know. Lifting my Bud in a silent toast to the bartender and receiving only a snarl in return, I pushed my way through the crowd to the door. They didn't block my way, but moved out of my path as if it were their idea in the first place. I found Tobe's car across the street, leaned against the fender, and tried sucking in a chestful of fresh air, nearly useless that close to the Corner Pocket, as the cigarette smoke and beer smell had drifted out to pollute the harbor atmosphere. I'd smoked more cigarettes than I care to remember until three years ago, when I quit cold turkey. After too many concussions in my life, my doctor told me to knock off the tobacco. No one is more obnoxious about smoke than an ex-smoker, and the stinky fog drifting from the Corner Pocket made me cough.

After a few minutes a woman came out, weaving slightly, a filtered Kool bobbing from her mouth, her unfettered breasts *almost* hanging out the sides of a sleeveless top. She slowed down, took a deep puff, and blew smoke in my direction.

"Fuck you, pig!" she said, and stumbled past me to her own car.

Pig. She didn't look old enough to remember that in the 1960s, when the war raged in Vietnam and people were just discovering the art of protest, law enforcement officers were called "pigs." Sad, too, because pigs are bright, highly sentient animals who do *not* love wallowing in mud, and are generally as intelligent as a human three-year-old. I'd thought that expression dissing cops had gone out of style decades ago—but apparently not at the Corner Pocket.

I turned in the direction of Lake Erie. The lake was especially beautiful in this semirural area, which was as wild and woolly as Tombstone, Dodge City, and Wichita had been more than a century earlier, when Wyatt Earp, Doc Holliday, and Bat Masterson were the fastest guns in the West.

Two men came out carrying their beers, looked up and down the street for me, and sauntered over to where I stood. One smoked a Camel and the other a fifty-cent cigar that smelled worse than anything else one could smoke. They both looked at me without saying anything. One of them, the cigarette guy, seemed reluctant, as if I were the last person in the world with whom he wanted to converse. He sighed and looked up at the sky, searching for the moon.

The cigar man said finally, "We wanna talk."

"I want to listen."

He shuffled his feet, and moved the cigar from one corner of his mouth to the other without using his hands. "Okay, then. Yeah, we knew the ones who got killed." He pronounced the last word "kilt," like a plaid garment worn by Scots. "Her not so much. The two guys, though—sure we knew 'em."

"Fontaine and Poole?"

He nodded. "Two living pricks."

"Why is that?"

"I don't think either of 'em could say a whole sentence without mentioning J. C."

"J. C.?"

Cigar said, "Where the fuck you been living, man? In a coal mine? J. C.—Jesus Christ."

"They talked about Jesus?"

Cigarette puffed, coughed, flipped the butt away; it scattered midair sparks until it hit the ground about ten feet away. "Sure they did, when they weren't talking about hating fags and hating nig—uh—minorities and hating the prez."

Cigar with a clarification: "President. Of the U.S.A."

"Thanks for explaining," I said.

"I gotta admit," Cigarette said, "we none of us are crazy about homos or black people either. Nothing against your partner or anything. Hate, though? We don't hate nobody—except maybe the Cleveland Browns, where you come from. We're Steelers fans."

"So," Cigar jumped in, finally taking the spit-soaked cigar butt from his mouth, "we didn't like those guys who got killed, or hang out with 'em, or with the broad, either. But if you're thinking it was *us* done it, you're full of horse puckey."

"I'm not looking for a confession," I said. "Just some help."

"People gettin' iced up here, it makes us all nervous. But don't get the idea we got much use for you, either."

"Yeah, cuz you're a cop," Cigarette said. "Cops always give us shit."

"Does Chief Koskinen give you shit?"

Cigarette snickered. "Nah. We don't have to drive home through his town when we've had a few too many."

"Which is damn near every night of the week," Cigar said, and they both yucked it up over that.

"Very amusing," I said, "but before you get too hammered—how did everyone around here get the idea to hate blacks and gays?"

"Maybe in the church," Cigarette offered. "I hear the preacher goes on and on about that."

"Reverend Urban?"

"Is that his name? I di'n' remember that. Jeez, man, do we look like two guys who go to church?"

"That would've been my second guess," I said. "All right, I know meth is a thriving business around here. Did the victims have anything to do with that?"

The two men conveyed a silent message between them. Then Cigarette said, "Hot damn! You poke a stick into *everything*. Stirring up a hornet's nest is what you're doin'." He glanced over his shoulder, but no one was coming out of the tavern. "Listen, as far as we know, none of them three people who got kilt cooked meth at home. Fontaine, though—hell, he makes a lotta money a lotta different ways, whether it's legal or . . . What word am I lookin' for?"

"Ethical?" I suggested. "Moral?"

"Let it go, why doncha?" Cigar said. "If you come back here, you're gonna step in it. We saw what you done to Harvey in there."

"Harvey?"

"With the big beard—the one you cold-cocked. But you ain't big enough to hold off thirty pissed-off drunks wanting to fight. They'll stomp you flat."

"Why would I want to fight?"

"Because," Cigarette said, lighting another one. "This is a small burg twenty steps south of nowhere, an' everybody knows everybody else. We don't like strangers, because it's our town—our *place*. What happens here is our business, and none a yours."

"Asking questions *is* my business," I said.

"And we answered enough of 'em," Cigar said. "Go ask someplace else."

"Like where?"

"Like back to Cleveland." He tossed his soaked cigar butt on the ground and smashed it dead with his heel. "Where you and your whore belong."

CHAPTER SIXTEEN

K.O.

K.O. parked his car near Ashtabula's downtown area, rolled down the windows to get a breath of fresh air off the lake a few blocks away, and wondered if he was wasting his time. There'd be many more interesting things to do on a Saturday night besides hanging around a half-dead city mini-park talking to teenaged punks.

Then again, it was Ashtabula County. There were social get-togethers and church dances, but not many places where a local kid could go to kick up his heels. Too far to drive to Cleveland, or in the other direction to Erie, Pennsylvania—not that K.O. had an idea of what Erie was like, having never been there. He recalled there had been little to do with his weekends before he entered the army and was shipped overseas to watch his buddies step on land mines—buddies too young to drink or vote or get anyone to listen to them or care what they said.

Coming back to Ohio after three years of eating sand and hauling around sixty pounds on his back, K.O. had felt lost and out of place. Three years in juvenile detention—in his father's day they used to call it "reform school"—and three foreign army tours that taught him to kill people apparently disqualified him from wearing a badge.

Then Suzanne Daniels, a private eye from Lake County, introduced him to Milan Jacovich, who had hired him full-time to get him his own private investigator's license. He could hardly wait to have that precious license laminated and stuffed into his wallet.

K.O. and Milan were not cut from the same cloth. Milan was mild-mannered and gentle, unless he was pushed. K.O. was an angry man, his simmering rage only millimeters beneath the skin. The two worked well together for the most part, but sometimes they bumped heads. Milan was the boss, and K.O. had a problem with anyone telling him what to do. But still in his mid-twenties, a stranger to college classrooms, and inexperienced in the profession in which he now found himself, he knew he still had much to learn.

He'd already learned a great deal from his boss and mentor—things like not losing his temper, not sulking, and the thing at which Milan was a light-heavyweight champ, the carefully placed sarcasm that often hurts worse than a punch in the mouth.

Then, of course, in one of his first cases, K.O. had met Carli Wysocki, and fallen hopelessly and completely in love.

On this particular Saturday night, Carli was having a good time someplace else with Tobe—possibly out exercising Milan's Herbie, who would invariably leave his personal signature on the grounds of the motel. K.O., missing Carli with more emotion than with lust, was sitting alone in his car near a sagging, half-empty park, waiting for any teenybopper creep from Queenstown High School wearing his pants six inches too low who would deign to talk with him. Any or all of them might decide this was a perfect time for a gang beat-down. K.O. could take two or three of them—but not all of them. On the other hand, there could be one who might—just might—cast a light on the triple murders.

Finally he walked around, stretching his muscles, waiting to feel that brief gust of lake air. Though more of a cat lover than a dog person, and though missing smoky gray Rodney, he found himself wishing he had Herbie with him at the end of a leash. At least Herbie would be someone to talk to—even if he didn't answer back.

K.O. saw a car at least a decade old heading toward the park, cruising to where the high school guys had congregated the other night. The headlights clicked off and the engine stilled. Through the windshield, the flame of a Zippo lighter illuminated the face of Jason Fontaine, who sucked in all the smoke from his Camel and didn't exhale it until he'd gotten out of the car, leaning against the front fender, waiting for his pals to arrive. He was startled when K.O. approached him.

"Gonna hang around with us again?" Jason demanded. "Bad idea. We're sick of you already."

K.O. said, "I want to talk with all of you, one on one."

"Man, I got nothing to tell you. I didn't kill my own father! I didn't like him, and pretty much ignored him, or tuned him out if he yammered at me—but he was my father." He hunched his shoulders against a chill wind that wasn't there, shivering. "If I knew who did kill him, I might take the law into my own hands."

"Don't be dumb and get yourself killed, too. If you know, go to the police."

"Go to Koskinen? Don't make me laugh, okay?"

"Talk to me, then."

"You're no cop."

"Close enough," K.O. said. "I'm a private eye in training."

"Why are you here?"

K.O. shrugged. "Koskinen couldn't handle multiple killings, and I can't blame him. Queenstown isn't Detroit."

Jason sucked on his Camel and blew the smoke out through his nose. "But why talk to me? I'm supposed to be crying my eyes out because I'm a half orphan. I don't know anything."

"You said your dad had lots of enemies."

"Everybody's got enemies, him more than most. But nobody hated him enough to . . ." He stopped, shoulders heaving with a sigh. "Well, I guess somebody did hate him enough," he said quietly.

"Jason, your dad dealt with lots of people who resented him." Jason began to protest, but K.O. held up a hand. "I know about his horse deals. I know he sold horsemeat to the prison and the cons were supposed to think it was beef. What about meth?"

Jason looked puzzled. "Methamphetamine? Look, man, I drink too much and I do too much weed. But meth? I wouldn't touch it. That fucks you up good."

"We're not here about meth or weed or crack or any other drugs, okay? That's not our job."

"What is your job, then?"

"We're with Detective Sergeant Tobe Blaine of Cleveland Homicide. Did your dad have anything to do with the meth trade?"

Jason looked away, over K.O.'s shoulder. "I doubt it. Look, lots of parents are understanding about dope. Some of 'em even give parties for us teens and let us drink or smoke weed in their homes, and the cops know and don't do squat about it." Smiling. "They probably smoke it themselves."

"Did your parents give parties like that, Jason?"

Long pause. Then: "Sometimes."

K.O. said, "Was your father supplying the drugs?"

"Hell, I don't know how he made his money. I know he was raising horses, but . . ."

"Jason," K.O. said, "you're living in some alternate heaven. I know your dad didn't cook Chunky Love in your mom's kitchen, but he might have been the middle man—a broker. And if that's even close to true, maybe he pissed off some of the big guys, just like the farm customers he screwed over." K.O. paused to swallow. "Nobody'd want the meth crowd mad at them."

Jason shifted from one foot to the other, considering. "Even if he did, Cordis Poole and Annie Jokela wouldn't've had anything to do with any drug. They were so damn straight that you could slide 'em under the door. Annie'd send a girl home from school if her jeans were too tight and you could tell where her panty line was, or she'd give detention to a guy who needed a haircut. And Cordis Senior? If you asked him what the weather was like, he'd quote some chapter and verse out of the New Testament. Neither of them would talk to a meth cooker, much less sell their shit for them."

"Who're the meth cookers in Conneaut or Queenstown?"

"I'm tellin' you, man, I don't know."

K.O. would have pushed him further if not for the arrival of another car, which pulled up beside Jason's. Cord Poole unwound himself from beneath the wheel and slid out of the car. On the passenger side, Patty, wearing darker Goth makeup complete with a black-handled dagger stuck into the waistband of her black jeans, lit up a long, skinny black cigar before she wriggled out and stood next to Cord, one hand perched on her cocked hip. Her eyes, outlined in kohl, burned into K.O.'s.

"You buyin' us dinner again tonight, K.C.?" she purred.

"It's K.O. And no, I'm not."

She wrinkled her nose. "Then go fuck yourself," she spat, words following her cigar smoke, and she strolled off, buttocks undulating beneath her jeans.

Cord said, "We're done talking to you, man. Understand? We're tired of it. Tired of you."

"Tired of us trying to find out who killed your father?"

"Let it go!"

"Your father and my father, too," Jason Fontaine said. "Take it easy, Cord."

"It's too late to take it easy!" Cord came close, shaking a fist under K.O.'s nose. "I don't wanna see you around here again. If you're not out of town by tomorrow morning, I'm gonna make you fucking sorry you were ever born."

K.O. turned his head slightly away and stepped back. "Why wait until morning?" he said.

It was all Cordis Poole Junior needed to hear. Roaring "Fuck you," he led with a right uppercut, his fist beginning below his hip and traveling upward. K.O. sidestepped easily, and while Cord was momentarily off balance, hit him with a clubbing, overhand punch, pushing off his back leg and twisting his hips for more power. The side of his doubled-up hand hit the top of Cord's shoulder so hard that it dropped him to his knees. Then K.O. kneed him in the face. When Cord tipped over and sprawled on his back, K.O. was over him, the heel of his shoe pressing against his Adam's apple. Cord twitched beneath K.O.'s foot like a goldfish who'd leaped out of his bowl onto the floor.

"Don't get up, Cord," K.O. said. He wasn't out of breath, and his face was barely flushed.

Jason had watched in silence. K.O. wondered if he'd have to fight both of them, but Jason was just observing. Now he moved forward and said, "Take your heel off his neck. He's through."

Jason knelt next to his friend, speaking too low for K.O. to hear him. Two minutes later he was able to help Cord to stand.

"He's all right," he said to K.O. "Banged up but okay."

"Are you going to take him somewhere," K.O. asked, "or is he planning for round two?"

"Not tonight." Jason Fontaine managed to get Cordis moving. "Stick around, okay? I'm not finished talking to you."

"Best news I've heard tonight." K.O. moved out of the way as the two teens and Patty maneuvered past him toward whatever public restroom was open on the main street, shaking his head at himself. What was there about him, he wondered, that made people take a swing at him? He hadn't come here to fight, just to talk.

He waited. Finally, Jason Fontaine came back, alone.

"Patty will take care of him until he can drive. Y' know, Cord's not such a bad guy."

"He threw the first punch. I don't negotiate with a guy trying to deck me."

"I'm not going to swing at you."

"Good choice."

Jason battled with himself for a long moment, searching for the right words. K.O. waited patiently. It's not as if there were anywhere else he had to be.

Jason said, "Could we walk? I need to move."

They strolled counterclockwise around the park. Jason offered a cigarette to K.O., who shook his head at one vice he'd always avoided. Jason fired up, took a deep puff, and coughed.

"This isn't easy," he said. "Look, I loved my dad. I didn't like him, but I loved him. You get that?"

K.O. did not get it. He didn't love his own father, didn't like him, hardly thought about him—and barely remembered his mother. But he loved Carli, as much as someone who'd never been in love before could. He loved his Russian blue cat, Rodney. And he loved the men and women with whom he had soldiered in Iraq and Afghanistan. They were his brothers and sisters in war, and he loved each of them equally, even if he couldn't remember most of their names.

He remembered the names of the ones who didn't make it home, though.

"I doubt my dad was anywhere near the drug trade," Jason went on, "but he knew people who knew people, if you get my drift."

"Are you going to 'drift' into a name, Jason? Otherwise, I'm just wasting time—and Cordis got beat on for nothing."

They were still walking, and even though they weren't near

anyone who might hear them, Jason glanced furtively around. Then he said, "There's a family, see? Their house is right on the river, out near all those wineries just outside Geneva. The old man—he must be around fifty or so—is Bobby Jeff McInerny, and his boys are Jimmy John and Wyatt. They're bad fuckin' news."

"They cook meth in their kitchen?"

Jason shrugged. "I couldn't tell you for sure. Mrs. McInerny took off a long time ago, so I don't know what those guys use the kitchen for. You hear things, though."

"Bobby Jeff, Wyatt, and Jimmy John McInerny."

"Right." Jason stopped walking. "You're not gonna go out there by yourself, are you?"

"Why? Do they shoot first and say hello later?"

"Sure, they have guns. They shoot ducks and wild turkeys—deer, too. Sometimes they shoot stray cats, just for the fun of it."

K.O. felt his insides twist. "Cats, huh?"

"Like I said, they're skeevy pricks. You're going out there?"

"Tomorrow," K.O. said. "After church."

CHAPTER SEVENTEEN

MILAN

Sunday morning was overcast, cooler than the past few days. None of us was dressed-for-church elegant. I wore no tie; Tobe thinks they're all ugly. K.O.'s only jacket had a zipper on it. Tobe wore slacks and a tailored vest. Carli's khaki Dockers, enhanced by a bright red shirt, would have made her the most looked at of all of us, if not for Tobe, who would've received less attention from the congregation if she'd arrived as a twin sister of E.T. There were at least three hundred worshippers in attendance, with a few over eighty and even fewer under forty. They were all Caucasian, and obviously shocked by the appearance of all of us.

A man wearing a sports coat and patterned shirt with no tie, who seemed to be looking for us, came forward in the lobby and shook my hand—not Tobe's or anyone else's—and said we were more than welcome to the church. He gave me a six-page brochure about what the church *does*, suggested we stay around after the sermon for coffee and cookies, and introduced himself as Tom Brady. I don't think, however—with his potbelly, his thick glasses, and his hair, which was disappearing faster than mine—that he was the quarterback for the New England Patriots.

An elderly lady with cotton-white hair and pink cheeks looking as if they'd just been pinched guided us to a pew about two-thirds of the way back, next to a young man who resembled the Sheldon Cooper character on *The Big Bang Theory*. I couldn't tell whether the woman with him was his wife, his girlfriend, his mother, or someone he'd picked up twenty minutes earlier at a Burger King.

Whoever she was, her T-shirt must have been purchased at a Discount Drug Mart. She looked profoundly uncomfortable with him.

I couldn't miss Philo Ackerman. The motel manager, who disliked us even more than we disliked him, was sitting between a woman one might forget thirty seconds after seeing her—perhaps Mrs. Feelo—and a geeky early-teen boy who looked just like him. Ackerman seemed surprised when he saw us. He clearly hadn't expected to find us in a Sunday go-to-meetin' at his Baptist church.

They began the ten thirty service singing songs from the hymn book, led by the assistant pastor, a woman whose name I didn't catch. She beseeched us to stand, of course, and everyone sneaked a glance at Tobe as they rose. Tobe met their eyes defiantly—she never allowed anyone to outstare her.

The assistant pastor was in her late sixties and seventy pounds overweight. She didn't look like a murderer—but one never knows.

I'd never heard the hymns before, but was more interested in the parishioners, who didn't look as pious as I thought they might. They seemed anxious and nervous. The third member of this congregation to die violently—Annikki Jokela—hadn't even been buried yet. They might be right to worry; was one of them targeted to go next?

Tobe had actually opened the hymn book, but I could tell she was on the wrong page. She was busy checking the faces around her. She pretended to sing, moving her lips but not making a sound.

It occurred to me that Tobe and I had been lovers for almost two years, and I had no clue as to whether or not she *could* sing.

Everyone else bellowed merrily, though none would qualify for the Mormon Tabernacle Choir. Many waved one or both hands around in the air, some in rhythm and some not—almost like kids in school, raising their hands, hopeful that God would notice them. Most wavers were women, but one octogenarian man in the front row was rockin' hard.

After everyone replaced their hymn books in the pews and sat down, the woman gave a short talk about various scheduled activities. What got my attention was an announcement of a monthly meeting for teenagers who, she said firmly, were "pro-life." I guess if you were "pro-choice," you wouldn't be admitted. Rather like sending out an open call for only people with blue eyes, or liver-and-onions lovers, or those with master's degrees in paleontology.

When she completed reporting the church "business" topics, she offered a short prayer. When she finished, I managed to say "Amen," and felt silly afterwards.

Then Pastor Thomas Nelson Urban Junior stepped up to the podium, a microphone and earpiece at the side of his face like the one always worn by the title actor in *Phantom of the Opera*. He'd traded his gardening outfit for khaki Dockers and a pink dress shirt, open at the neck so a yellow T-shirt peeked through.

I whispered to Tobe, "Some new kind of preacher drag! I'd expected him to be in an all-white suit."

She hissed back, "He's a Baptist minister, not Wayne Newton."

Urban began by welcoming all first-timers to the church. Then he zeroed in on us. "We have *official* visitors here, all the way from Cleveland. They've come to assist our local police in solving the shocking mystery of who foully murdered three of our own parishioners. I'm sure you knew all of them: Cordis Poole Senior, Paul Fontaine, and our beloved Annie Jokela."

I tried to remember from what Shakespeare masterpiece Urban poached "foully murdered." Every great quote we've ever heard in our lives comes from Shakespeare.

And then Urban said, "We thank you, friends from Cleveland, and pray for you all. Will you please stand so everyone here can see and appreciate you?"

I happened to look at K.O. as we were rising. I think he said, "Unfucking believable" under his breath. Everyone turned and stared at us, and I heard more than a few gasps from attendees who hadn't noticed Tobe earlier. Carli blushed; she wasn't used to being in the limelight.

There was a smattering of applause from somewhere, but it stopped quickly. Gratefully we resumed our seats. The preacher said, "We live in difficult times, my friends. I pray several times a day that this difficulty stops! We are Christians. We live in peace. We live within the embrace of Jesus Christ, our Lord and Savior, who loves us all and watches over us."

Jesus apparently hadn't watched over Poole and Fontaine and Annie Jokela, but Urban didn't remind anyone of that.

After a few more moments of clucking and tsk-ing over the murders, Urban began his sermon. It had a great deal to do with believing that every single word in the Bible is the word of God. He insisted the good book says we *must* support the church with both money and service, i.e., telling everybody we know all about the Gospels, presumably so *they'll* kick in a buck or two as well. He pointed out that whatever we have was given by God, and now it's our turn to pay it back. Urban said that when Jesus shows up to reign over the earth for the Millennium, he'll know if we didn't pay up front, and we'll be sentenced to wear crappy clothing and sweep up the streets or peel potatoes for the next thousand years.

"You've been warned," Urban told us. "This is your warning."

If we're smart, he said, we all should be on Jesus's side. "Well, you'd better be! Because some people," he said, beginning to thunder, "hate Jesus. Did you know that? They hate Jesus and they hate Christians. So they defy Jesus by sinning." He sighed. "Well, we're all sinners, we know that. But I'm talking *big* sins. Murder is a sin. Abortion is *murder,* and therefore a sin. Loose women and the men who use them actually roll and sweat in carnal sin. And those who know the Bible forbids a man lying with another man— and that goes for women, too—they go ahead and do it anyway, because they *hate* Jesus. Homosexuals—" and Urban carefully pronounced every syllable—"hate Jesus!"

"So you know what y'all should do, friends? Abortion should lead to arrest and prosecution. If you know anyone who's done that, report them to the local police! You know any loose women who've had carnal relations outside of their marriage? Shun them! Turn them away. Don't speak to them or associate with them, because their filth touches all of us. Homosexuals?" Urban over-pronounced it again. "If you have a child who's sometimes exhibiting homo behaviors, like boys flouncing around, or playing with dolls, or having a limp wrist or something like that? *Punch* him! Punch him right in the face, *hard*! Same goes for a little girl who plays with trucks, and dresses like a boy all the time. Every time you see them do that, punch them again—and each time explain *why* they're being punched.

"If they're too big to punch, humiliate them. Make fun of them.

Embarrass them in front of everyone, and make your friends humiliate them, too. Because being a homo, friends, is a sin!"

Tobe whispered to me, but I'm sure several people seated close to us heard her, since they turned to glare wickedly: "I'm ready to puke!" Even Pastor Urban, who was too far away to hear the words, caught the attitude and looked directly at the four of us.

After what seemed like a lifetime, he once again urged us to thank Jesus for taking care of the three murder victims now in heaven who'd belonged to the church. And then finally—*finally*—the sermon was over, the last hymn was sung, the last short prayer thanking God was intoned, and it was time to leave. We didn't get away cleanly, though. Pastor Thomas Nelson Urban Junior made it out to the lobby quickly, and stopped us at the front door.

"Surprised to see you this morning," he said, rubbing his hands together. He'd worked up a sweat, and downwind of him we were instantly aware of it. "If you're ever in the neighborhood again, you're always welcome at this church. You're welcome to love God."

He was extra polite, but he never looked at Tobe. Not once!

As we headed out to the parking lot, Philo Ackerman waved at us and came rushing over, leaving his wife behind.

"I didn't know you were coming here," he whispered. "I would have told you not to."

"Why?"

His shoulders were raised as if to hide his face from others as he glanced surreptitiously at his fellow parishioners heading for their vehicles. "This is not like a lot of other churches. They have—funny ideas. Difficult ideas. I'm sure you heard some of them just now."

"Why don't you find another church?"

He looked as if he might cry. "I'm a businessman," he said. "Being a churchgoer around here is just good business. I just don't think it's good business for you."

"No?"

He shook his head. "Forgive me for bothering you. I know you don't much like me—and frankly, I don't like you, either. But I wouldn't want to see any of you get hurt or anything." He sucked in more air than I dreamed he could, and said, "I've got to get back to my wife. Just be careful."

"Thank you, Philo," I said, pronouncing his first name correctly. "I appreciate your concern."

I watched him scurry away, faux-smiling and shaking hands with everyone. I couldn't help feeling a little sorry for him.

In the car, heading back to the motel, Carli Wysocki said, "If you guys ever make me go someplace again where I have to stand up and be stared at, I'm going to murder all of you."

"People stare at you all the time," K.O. hastened to assure her. "You're as pretty as any movie star."

"Right," she said. "The Wicked Witch of the West."

"I don't want to screw up your fantasy, Carli," Tobe said, "but they were mostly looking at me. Not because I'm any movie star— unless maybe Angela Bassett. I ruffled their feathers."

"We noticed." K.O. leaned forward from the back seat. "Other than that church being a bigot hotbed, did we learn anything today?"

I announced, "I have a theory. Pastor Urban . . ."

"*Junior*," Tobe said.

"Junior. Pastor Urban Junior, and presumably everyone who goes to that church, thinks abortion is murder. Secondly—they have no use at all for 'loose women.'"

"Then this should be a ghost town," K.O. suggested.

"Not seeing one single black face in that church besides Tobe's tells me bigotry and racism runs pretty deep," I said. "Therefore . . ."

"Colonel Mustard did it in the library with a candlestick," Carli giggled. K.O. looked bamboozled. All his years in juvie and then in Middle East combat, and he'd never played the game of Clue.

"Maybe the killer, or killers, have a hard-on for that church and its members," I said. "These holy holies walk around with a big target on their backs. And who's wearing the biggest target of all?"

"Pastor Urban!" K.O. and Tobe chorused it together.

"*Junior*," I said.

CHAPTER EIGHTEEN

MILAN

Joe Platko was on duty at the Queenstown police department because it was not a good day for Eino Koskinen to be hanging around his office—not in his state of mind. It's sad that not everyone whose loved ones are taken by death is given the same consideration, nor the time for grief, as someone who's legally part of the family.

"Bobby Jeff McInerny," Platko repeated when K.O. and I mentioned his name. "Scraping the bottom of the barrel, are you? You think he's the serial killer?"

"If we thought that, we'd march in there with the Bureau of Criminal Investigation or the Highway Patrol," I said. "The McInernys *do* cook meth, don't they?"

Platko shook his head. "It'd be unethical for me to tell you. You're not police officers."

"Detective Sergeant Blaine is a police officer."

Platko said, "But she's not here." He settled back in what was usually Eino Koskinen's chair. "You don't seem to understand the police don't talk about open cases to *civilians*."

"I've been a licensed private investigator for most of my adult life," I said. "Before that, I was a Cleveland police officer. And before *that*, I was a United States Army military policeman in Saigon, ducking Vietcong snipers shooting at me before you were even an infant sitting in your own shit. Detective Sergeant Blaine was assigned here by the Cleveland chief of detectives, and she's asked experienced investigators like Mr. O'Bannion and me to accompany her—to help *you*." I threw one haunch over the corner of his desk. "So I'll ask you again, is the McInerny family cooking and distributing methamphetamine in their kitchen?"

Platko nervously reached up to fiddle with the open collar of his uniform shirt. "Well—yeah, I suppose so. I haven't actually seen them do it, though."

"So," K.O. said, "this department just doesn't give a damn?"

"It's not that at all!" Platko got defensive. "We're a three-man department. We can't go arresting everybody because they might have—illegal tendencies, especially if they don't live in our village. We worry more about serious crimes, like rape. Or murder."

"When's the last time," K.O. asked, "you had a rape here in Queenstown?"

"Uhh . . ." Platko gave a quick glance at the file cabinet. "A long time ago. Maybe ten, fifteen years."

"Before Paul J. Fontaine, when was the last Queenstown murder?"

Again, Platko looked stricken. "I—don't think there's been a murder here since the nineteenth century."

K.O. observed, "You don't bother drug dealers because you're too busy solving serious crimes that never happen?"

"This is a peaceful town, and we like it that way. If bad shit goes down in Geneva or Conneaut, that's their problem, not ours."

"We won't talk to Bobby Jeff McInerny about cooking meth. We're going to ask him about murder," I said. "Are you going to give us his home address, Officer Platko? Or not?"

Tobe had decided she'd spend the day trying to talk more to the widows, Gwen Poole and Maude Fontaine. Neither of them had shown up for church services that morning. That meant K.O. and I were on our own that afternoon.

The McInerny farm wasn't much of a farm at all. I could see nothing planted anywhere, which was strange, I thought, on a road where farms and vineyards were common. At one side of the house, set back about two hundred feet, was a falling-down shack, surrounded by chicken wire, and from the sound and smell, it was indeed occupied by chickens. From its look, it wasn't the Ritz-Carlton of chicken coops.

The house itself was unkempt and disheveled, probably not painted for at least two decades, its roof carelessly patched. Two of the windows were broken, and the cracks had been "fixed" with duct tape. On a May day when the temperature was somewhere close to seventy degrees, smoke poured from the chimney.

A huge dog the color of a pair of worn-out Dockers was hooked to a relatively long chain attached to one of the pillars of the bedraggled porch whose swaybacked floor swooped in on itself in the middle. One of the four wooden steps was broken in half. The dog, reclining in the dirt amidst his own droppings, was nearly as big as I am—some sort of patchwork made up partly of rottweiler, mastiff, possibly Saint Bernard or Newfoundland. My dog Herbie, a pit bull mix, was not exactly exalted for his beauty, but compared to the giant dog guarding the McInerny manse, he could have won the Westminster Kennel Club Best in Show.

When K.O. and I got out of the car, the dog rose on all fours, arching his back and lowering his head. He didn't bark. Shaggy hair stood up all around his neck, though, and he treated us to a scary view of sharp yellow teeth. His low rumble of a warning growl reached us from thirty feet away.

K.O. mumbled out of the side of his mouth, "That's the first animal I've ever seen that makes me nervous."

"I bet he's a sweetheart if you throw balls for him to chase."

"Whose balls?"

From behind the chicken coop appeared a young man with an old rifle. It might have been made in 1878, but that didn't make it any less threatening, since it was pointed right at us. The man himself was nearly as tall as me, but easily weighed seventy pounds less. His deep-set eyes were as empty as a haunted house.

"Welcome wagon," K.O. said quietly.

I nodded. Then I waved at the young man and called out: "Wyatt? Wyatt McInerny?"

The young man shook his head. "I'm Jimmy John McInerny."

I had to wonder where the family came up with the name "Jimmy John." Hopefully not inspired by the chain of gourmet sandwich restaurants, nor by the man who owns those restaurants and brags of having fun shooting African elephants for "trophies." Because this particular Jimmy John looked as if he hadn't eaten since a week ago Thursday.

Wyatt, the other brother, came around from the back of the house and was armed, too—with a much newer weapon, some sort of Glock handgun, and also pointed at us. Another skinny-minnie, somewhere in his mid-twenties, although he looked twice his age. Habitual use of meth does that to you, although it looked like if anything swallowed, smoked, inhaled, or injected, Wyatt McInerny had made it his full-time hobby. His eyes were not empty at all; demons lurked behind them.

"Think they'll shoot two unarmed men?" K.O. whispered.

"No. They look like such nice people."

Emerging from the front door of the house onto the sagging porch was Bobby Jeff McInerny. Both boys closely resembled their sire—but if you've seen *one* McInerny . . .

Bobby Jeff wore faded overalls with no shirt, and probably no underwear. I chose not to think of where he might be carrying a gun.

"Y'all's trespassin'," Bobby Jeff said, his voice a crow's caw. "You kin walk off'n my propitty now, else you stay *on* my propitty for the rest of eternity."

"We mean you no harm," I said. "We just want to talk to you. We're from Cleveland—"

"I know who's y'are and where y'all's from."

K.O. whispered, "Who told him about us?"

"Three guesses." I raised my voice. "We're not police, and we don't care what you do for a living." I held both arms out to my sides, hands open. "We're not armed, either."

"You're damn lucky sons a bitches, then. Why you here botherin' us?"

"If your boys put up their guns, we'll tell you."

It took Bobby Jeff a while to decide, almost as if he was agonizing over which brand of canned corn to buy. Finally a jerk of his head, and his sons reluctantly lowered their weapons.

He came down off the porch, moving toward us. The dog, no longer growling, apparently got in his way, because Bobby Jeff sent him scurrying with a kick to the ribs, eliciting a yelp of pain. K.O. tensed next to me.

"Let it go," I said softly.

Wyatt and Jimmy John stayed where they were. The dog slunk

back toward the house and lay down noisily in the shadow of the porch. Bobby Jeff stood in front of us. It was obvious he'd been nowhere near a bath recently. Fists on hips, he squinted at us through one half-closed eye. "So talk," he ordered.

K.O. took the lead. "You were friends with Paul Fontaine."

"Knew him. Weren't friends, though. I don't got no friends."

"Understood," K.O. said, and McInerny didn't catch his sarcasm. "You were in business with him?"

"In bidness?" McInerny snorted, hawked, and spit. "Do I look like some banker to you? Me an' him, we had a couple things goin' once in a while, but we weren't no partners nor nothin'."

"Did he cheat you?" K.O. pushed. "Did you hate him for it?"

"He cheated some, like ev'yone else cheats. But I didn' hate him, nor nobody else. I don' get mad, young feller. I get even."

"Well, somebody hated him," I said. "Enough to stick a knife in his heart."

"Sumbitch didn' *have* no heart," Bobby Jeff said, "but it weren't me that stuck him."

"Who did, then?" K.O. asked.

"That what you come out here to ask me? Who done it? How'm I s'pose to know that?"

"How did you know who we were?" I said.

"Think I live in a cave? I got a telephone, y'know. Ev'ybody in town got a telephone! We all know about you."

"Mr. McInerny," K.O. said, trying not to glance at the two sons, who no longer pointed their guns at us but still held them at their sides, "we're hoping you can shed some light about Fontaine. There must be somebody in town who wanted him out of the way. Maybe you know who that somebody is."

"Most folks hated him. Screwed everybody. Screwed me, too, but it was small pertaters."

It took me a moment to figure out *pertaters* meant *potatoes*. I said, "Fontaine was involved in your business?"

McInerny twitched. "He was—a customer."

"Fontaine did meth?" K.O. said.

"Naw. He was a nutcase Jesus guy, he went to that church all a time, an' he never touched no drugs. I think he bought it an' sold it to somebody else."

"Somebody who didn't have the balls to buy it himself?"

"Didn' ask, didn' care." He cocked his head. "You-all were at that church today, right?"

K.O. and I exchanged quick glances. McInerny had at least one thing right: everybody in this part of Ashtabula County knew who we were and what we did.

"That hadda be funny. That preacher, he hates just about ev'ybody—big city people like you, faggots, abortion docs, women in general, even children. I bet when he saw your colored woman, he musta shit a brick. He ain't no big fan of the coloreds."

K.O. said, "You got a phone call about us today already?"

Bobby Jeff McInerny preened, sounding almost proud. "I got a hell of a lot more than one phone call, pal."

We headed back toward the motel in K.O.'s car. I hadn't been behind the steering wheel of a car for several days, which I found pleasant. The view is much better when someone else is driving.

K.O. said, "I didn't know we had hillbillies in Ohio."

"They're in New York City, too. So, if Fontaine never used drugs but bought meth from McInerny, who was he buying for?"

"Could be anybody."

"Everyone in town knows where they can get meth, or any other kind of drug. If it's not from Bobby Jeff, then from somebody in the Corner Pocket or somewhere else."

I let it hang until K.O. said, "Somebody in jail?"

"Bingo! There are a few hundred men in that prison, but Fontaine didn't sell dope to some down-in-the-dumps schmuck who got put away for smoking boo. It had to be some con who actually runs the joint from the inside."

"The prison boss."

I nodded. "The Prophet."

CHAPTER NINETEEN

K.O.

It was nearly impossible to find a decent restaurant in the immediate vicinity that was open on Sunday. The Cleveland trio considered a trip back to Lake County for some good food and pleasant surroundings in Mentor, but it had been a long day, and they all were tired. K.O. drove to Geneva-on-the-Lake and picked up two pizzas from a so-called Italian restaurant that was painted lime green, inside and out, and back at the motel, they feasted in Milan and Tobe's room. There was a historic pizzeria in Conneaut, Pizzi's, in the same location for almost eighty years with possibly the best pizza anywhere outside New York City, but it was closed on Sunday.

K.O. watched Milan and Tobe side by side on the bed, their feet discreetly touching, and when they looked at each other, their feelings of affection were obvious. K.O. was jealous they would spend the night together and he, having waved good-bye to Carli right after church and even watching as her car disappeared down the road, would sleep alone.

It was a different kind of job than most men had. Working nine to five, Monday through Friday, two weeks off in the summertime, time-and-a-half for overtime, and coming home to the woman he loved every single night? He'd never hung out with other guys. He had never gone to ball games with them, or cruised singles bars, or played pickup basketball. He'd been lonely since childhood, and now that he'd found someone more important to him than his own life, he treasured every moment he could be with her.

Between bites, Tobe related her meetings with recent widows Gwen Poole and Maude Fontaine.

"When Gwen found out I'd been to Urban's church this morning, it was her first real laugh since Cordis got killed."

"She must have had an unhappy marriage," Milan said.

"Unhappy life." Tobe flipped open her notebook. From her shirt pocket she removed a pair of drug store reading glasses, popping them onto the end of her nose. "Cordis Senior was a big man, and he was strict about everything. Almost like someone from a Third World country who didn't want his wife ever talking to another man, for any reason, unless he was right there."

"No veil?" K.O. asked. "No burka that covers women from head to toe in some oil republic?"

"Well, he didn't go that far," Tobe said. "He did insist she wear long sleeves all the time, even in summer, always in a dress or a skirt, and minimal makeup. The only TV he let them watch besides sports was religious programming. Ernest Angley, Joel Osteen—and Cordis insisted they all watch."

K.O. said, "That sounds abusive to me."

Tobe continued, "Gwen said that when Junior was young, his father would punish him by making him kneel on the floor on sprinkles of hard, uncooked rice until his knees would bleed. When he got bigger, a smack in the mouth was the best way to control him."

Guilt tugged at K.O.'s guts. He rarely felt guilty, because he learned early to do what he had to do. But now he was sorry he'd roughed up Cordis Junior in the park. The kid had been hurt enough.

Milan said, "Gwen told you Cordis never abused *her*."

"Mental and emotional abuse," Tobe told him, "doesn't leave marks you can see, except maybe scars on the soul. There's one other thing I found out, which has nothing to do with the killings. When he wasn't going to church, or praying, preaching, or listening to Ernest Angley, Cordis played on his computer, cruising porn sites."

K.O.'s eyebrows jumped. "Porn? Kinky stuff?"

"I don't think so. The few times she caught him, he was watching straight old-fashioned fucking." Tobe chuckled. "She didn't use that particular word, though."

"Any man with a computer looks at porn *sometime*," K.O. said. "Do you?"

"Not since Carli and I have been living together. I'd rather die than have her walk in on me."

"Boys," Tobe said, "I still have lots to say about our other victim's widow."

"Mrs. Fontaine?"

She flipped over a page in her notebook; her handwriting was large and bold. On the job, she probably went through one notebook per day. "Maude Fontaine. She cries over her dear departed, but she wasn't that crazy about him."

"Why?" Milan said.

"Because he was a crook and a cheat. She knew it, and lived nicely on his ill-gotten gains, but it made her nuts every day of her life. And it disturbed her that he pranced around like the BFF of Jesus Christ at church, but was an anus the rest of the time."

"He must have been a good actor," K.O. said.

"He got pissed off on abortion, on gays, on race. And he constantly chased after women. Maude said she could even understand it if he had a mistress, but he'd jump on just about anything that moved."

"Names?" Milan said.

Tobe shook her head, put down her notebook, and reached for another slice of pizza. "She stopped short of naming names. She said there was no point in 'outing' the sluts now."

"Both Poole and Fontaine," K.O. mused, "were religious fanatics. One was a porn freak and one was a playa."

Tobe laughed. "Okay. Then explain Annikki Jokela."

"Jealous chief of police," Milan said, "who could've killed both men for messing around with his girlfriend, and then killed her, too, out of jealous rage."

"Koskinen was more messed up than that," Tobe said. "People shatter when someone they love is murdered. He's a broken man."

"So we're eliminating Koskinen altogether?"

"Unlikely—but possible."

"So is the Tooth Fairy," K.O. said. He reached for another slice of pepperoni, onions, and green peppers, wishing that legendary pizzeria in Conneaut had been open on Sundays. "What're the plans for tomorrow?"

"In the morning," Tobe said, "a chat with Koskinen. Then a second visit to the beautiful scenic prison. Maybe you could join us, K.O. You shouldn't miss this idyllic vacation spot."

"I've been in prison," he muttered.

Milan stopped chewing. "Did they keep you in shackles whenever you were out of your cell?"

"No, but . . ."

"If you had a visitor, did they chain your hands to the table?"

"I never had visitors!"

"Your cop mentor—Jake Foote—didn't he come to see you all the time?"

"That was different!"

"*This* is different," Tobe said severely. "I've been in uniform a long time, K.O. I've nailed murderers and rapists and child molesters and human traffickers who never went to a pussy juvie facility like you. You got to wear your own clothes. They sent you to classes. They let you play sports. You wouldn't know a real prison if it fell on you."

"You're on our side," Milan told him. "Remember? You're one of the good guys."

"Right," K.O. said. "I'm the good guy who goes to get the pizza." He shook his head bitterly. "And then you two guys snuggle up together all night long in a motel, and I have to go sleep alone."

"Well," Tobe said, "that *is* prison."

K.O. would have preferred a root canal to visiting the prison the next day. Too many memories that might never go away, like the sound of the lock on the juvie detention door at night, the morning roll call, the eyes of someone in authority drilling through him every waking moment.

A prison is a prison, Alcatraz or not.

He was still bummed that Carli had gone back to their apartment in Beachwood. She was the first woman with whom he'd ever cohabited, and he hated not being with her, even for a single night.

It's not that they had sex *all* the time. But for her to fall asleep with her head on his shoulder, or failing that, just drifting off as they held hands, was for him the most important thing in the world. For the first time in his life he was a vital part of someone else.

He walked on the highway for a while before turning in, hands in pockets, jacket zipped up to his neck against the cold breeze blowing off the lake. A passing car slowed, then stopped on the berm in front of him.

The driver opened his window and called, "Hey, you! Hold up there!" Two other men, one from the passenger seat and one from the backseat, got out. Big men.

One of them said, "What's the deal—you wandering around on foot in the middle of the night? Casing a joint so's you could rob it?"

"Why? Are you writing a book?"

"Don't get smart with us, punk," the other one growled.

"Getting smart with you is easy," K.O. said.

The driver climbed out of the car, and K.O. thought he might have seen him in church that morning, singing louder than anyone else. Maybe the other guys had been there, too. "You one o' those people from down in Cleveland, right?"

"I'm a Browns fan, if that's what you mean."

"You with the nigger woman and that old guy."

K.O. almost smiled. He wasn't sure which amused him more, coming from a perfect stranger: the racial slur to Tobe or the zing on Milan's age. He was glad neither of them were there to hear. "I'll be sure to give both of them your regards," he said.

The Don't-Get-Smart punk slowly moved to K.O.'s side, standing close. The driver said: "You fuckin' people are all over our town, stickin' your noses where they don't belong, causin' trouble."

"We don't cause trouble," K.O. said. "We look for it and then fix it."

The first one who'd spoken said, "You walk soft around here, or *you* gonna be the one that gets fixed."

"That sounds like a threat."

"We don't threaten people. We *do* it!" the driver said. Don't-Get-Smart grabbed both K.O.'s arms from behind him, and the driver drove his fist deep into K.O.'s stomach.

This was not K.O.'s first fight—not even close. From experience, he knew what was coming, and managed to tighten his stomach muscles so the blow, which hurt like hell anyway, didn't knock all the breath out of his body. He lifted one leg and raked the edge of his shoe heavily downward on the driver's shin, stripping much of the skin off his leg and then smashing into his foot. He snapped his head back and broke Don't-Get-Smart's nose with a loud crunch, which easily freed his arms as the man staggered, his hands up to stanch the sudden bleeding of his nose. Then K.O. took one step forward and kicked the driver in his stomach. When he howled in agony and bent over, clutching his gut, K.O. clubbed him on the back of his neck.

The third trio member came up quickly on K.O.'s blind side and hit him, hard, at the corner of his left eye, snapping his head around. Then he punched him in the kidneys, putting K.O. on his knees and in perfect position for the kick that would break a few ribs. But as his attacker's foot came up, K.O. captured it, twisted, and stood up with the man's leg in his hands so that he balanced on only one leg.

Then K.O. punched him in the testicles—a straight right-hand blow that traveled less than twelve inches, but the scream could have been heard across the Ohio–Pennsylvania state line.

K.O. had only hit someone like that once before, when he was fifteen years old and beating up the two kids who had roasted a stray dog alive inside a Weber Kettle. That punch probably sent him to juvenile detention faster than anything else he did to them that day, broken bones included.

Now one of his attackers was flat on the ground, blood gushing from his nose. One was *sitting* on the ground, grimacing as he attempted futilely to put his kneecap back where it belonged. And the third staggered about, moaning in the key of E above high C. Surprised and outnumbered, K.O. figured he'd done all right, despite the thin skin between the corner of his eye and his cheekbone being split open and dripping blood down the side of his face.

A permanent scar? He didn't know, nor did he care. He had quite a few scars already, but he didn't think anyone noticed them unless they got close. Even when she'd been close many times, Carli'd never asked about those scars.

He took a small pack of Kleenex from his pocket and pressed

one against the cut, looking once more at his vanquished foes. All were conscious, but none seemed anxious to continue the fight.

If they were packing heat, however, they just might shoot him in the back as he walked away.

His kidney aching from the sucker punch and the side of his face throbbing, he trudged back to his motel, probably five hundred yards or so from where the fight started. When he got into the room, he washed away the blood with soap and cold water so he could see in the mirror just how bad the injury was, and tried to stop the bleeding with a styptic pencil he'd brought from home.

Just in case he cut himself shaving.

CHAPTER TWENTY

MILAN

The first thing I did, even before breakfast, was to drive across the road to the Love's store to buy some big square bandages for K.O.'s injured face. K.O. begged me to go so he wouldn't run into Kathy Pape behind the counter.

She was there, all right, but she didn't know who I was, and considering my age, she didn't give a damn, either. Her wish that I have a nice day was approximately as sincere as "Y'all come back and see us, hear?" is in rural gas stations in Georgia.

Then I went next door to McDonald's and ordered three coffees to go from the attractive young woman K.O. had told me about, the one whose father worked directly inside the prison, mostly running a janitorial and maintenance service. I remembered her name was Mia, and also that she never smiled. She *tried*, but it was like smiling with an infected wisdom tooth. I thought if I worked at a fast-food joint for minimum-wage subsistence, I'd look sad, too.

I delivered one of the coffees to Tobe as she was getting dressed and then took the other two into K.O.'s room.

"I don't *know* who they were," K.O. told me for the tenth time or so as I was affixing the bandage just beyond his eye. "I might have seen them at church yesterday, or maybe not. I didn't memorize everybody's face. Whoever they were, they were coming after me."

"After the three of us," I said. "When they saw you alone, they figured to cut their odds a little and then hunt for Tobe and me later."

He winced at the pressure of my thumb on the plastic bandage. "I saved your lives, huh?"

"Not exactly. Tobe always carries a weapon."

"In bed?"

Fifteen minutes later we were in Tobe's car, heading for the Queenstown police station. She caught sight of K.O. in the rear-view mirror. "How're you doing, Scarface?"

K.O. extended his middle finger and spoke with a phony Al Pacino Cuban accent. "Say hello to my little friend."

"You suppose Chief Koskinen knows those guys who messed up K.O. last night?" I said.

"I've been thinking the same thing, Milan." Tobe took off her sunglasses, as the sky was still somewhat overcast, and hooked them into the opening of her jacket. "The chief says he's not religious, but the service we attended was at his late girlfriend's church. I don't know why he's pissed off at us trying to find the killer."

"These guys who jumped you, K.O.—they had no knife?" I said. "No weapon at all? You can't murder someone by punching them in the stomach."

"Probably right, Milan. And now, to change the subject just slightly . . ." K.O. leaned forward, his head between mine and Tobe's. "Do you think Koskinen knows the McInerny family cooks meth in their kitchen?"

Tobe said, "If I were the police chief around here, I'd damn well know about every drug lab in the county."

"Annie Jokela's funeral is tomorrow," I said. "Do we attend?"

"I won't go near that church again," K.O. said. "It creeps me out. And they'll pay more attention to Tobe than to the preacher."

Eino Koskinen was at his desk when we arrived at the police station. From the look of his reddened, sunken eyes and his almost blank stare, I doubted he'd slept much. On the desk, his mug was almost full, and I saw he'd spilled a few drops of coffee onto his shirt.

"You people," he said in the way of a greeting, "better hurry up and solve this goddamn thing before somebody else gets killed."

"You should be home, Chief," I said. "You're in mourning."

"I'm not *entitled* to 'mourn.' Besides, I'm one-third of this police department. I need to be here."

"You have the three of us," Tobe said. "I'm assigned—and Milan and K.O. are with me."

"Do what you want, then. I'm whipped." Koskinen resignedly shook his head. "I don't belong in this job anymore. No guts, no brains, no backbone. Why don't *you* take the job, Detective Blaine?"

"I already have a job, Chief—and I want to get back to it. That's why we're anxious to clean things up for you ASAP."

"So? What do you want from me?"

"Another phone call to the prison warden," I said. "We haven't finished with the Prophet."

Warden Glasser was annoyed the first time we visited the prison. On this trip he was downright furious.

No greeting at the door, as he'd done the first time. He summoned us to his office—and didn't invite us to sit down, either. "What do you think this is? A rest home for the elderly? It's a prison. These men are here because they broke the law. They're being punished! They don't *get* privileges, like getting hauled out of their cell to talk to complete strangers. They pay their debt to society, then they get released, and after that I don't give a damn what they do."

"Or what happens to them," Tobe said.

"Damn right! You're a police officer, you know better than anyone. You're one of the ones that put 'em in here in the first place."

"Maybe so, Warden—but they're human beings."

"Not to me, they're not!"

"No," I said. "To you, they're profit."

His enraged scowl could have fit some being threatening to hurl a vengeance-seeking lightning bolt at us. "Be careful what you say, Mr. Jacobson," he warned.

Jacobson again? I sighed.

"I can refuse to allow you on this facility. I can throw you the hell right out of here."

"Be my guest," said Tobe. "I'll just call the state attorney general and tell him we're investigating serial homicides and you refuse to cooperate. Within minutes he'll be up your ass faster than a proctologist."

He sputtered like oil dropped on a hot broiling pan, his face purple. I just grinned, K.O. muttered, "Wow!" under his breath, and Tobe stared the man down. Finally the warden picked up his desk phone and barked an order or two.

When he hung up, he said, "You got to stop coming here. You got to leave Elijah Jackson alone. He does his time and don't bother anybody. He don't know anything except what goes on in this prison, and that's nobody's business except mine. You'd best remember that." He looked at the wall clock. "Again, you got exactly fifteen minutes."

"Warden Glasser," Tobe said, "we'll take all the time we need, and you can't do a damn thing about it. Are you going to arrest me? I *am* a cop, and the prison guards in here are *not* cops. And I know so much about how you run this Devil's Island that with one phone call to the AG's office, you'll be sitting on the other side of these bars eating horsemeat for lunch. Just think about how glad your cons will be that you're one of *them*. I figure you'll last three weeks. Still want to stick with this fifteen-minute bullshit?" She looked at him until he tore his eyes away.

Within five minutes a prison guard appeared at the door of the warden's office to accompany us to the visiting room, glowering almost as darkly as the warden. It was a relatively cool morning, temperature in the high sixties, but there were half-moons of sweat stains under the arms of his prison-blue uniform. He marched ahead of us, his lower jaw extended and antagonistic.

Eventually he unlocked a steel door and led us down a long hallway. "Another two years," he murmured, shaking his head angrily, "and I can retire."

"Don't like your job?" K.O. said.

"Corrupt. Everything about this place is corrupt. The warden, the cons, the people who own it. And you know who's worst of all?"

"Who's that?"

"The guy you're visiting. The Prophet. I tell you, he scares the shit out of me—and he's all chained up." His heavy sigh almost emptied his lungs. He got us to the visiting room and unlocked the door, standing aside for us to enter.

Elijah Jackson was already there, colorful beads entwined in his Rastafarian curls and his beard. When he saw us—check that, when he saw *Tobe*—his smile lit up like a Christmas tree.

"Yowza!! My favorite cop! Couldn't stay away from me, could ya, sugar-buns?"

"I dream about you, Prophet," Tobe said.

"An' you brought your two boy toys along with you so they could watch! Hey, more's the merrier, *I* say." He waved a manacled hand at the three chairs on the other side of the table from him. "Make yourselfs comfy. I'd make a pot of tea for all y'alls, but . . ." He laughed aloud. "My hands are tied—at the moment."

Jackson watched us as we sat down, especially Tobe, whom he favored with a lascivious up-and-down examination. "What kinda bra you wearin' today, copper? Shit, I jus' *love* watchin' them boobies bouncin' around under your shirt."

And then he said "OW!" loudly, because Tobe kicked him in the shin, very hard, under the table.

"Count your lucky stars," she said, "that you're handcuffed like that, because if not, I'd knock out every one of your teeth, and then reach down your throat and pull out your fucking liver. We understand each other now, Jackson?"

"Woof!" Jackson said. "Man, you are one tough bitch. Okay, okay—I be very polite now, so's you won't scare me no more." He let a deep breath whoosh out of his mouth. "Anybody here got a ciggie?"

K.O. said, "We left you a carton at the gate. You'll get it."

Jackson noticed K.O. as if for the first time. He hadn't been with Tobe and me on our first visit. "Well, that's mighty kind of you, whoever you are. You're the other guy got sent up here to find a killer too, eh? Look like you still in high school. Well, welcome to *my home*." He laughed again. "Your first time inside a prison, huh?"

"I visited one," K.O. said. "Liked it so much, I lived there for almost three years."

"Where'd you get the beads, Prophet?" I said. "You're all dolled up. Going somewhere today?"

"Nah. I got a bunch of beads in my li'l stash. Wear 'em when I feel like it. Didn't know the sexy cop lady was comin' to see me today, or I woulda *really* dressed up. Bracelets, necklaces—I got 'em all." Elijah leaned back in his chair, stretching the manacle chains. "So what's it this time, Sexy Cop Lady?"

Tobe said, "I'm wondering why you have all that bling. Why you scare the guards. Why the warden says to leave you alone."

"Lots a questions," the Prophet said.

"You can't catch a fish, Elijah, unless you bait the hook."

"We know you deserve being locked up," I reminded him, "and so do you. But you get all sorts of privileges."

He grinned. "Guess I'm just lucky, huh?"

"That," Tobe said, "or you *do* something to *get* something. What could that be, I wonder?"

"You right, cop lady. So if you wanna ask me questions, *I* gotta get something out of it if I answer."

"How about my unending thanks and respect?"

Elijah Jackson laughed. Actually K.O. and I laughed, too.

Tobe said, "You know damn well I can't get you pardoned. And you already have all the perks you need."

"No nice warm snatch, though. I surely do need summa that. And some a those yummy titties like yours."

"Do I look like a pimp to you?"

"I don't do no hookers. Never paid for it my whole life, an' never will."

"Everything costs," I said. "Everything. You don't have to pay money all the time, but it still costs."

"Oh yeah? Look, I know you're shaggin' this pretty lady here. Massa visitin' the slave quarters, huh? What's it cost *you*?"

"Coming here," I said, "and talking to assholes like you."

That didn't seem to upset him in the least. I'm sure he's been called worse. Tobe said, "All right, Elijah—let's negotiate. You're right, I can't get you pardoned, and I can't get you more prison privileges. I can't even talk to the warden about you, because you and he are evidently best friends forever.

"But I *can* talk to the attorney general of the State of Ohio. I can call up the head of the Highway Patrol. I can even get in touch with the ATF, who are really anxious to find out who makes all the money on drugs in this county, and tell them all that you actually *run* a major drug ring right here in this corner of the state from prison, and you get to keep your bling and your beads and your tight, firm grasp on the balls of everyone in here. That's because for every dollar your drug crew brings in, you give a little off the top to Warden Melvin Glasser. Don't you? And that's *why* you're the boss man in here, Elijah. Otherwise you'll be cleaning out toilets and going out with the other cons to dig ditches and cut weeds for big corporations who pay Glasser and *his* bosses, and the cons don't see one red cent of it."

Elijah Jackson spoke not a word. But he gulped. Loudly.

"I think," K.O. said quietly, "you better start talking to the cop lady, Mr. Prophet."

"And talk nicely," Tobe warned him. "Because you ask me to flash my tits just once more, you'd better get your personal toothbrush ready to scrub out those urinals."

"Eew!" I said.

CHAPTER TWENTY-ONE

K.O.

K.O. had always thought of Tobe Blaine as Milan's girlfriend, because most of the time he'd see her socially and not professionally. But more and more he realized what a good police detective she was. Smart as hell, she had an unerring "gut feeling." She went after whatever she wanted, and she had intuition that just wouldn't quit.

That's probably why she got the Prophet, Elijah Jackson, to spill the beans.

The prison was actually owned by some corporation in Florida. Owning prisons was their only business, which meant that their first and only aim was profit. The warden, Melvin Glasser, worked directly for them—and the guards, cooks, plumbers, janitorial guys like John Aylesworth, and other personnel got their paychecks from Florida, too.

When Jackson had gotten busted years earlier, he was already a kingpin in illegal drugs in the county, and *rolling* in money, so it didn't take him long to make a deal with Glasser, who wasn't an owner, but simply an employee looking to make a few extra dollars. If the Prophet were allowed to continue running his racket from his cell, his pals on the outside would deposit meth money into Jackson's private bank account in the Cayman Islands, with a small chunk of it going directly to Glasser, and Jackson would be served the food Glasser enjoyed every night instead of the horsemeat the rest of the cons ate.

The Prophet also had a busy schedule of visitors, some of whom he met with in a private room somewhere. Many of those visitors were female.

There've been many similar stories, probably true, about high-level gangsters like John Gotti and Al Capone who were sent to jail in luxury, as well as some politicians who've been caught with their hand in the till or with their pants down when they should have kept their zippers up. It was surprising, though, that these privileges had been awarded to a drug kingpin in a rural Ohio county prison.

Although he had met the late Paul J. Fontaine in person only once before his incarceration, Elijah Jackson's "people" did meth business with him on a regular basis. That meant they did business with the McInerny family, too. K.O. wondered whether the three goons who'd called him out had been sent by Bobby Jeff or by someone else who had worked for or with Fontaine.

It was a good thing they had caught him, and not Milan or Tobe. She wouldn't have bothered fighting them; she'd just blow them to hell and gone with the Glock she carried at all times.

The Prophet's confessions rang true, but he swore he knew nothing about who had killed Paul Fontaine, or Annie Jokela or Cordis Poole. "Why'd anybody want to ice them?" he said. "An' Fontaine? Shit, man, I do *business* with him. Now he's dead an' gone, it's *costin'* me money!" He leveled a slim, graceful finger at Tobe. "Now you can get me in any kinda trouble you want, cop lady. Rat me out to the prez of the U.S.A. if you feel like it. But I'm tellin' you true."

K.O. shrugged. "It *sounds* true."

"Don't get all worried, Prophet," Milan said. "We're not here to shut down your—enterprise. We want to stop whoever took out Fontaine and Poole and Ms. Jokela before they kill anyone else."

Frowning deeply, Elijah thought for a while. He even ducked his head down so he could scratch his nose with one of his manacled hands. Then he said, "If I was you—an' I *ain't* you—but if I *was* you, I'd shut down that damn church."

When the three of them got back to the motel, Tobe whipped out her smartphone and Googled to find a good restaurant not far from where they were. "Most restaurants are closed on Monday," she complained. "What the hell is that? People have to eat!"

"It happens in Cleveland, too," Milan said. "Sundays and Mondays are not great restaurant days."

"I don't give a damn what happens in Cleveland," Tobe snapped. "I can fix my own dinner in my own apartment in Cleveland. Think I can whip up something like a coq au vin tonight in this dungeon they call a motel?"

Milan sat on the edge of his bed. "Worst-case scenario, there's always pizza again."

"I'm *sick* of pizza," K.O. said. "I'm turning into a pepperoni." He looked at his watch; it wasn't quite five thirty. "You guys do what you want. I'll just run over to McDonald's."

Milan shuddered. "That sounds like a death wish. You're actually going to *eat* at McDonald's?"

Tobe said, "Did you know that only forty-four percent of the meat in those McBurgers is really *beef*?"

K.O. laughed, although he didn't find it funny. "What's in the rest of it, then?"

She shook her head. "You don't want to know."

K.O. started his car but didn't put it in gear. Hands on the wheel in the standard ten o'clock and two o'clock position, he was thinking hard. He still wanted to go to the McDonald's across the road, and not just because it was evening and he had no restaurant at which to eat.

He took a deep breath, exited the motel parking lot, and drove across the highway. For a moment he felt a flash of panic, a fear with which he was hardly familiar, when he saw Kathy Pape's car parked in front of Love's. He shook his head to clear away the cobwebs; after all, he wasn't planning to visit Love's anyway. He was heading directly for Mickey D's to talk with Mia Aylesworth.

He did drive his car around to one side of McDonald's, just in case Kathy Pape glanced out the window at the parking lot.

It was too early for the dinnertime crowd. Two unshaven men, truckers by their look, sat alone at separate tables, and an upper-middle-aged woman was just coming out of the ladies' room. Otherwise, K.O. had the place to himself.

Mia Aylesworth was behind the counter, and allowed herself the smallest of smiles when he said, "Hi. Remember me? K.O., from Cleveland?"

"Uh—sure. Hello."

"Hi, Mia. Am I too late for coffee?"

She shook her head. "No, I just made some, fresh. Want anything with it?"

"No, thanks. I live on black coffee."

She nodded, moved back to the coffee machine to pour. When she returned, she tried handing K.O. a plastic top, but he said, "I'll drink it right here." He lifted it in a toast before sipping. "Cheers."

"Aren't you going to eat *anything*?"

"Maybe later. Where are *you* going to eat?"

"Home," she said. "I leave here in about half an hour. Then I go home and cook dinner for my father." She shook her head. "I'm around food all day."

He nodded. "I saw your father today."

Whatever tiny smile she'd displayed vanished into the mist like Brigadoon. She pressed her lips together and began wiping down the counter for no particular reason, as he hadn't spilled his coffee.

"He doesn't like his job much, does he?"

"I don't like mine, either," Mia said. "But I don't hang out with violent criminals all the time." Sigh. "He'll retire soon, and then we're both out of here. Out of this damn town."

"You're not going to college?"

She took a long moment to decide. Finally: "Not now."

"Your friend Kathy," and he jerked his chin toward the archway separating McDonald's from Love's, "says you were an A student. You could have gotten a scholarship, right?"

"It's not just the money," she said. "My father needs me right now." Her sigh was ragged. "I need him, too."

"Do you have a boyfriend?"

All at once she was bellicose. "Why? Are you hitting on me?"

"No," K.O. chuckled. "I have a girl of my own in Cleveland. I'll only be around a few more days. But you must have some friends here—*friend*-friends, I mean."

She hesitated. "I have acquaintances. That's all."

"I've met some people you went to high school with, though. Cord and Jason and Cannon and . . ."

Her brow furrowed and her eyes grew small and glittering hard. "They're not friends. They're pathetic bullies," Mia said. "When someone fights back, bullies and cowards wither away. Why are they bullies, Mia?"

Her voice grew louder. She was on a roll. "Because they're dumbshits. They don't have an original idea in their heads. They just learn from older people, like their parents and their teachers. They're all bullies, too, except they're careful enough to get kids to do the bullying for them so they can keep their own skirts clean."

"How does that happen?"

"I don't want to talk about it, okay?" She glanced around, but neither the other workers in the kitchen nor the day manager, a guy actually wearing a McDonald's necktie he hoped would make him look important, were paying any attention to her.

"Mia, we don't know each other very well," K.O. said gently, "but if it helps, I'm a pretty good listener."

She took a deep, thoughtful breath, fighting her own emotions. Then, finally: "When I was just little, my mom died of cancer."

"I'm sorry for your loss."

"And . . ." Mia stopped, flustered, almost walking away. Then, shaking her head, she changed her mind. "Two years ago—my brother committed suicide."

K.O. nodded sympathetically; he'd heard of Tate Aylesworth's suicide from Kathy Pape. "I'm so sorry. Any idea why he did it?"

Mia's face grew almost stormy. "Because he was bullied. He had to swallow a lot of shit from people he knew, and a lot of shit about a thousand times worse on Facebook and Twitter." Her chin was quivering. "Tate was gay, which is pretty rare in a place like Queenstown. He came out to us—my dad and me—a year earlier." Sniffling, she took her McD's cap off and ran her hand through her Mohawk crest. "It was fine with me, one way or the other. My father is a nice man when you cut through all the crap he gets from his job; he loved Tate and accepted it. The other people around here, though? Not by a long shot!"

"People here bullied him?"

"The guys he went to school with—all the younger guys."

"Did they ever beat him up?"

"Not really," Mia said. "They pushed him around some. They'd bump into him and knock his books out of his hand, or they spilled

Cokes on him. But the worst stuff was mostly on Facebook and Twitter. They'd type awful things to him. *'Get out of town, you faggot!'* Things like that, fifty, a hundred times a day."

K.O. said, "I met with some of those kids. They called me the same thing. I didn't give a damn what they said."

"Well, Tate gave a damn, because he *did* live here, and he *was* gay. Besides, those shits said a lot worse than that on Facebook."

"Worse?"

K.O. noticed her chest was shaking as she tried to disguise a sob. "They suggested that he should kill himself." Her eyes teared up, and a single drop ran down her cheek. She didn't bother brushing it away. "So finally, when he just couldn't take any more—he *did*. I was the one who found him. He was hanging, in the garage."

K.O. touched her hand, but more rapidly than he expected, Mia wrapped her fingers around his wrist, hard, and wrenched it away. Her grip was incredibly strong.

"Jesus, I'm sorry," he said. "I didn't mean anything."

She backed away from him. "I don't like being touched."

"I won't touch you again, I promise."

She gave him a reluctant nod.

He let moments go by. Finally, he said, "Did you talk about your brother afterward with Pastor Urban?"

Her lip curled into a sneer. "That son of a bitch! All those people who come to his damn church every week and wave their arms in the air trying to get God's attention while they sing hymns, listening to every word Urban says, trailing after him all week long, bringing him dinners and baking him cookies and kissing his ass like he's some sort of divine being or something—they were the ones who talked the high school boys into bullying Tate in the first place."

K.O. nodded, sipping McD's very hot coffee. Recalling Pastor Urban's homophobic rant during his sermon, he said, "I spoke with Jason Fontaine. Was he one of the bullies?"

Mia considered it. "Maybe—at the beginning, but he's not like the rest of those creeps. His father, though? One of the worst."

"His father got killed, Mia."

"He gets no tears from me, the shithead!"

K.O. tussled with his own thoughts. Then he said, "Paul J. Fontaine went to Urban's church, didn't he?"

She nodded. "He was on the board of directors."

"How about Cordis Poole? Senior, I mean."

She squeezed her eyes shut. "A churchly maniac!"

"And Annie Jokela?"

Mia put her McD's cap back on her head, covering up her semi-Mohawk cut. Like every other worker in McDonald's, the cap made her look slightly ridiculous. "Jokela never missed a Sunday. She always sat up near the front so when she yelled 'Amen' all the time, she would be sure Urban heard her. She worked at the high school—she was no teacher, just somebody in the office. And if you'd go in to ask for something—supplies for your classroom, like board markers or paper clips—she'd always say, 'God bless you' or 'Jesus loves you.' Whatever you wanted, you wouldn't get it unless you said, 'God bless you' back to her. And that's a *public* school."

"So Jews could go there. Muslims, Buddhists, atheists—anyone, right?"

"Are you kidding?" Mia laughed a mean laugh. "If you find any Jews or Buddhists in Queenstown, let me know so I can go find out what they look like." Then her deep sigh practically emptied the room of oxygen. "You can't hide being a bigot behind your religious convictions. It doesn't work like that. It's all hate. Hate keeps people going. Even my dad. I don't know who he hates more— the murderers and rapists he cleans up after every day, or these goddamn Bible pounders."

"Three of these Bible pounders, as you call them, were murdered."

She rubbed her eyes as if scrubbing away the dust bunnies in her brain. "Look, the manager's glaring at me. I have to get back to work."

K.O. watched her head toward the kitchen under the disapproving gaze of the manager with the bad tie. Mia was a pretty girl, or would be were she not so furious about everything. Obviously the Mohawk hair and her clothing choice were signs of rebellion—against her schoolmates, their parents, their church, and everything else in this corner of Ohio.

It was none of his concern. He dumped the rest of his coffee on his way out. He sidled around the building to his car—but as he was unlocking it, someone called to him, and he knew exactly who it was.

"Where you going, shit-for-brains?" Kathy Pape marched toward him, a snarl on her lips and fire in her eyes. "Running away, you gutless fuck?"

He didn't answer until she reached the car. "Your girlfriend's not half as pretty as me," she said, "and she's a bitch cunt."

"Watch your mouth, Kathy."

She actually snorted. "You could of had my mouth anywhere you wanted it, but you fucked up *bad*. And then you had to *tell* her what happened!"

"You told her things, too—but you lied."

"So?" She flipped her blond hair. Every pretty young woman knows how to flip her long hair; it's in their DNA. "She threatened me! She threatened me with bodily harm. I should of called the cops right then and there."

"I'd love to've heard your side of the story."

"Yeah? Well, I'd tell all my stories about *you*. Cordis and Cannon and them, they were right about you in the first place. Fag! Dirty faggot! Fudgepacker!"

K.O. slid behind the wheel of his car. "Kathy," he said quietly, "I hope I'll miss you."

That threw Kathy for a loop. "Huh?"

"Yep. I'm going to put this car into gear, back up a little bit, and then drive it right at you. So I hope I'll miss you—for your sake."

Suddenly frightened, Kathy Pape backed up quickly, stumbling over the curb, then straightening herself to hop up onto the sidewalk and half run toward the door. K.O. backed the car out, shifted into drive, and roared off, leaving skid marks in the parking lot.

That was a lot of hatred for one person, he thought. He tried to remember if anyone had ever really hated him. No. Disliked him? Sure. Wanted to fight him, maybe hurt him? Yes—too many times already in his young life. But hate?

Hate is a word that gets thrown around too often. "I hate the Pittsburgh Steelers." "I hate broccoli." "I hate Fox News." But those who say it don't really *hate*. It's just a word.

Except some people go to bed each night and wake up to tend to their hatreds like campers tend a small cook fire.

Mia was right. *Hate is what keeps people going.*

CHAPTER TWENTY-TWO

MILAN

At about 7:30 the next morning, the three of us sat in the lobby of our motel. Both K.O. and Tobe were sipping coffee that I'd had to drive across the highway to Mickey D's to collect because K.O. didn't want to run into Kathy Pape again, and I was drinking tea.

We had to talk loud enough to hear each other over the thrum of the rush-hour cars going by on I-90, but softly enough so we wouldn't be overheard by the night clerk, Mrs. Hiatt, who looked exhausted after her all-night stint, and who kept disappearing back into her office only to pop out again, hoping her disapproving grimace would dissolve us all into dust.

K.O. did most of the talking, mostly about Mia and her father.

"The Aylesworth family is bitter about lots of things," he said. "The father hates his janitorial job at the prison, and hates the cons like poison. As for Mia—her panties are in a permanent twist over the high school kids who bullied her brother into hanging himself in their garage. That was two years ago, but she acts like it was the day before yesterday. So both of them hate their church, hate where they live, and hate everybody in it. Just about every night after work, Aylesworth stops to have a drink or two someplace in Ashtabula, and then goes home so Mia can cook his dinner. So—what have we got? The magical world of methamphetamine?"

"Paul Fontaine was involved with meth, with the McInernys. If Koskinen wasn't in on that, too, he sure knew about it and did nothing."

"Which means," K.O. suggested, "he was on the take."

"And Koskinen was sleeping with Annie Jokela," I said. "I don't know how all that connects, but—"

"Annie Jokela," Tobe continued, "probably had nothing to do with the McInernys because she was a first-class holy roller."

"So was Cordis Poole," K.O. said. "I don't think Cordis Junior shed a tear that his old man got brained to death. Jason Fontaine didn't like his father, either."

"And neither had anything to do with Annie," I said, "except they all went to the same church."

"And Aylesworth hates that church and its members." K.O. looked at Tobe. "So it *is* him."

"Still a person of interest," I said. "But if he'd decided on a killing spree, he'd lose it all at once. Ka-boom! Like those insanities who walk into a school and start blasting away—not somebody who carefully plans three killings of people he knows well and spreads them out over a couple of weeks."

"So we're at square one again, Milan?" K.O. said.

"Not necessarily. I'll go see the McInernys—if the dog doesn't eat me. K.O., ask Amy Comunale Klein at the newspaper about all three victims—and about Nowicki, too, for the hell of it. Maybe Tobe can press Koskinen more; he hasn't been really cooperative since the night Annikki Jokela died."

Tobe finished the rest of her coffee. "I hate to bring this up, Milan, but I'm the cop in charge of this case. So we're changing things around a little. You go in and lean on the chief. I'll be the one visiting the McInernys."

"Sounds dangerous for you."

"I'm the only real police officer sitting here—and I'm the only one carrying a weapon."

"I don't like you putting yourself in harm's way . . ."

"Don't make me flash my badge at you."

I'm crazy about Tobe—I have been from the beginning—but I had second thoughts about arguing with her. Tobe never went anywhere without a loaded Glock. Who was I to tell her not to visit three illiterate hillbillies who didn't wear underwear, cooked meth in their kitchen, and might accidentally blow themselves off the face of the earth?

Philo Ackerman walked through the door, stopped cold, and

stared at us like we were having an orgy in his lobby instead of just drinking coffee. He glared at Mrs. Hiatt behind the desk as if our being there was all her fault, and then marched over to us.

"What are you people doing?" he demanded.

"Curing cancer," Tobe said.

"You can't hang around in the lobby."

"No?" I said. "Then why have chairs and a table here?"

Feelo sputtered again—one of his favorite habits. "We can't have people making a mess in our lobby."

"Define mess,"

"If you don't leave," he huffed, "I'll call—"

"The police?" Tobe said. "Don't bother. I'm right here, Feelo."

Ackerman would have looked down his Pinocchio nose at her had she not deliberately mispronounced his first name. "This isn't Cleveland! Your badge means nothing; you don't even have the right to *be* here, throwing your weight around and playing your race card."

Tobe's tone was as frigid as Lake Erie when it's frozen. "But I can call the attorney general—I know him personally, by the way—and tell him you treat all of us like dirt in this craphouse you call a motel, and you have since we checked in. I'm a minority, Feelo, in case you didn't notice. An African American. So I suggest you knock off the 'race card' shit, because one word from me about your abuse of *my* civil rights, and the attorney general will close this place up tighter than your asshole."

Whatever color had illuminated Philo Ackerman's cheeks disappeared, leaving him ashen white, and he had to shove his hands into his pants pockets so we couldn't see them shake.

"And on the off-chance that the general isn't in his office, Feelo," Tobe continued, "and on the *off*-off-chance that you address me as 'woman' just one more time, I'm going to put my badge and gun on the table and punch you so hard in your kidney that you'll be pissing blood for a year."

That got an audible gasp from Mrs. Hiatt, who placed one hand at her throat as though choking on a chicken bone. As for Ackerman, he was close to fainting.

As we left the office, Tobe said, "Maybe tonight there'll be rattlesnakes in our pillowcases."

"There's enough deadly poison around here," I said, moving to the car Chief Koskinen had loaned us, while Tobe slid behind the wheel of the Cleveland P.D. unmarked and K.O. got into his own, "that Feelo wouldn't need rattlesnakes."

After several days, Eino Koskinen had finally shaved, although there was a scab half the size of a dime on his lower jaw where he'd nicked himself. He was also wearing his official police chief shirt instead of his Hawaiian luau get-up. He still looked like he was in deep shock; Annikki Jokela's murder had taken more of a bite out of him than anyone realized.

Koskinen was at his desk behind a pile of papers and files gathering dust that hadn't been touched in a few days. His shoulders slumped even further when he saw me walk in. He dropped his chin onto his chest and rubbed at both eyes.

"Why aren't you out there asking questions?" he said sourly. "It's your job, not mine."

"I have questions for you," I said. "If you're up to them."

He waved absently at his papers. "I've got lots of work here."

"The quicker you answer my questions," I said, "the quicker the problems get solved."

He shook his head; the smallest gesture of his looked heavy, overburdened. "I'm not your problem."

"Not so sure about that."

He raised his head, a bullmastiff being awakened from his nap, and glared at me. His squint and his angry jawline made him look more like a pissed-off cop. "Are you accusing me of murder?"

That threw me. "It never crossed my mind. We've talked with Elijah Jackson—the Prophet."

"You think I don't know that? It was me set up the meeting in the first place, calling the warden. Remember?"

"The Prophet said he knew Paul Fontaine and had done business with him."

Koskinen shrugged. "Why is that my affair?"

"Because Fontaine lived in your town and dealt with a big-time drug peddler like Elijah Jackson."

"Jackson's in prison, for God's sake. He's a criminal, but he's not your killer."

I nodded. "We went back and saw him again."

"What for?"

"To learn more about Fontaine." The chair opposite his desk was unoccupied, but I chose to stand; it issued an extra dollop of pressure on him. "He also told us about the McInerny family."

Koskinen blinked, then took a moment to compose an answer. "I know about them," he said airily, waving an arm in the general direction of where the family lived. "They're over in Geneva. Not my territory. We got the Tri-County Drug Task Force—Ashtabula, Lake, and Geauga Counties. They take care of all that."

"Evidently they don't take care of the McInernys," I said. "Put one foot on their property, and they're all over you."

The chief shrugged. "You've heard about that Stand Your Ground law? The McInernys, they're entitled. They got a right to protect their own property—specially if they don't know you. Stand your ground, you know?" He looked away from me for his next statement. Now he was sulking—a most unattractive behavioral choice for a chief of police. "I've never been there, never seen 'em cook up meth, and they don't live in Queenstown. Talk to the Geneva cops, not me."

"I'm talking to you because you damn well know about all of it," I said, "and you know about Fontaine's connection with them. You take a teensy-weensy skim off the top every week, too, don't you? At least that's what the Prophet hinted."

His mouth clamped shut like a wolf trap, and we had a stare-down for almost a minute. Then he said coldly, "You don't expect me to fall slobbering at your feet and confess, do you?"

"We're up here for three homicides—at *your* request," I said. "So I don't give a damn if you have a piece of the drug trade or you rob 7-Elevens at gunpoint. Fontaine got iced, and he was in meth up to his ears. Cordis Poole and your friend Annie also died before their time. I want to know what these three people shared with each other that might have anything to do with drugs—or with *you*."

Koskinen's sigh nearly shook his large body. "It's complicated."

"People say that about their Facebook relationships."

One more deep breath, Then: "Oh, what the hell. All right, then. Paul Fontaine was screwing Cordis Poole's wife."

"*What?*"

"They knew each other in a small town like this. And they all went to church weekly, if not more. Cordis was a mean man, especially to his family. I don't wonder that she—uh—what's the word I'm looking for?"

"Comfort?"

"Maybe."

"Solace?" I suggested.

"Yeah, I think that's it. Solace. Someone to make her feel better about herself."

"So you think Poole found out and killed Fontaine?"

"I don't know."

"Why the hell didn't you tell us this at the beginning?"

He looked sorrowful. "I didn't want to soil the wives' reputations any further. They've both been recently widowed."

"Okay, let's assume that's true. Poole killed Fontaine. Who killed Poole, then?"

Mystified, he just shrugged. "Could have been Gwen, avenging her lover's death. Or maybe Maude Fontaine—out of jealousy."

"You're stretching."

"Why?"

"Many reasons. Mrs. Jokela wasn't part of the so-called love triangle, as far as you know." His head snapped up angrily. "And she was killed *after* Poole and Fontaine were both dead."

He tried licking his lips, but his mouth had gone dry. His cheeks flamed, his head moments away from exploding. Eventually he managed to say, "Well, maybe Gwen Poole got furious because Annie was the senior official in high school that got Cord Junior suspended for two weeks last year because she caught him drinking beer and smoking pot under the stairwell."

"You think she single-handedly wiped out not only her husband *and* her own lover, but some big shot in high school who caught her son drinking and smoking on the premises?" I shook my head. "Detective Sergeant Blaine interviewed Gwen Poole; she didn't think the woman had lost her mind and turned into a serial killer."

Koskinen slammed his hand down on the desk, and the dust from his untouched files rose into the air and disappeared. "Damn it, if I knew the answer, Jacovich, I never would have called you."

I leaned forward. "Chief—pretty soon you and I are going to go fifteen rounds." And *I* slammed my flat hand onto his desk even harder than he'd done. This time some of his papers leaped into the air and wound up on the floor.

The chief jumped a little bit, too. I don't think anyone had ever raised their voice to him before, especially in his own office. And as I left, I wondered about whether he'd even called the Tri-County Drug Task Force, and whether they ever bothered with what goes on in this large county in the most remote corner of Ohio.

Once in the car, I took out my cell phone to call Tobe, but thought better of it. While at the McInerny place, she probably wouldn't want to stop whatever she was doing to answer a phone call. I'd wait and check with her later in the day.

In the meantime, I headed toward the home of Gwen Poole. I'd not met her before, though Tobe had. But after Chief Koskinen's speculations about murder, I thought it better to have a conversation with her myself—and try not to mention religion to her at all.

CHAPTER TWENTY-THREE

K.O.

The *Messenger* didn't sprawl out over a huge building, but occupied the ground floor of a two-story building on a side street in downtown Ashtabula, just enough space for the eight employees who readied the paper for its weekly appearance. The publisher, whoever he or she was, worked elsewhere, and the printing was done across town, as well.

There were only two offices that had doors that opened and closed—one for the editor and one for the sales department. The other members of the crew shared a large room with cubicles. Overhead a fluorescent light fixture hummed too loudly.

The woman K.O. talked to when he first entered must have been at least sixty and wore her mouse-brown hair long and straight, falling four inches below her shoulders on a dress she might have purchased, used, at a thrift shop sometime in the 1970s to wear when she cleaned out her garage. When he told her what he wanted, she couldn't quite figure out what to do with him. People just didn't walk into the *Messenger* "news room"—that's what she called it, anyway—and ask to check some old files. The paper didn't really *have* any old files. When they'd "gone computer" some six years earlier, they'd packed up their bursting file cabinets full of news stories and filler items about county residents from Geneva to Conneaut, and all the towns and cities in between. The *Messenger* wasn't exactly the *Washington Post*.

Eventually she found a computer in a cubicle that wasn't currently in use and told K.O. he could look up whatever he needed to that had appeared in the paper in the past six years. "You need the password to get into this stuff," she said. "Type in 'messenger-clips'—one word. Well, it's really two words, but there's no space between them. Messengerclips." She studied him as though she'd never before seen anyone nearly so young and shook her head as she walked away on her squeaking, down-at-the-heel loafers.

It took him a few minutes, but finally K.O. made it to the site he wanted, back stories from the *Messenger*. He leaned back in his chair, popped his knuckles, and typed in the name "Paul J. Fontaine."

It never did say what the *J* stood for. People rarely used their middle names at all, except perhaps at their own wedding. He did find several Fontaine stories. Hiring convicts to work his ranch land, with a picture of him, smiling, his arm thrown across the shoulders of a nonsmiling inmate in an orange prison jumpsuit, who might have been forced to work digging fence poles at the point of a shotgun. Fontaine and his wife sitting at a restaurant with several friends, a big hand-painted sign stretched out behind them: "Happy 20th Paul and Maude." Paul was drinking, and one of his friends was handing him a large cake knife so he could slice into a white cake with pink frosting and a burning candle on top. Maude was watching him with what appeared to be fear and sus-picion, looking as if she anticipated a root canal rather than an anniversary party.

Another photo of a more casually dressed Paul shaking hands with Pastor Urban in front of the church, both hamming it up for the camera. A picture of him astride his "new" horse, taken four years ago. A tiny paragraph about Paul being stopped for reckless driving on Lake Road a year earlier; he had gotten a warning and the officer, Joe Platko, had followed him until he pulled into his driveway safely.

There was another short piece about Paul J. Fontaine returning home after a two-week trip to Mexico—on "business." K.O. knew little about Mexico, but he was aware that two of its most profit-able enterprises had much to do with America: drug smuggling and horse slaughtering.

And that was it. Whatever Fontaine had been up to—and the stories regarding his illicit activities couldn't *all* have been fabricated—apparently never found its way into the newspaper.

Cordis Poole Senior was another story. There were several short items involving him with the church, with Pastor Urban, making a speech at an abstinence-only meeting, a trip to Little Rock for a Baptist convention, and a photo of him with his son, Cord Junior, in which he wore the same Steelers shirt he'd worn in the photograph in Koskinen's file. Junior, as he'd always been when K.O. spent face time with him, looked as though he wanted to be anywhere else but in that picture.

There was a one-paragraph story, though, published about eight months earlier, that caught K.O.'s attention.

> Police in Queenstown were called to investigate a report of a domestic disturbance at the home of Cordis and Gwen Poole at a few minutes after midnight Sunday night. No arrests were made.

Like many of the short news paragraphs, there was no author's name given.

As far as K.O. knew, "domestic disturbance" always involved some sort of violence between spouses—and knowing that Cordis Senior had been a large man and a high school football star, he didn't think this particular police incident involved Gwen Poole abusively attacking her husband. He scratched out a note to mention that information to Milan.

Naturally there were major reports of both Fontaine's and Poole's violent and untimely deaths, too. The length of the stories demanded an authorial identification; the woman who'd written the graphic reports was the one Milan suggested he originally contact: Amy Comunale Klein.

When K.O. looked up Nowicki, who had bought the horse Chocklit for his teen-aged daughter, he found he'd been mentioned almost every summer, around July Fourth, for throwing a large outdoor party at his ranch for his family, friends, and for the many laborers who worked for him. There were photographs of the festivity every year, and as Nowicki had said, many of his employees were African American. Otherwise, there was nothing about him in the vast file of *Messenger* stories on the website, a collection of news and trivia that in the old days of newspapers was called "the morgue."

When he trolled for Annikki Jokela, he found her name mentioned just once, in an obituary listing her as the sole survivor of Paavlo Jokela, who'd died four years earlier.

News story about Cordis Poole's temper problem. Rumors about Fontaine's illegal carryings-on. But Annikki Jokela? Nothing.

K.O.'s name was being called, and a formidable middle-aged woman with dyed red hair, and an expensive camera on a strap bouncing against her chest, was descending on his cubicle as if it were an invasion. "I hear you were asking for me," she boomed, extending for a handshake. "Amy Comunale Klein here. Sorry, I was out this morning scouting up news." She hovered, looking impatiently at him, until he realized he'd been sitting at *her* desk.

"I hope I didn't mess up anything on your computer," he said, standing up.

"If you did," she answered, unloading her camera, purse, and an overstuffed shopping bag onto the floor, "I'll be mad at you. You're one of the Cleveland cops, right? Well, I told one of your other people, I never met the first two victims. I don't get to Queenstown that often, and the stuff they did was more 'man stuff,' and I didn't cover it. I only got called by the chief to take murder pictures because it was late at night and I was the one on duty." She laughed. "We don't close this office at six o'clock every day. Small and dinky as we are, this *is* a newspaper."

K.O. said, "You didn't know the first two victims personally. Did you know Annikki Jokela?"

"Sure, from the Food Bank. And we were in a book club together."

"A book club?"

"A bunch of women of a certain age would read one selected book a month, and then meet and discuss it. Annie Jokela didn't stay in the book club very long."

"Why was that?"

"Because we were all reading novels, mostly by and about women. *The Joy Luck Club*, the *Ya-Ya Sisterhood*, things like that. After all, you read fiction to escape your own problems by focusing on someone else's."

"Okay. So . . . ?"

"So Annie didn't want to read novels," Amy Klein said. "She insisted we read all her religious stuff and then discuss it—which turned into an endless go-to-prayer meeting. Finally us members told her enough was enough, that this was a club for literary entertainment. So she quit the book club, as all she thought about was God and Jesus and her church."

"Do you go to church, Ms. Klein?"

"Not often. Christmas and Easter—because so many other people go. But Christianity was Annie's only interest."

He glanced down at his notes. "Do you know John Aylesworth?"

Klein still looked annoyed at not hearing a juicy secret, but she pushed on. "The name sounds familiar. Why? Who is he?"

"He works at the prison in Conneaut."

"I don't write about the prison. I hate the fact that there's one around here, privately owned by people who've never even *been* to Ohio." She placed a knuckle between her teeth and chewed gently on it. Then her head jerked up quickly. "*Yes!* John Aylesworth. I *did* do a story on him a few years ago after his son died."

"The one who committed suicide?"

"Sure. But my story was about the father. You can look it up on that computer if you want."

News stories in the local weekly paper rarely ran more than a few paragraphs, so K.O. said, "I'd rather you tell me—since I've got you here in person."

"Well—as I remember it," Amy Klein said, "he got suspended from his job for a while. He was going through some real emotional problems, what with his wife dying and then his son."

"We all have problems that don't get our names in the paper."

"Yeah, but he let his problems come out. Explode, is more like it. They made him see a psychologist for a while and take anger management classes."

"Why? Did he use illegal force against the cons?"

"I don't remember him ever assaulting the inmates, although he was pretty mean to them back then. He's got a crippled hand, so I'd think he'd stay out of fights. The reason for the suspension, though, was him actually taking a swing at the pastor of the Baptist church."

"Pastor Urban?"

Klein nodded. "They ran into each other outside Pizzi's Pizzeria in Conneaut on a crowded Friday evening. I never did find out what the trouble was about, but they jawed at each other for a while in the parking lot, and then Aylesworth hauled off and popped Urban right in the nose." She winked at K.O. "With his good hand."

K.O. shook his head in amazement. "He didn't get arrested?"

"No. Urban chose not to file a complaint."

"You were there when it happened?"

"No, but I was on duty that night, so I got the call. By the time I got out there, Aylesworth was gone, but Urban was milling around with some parishioners and a couple of Conneaut police officers, all making a fuss over him like he was a rock star or something, his face and his shirt all bloody. Well, it'd dried up by then, but—"

"Why wouldn't he file a complaint?"

"Who knows?" Klein said. "Maybe he didn't want publicity. In fact, he begged me not to print anything about it, to just let it go."

"But you did print something?"

"I'm a reporter, kiddo. This isn't the *New York Times*, but reporting is what I do." She pointed her forefinger at K.O. and then squeezed it shut as if pulling the trigger of a pistol. "So you watch what you do up here, or you'll be in the *Messenger*, too."

"I'll remember that." K.O. scribbled in his notebook. "Thanks for sharing this with me, Ms. Klein."

"Sure. But you owe me, now."

"What do I owe you? A drink? Dinner? Flowers?"

"No, you owe me the name of who it was Annie Jokela was shagging before she died. That's what you were trying so hard not to tell me, right?"

"No way. Until we find out more, it's too personal to have it blasted all over the county."

"I won't print it!" she said, crossing her heart and then holding her hand up near her face, as though swearing on a Bible in a court of law. "I swear to God I won't. It's just—off the record."

"There's no such thing," Kevin O'Bannion said, "as 'off the record.'"

CHAPTER TWENTY-FOUR

MILAN

"Give it up, Mr. Jacovich! I've answered enough questions to last me a lifetime!"

In her spacious Cape Cod colonial, into which Gwen Poole finally invited me when my visit that morning surprised her, she'd seated herself on a tall stool at her counter separating the kitchen from the living room, her legs dangling because they weren't quite long enough to reach the rung. The house was squeaky clean, but there were no signs of mourning anywhere—no flower arrangements, no photographs, no sympathy cards on the mantel, and no clue of Cordis Poole Junior. It seemed as though Gwen Poole had always lived here all by herself.

Although Tobe had talked to her before, this was the first time I'd met her in person. She wasn't pretty, nor homely either— neither sexy nor sexless. Her hair was neatly combed but bore no trace of a beautician's touch, and she wore no makeup save for a timid swipe of light pink lipstick. If it were the 1950s, her drab brown dress wouldn't have surprised me, but in the twenty- first century, middle-aged women rarely wore dresses unless they planned to go out somewhere.

She didn't appear unhappy, but she did seem annoyed that I was bothering her at home.

"Ms. Poole," I said, "the best way to solve this crime is to find out all we can about your husband. That's why we ask questions."

Her face, more or less passive before, turned wolf-mean. It's frightening when someone gets angry and all their teeth show when they speak. "Let me lay it out for you then, and save you all your questions. I didn't like my husband, not for at least the past ten years. He was pushy, domineering, and abusive in every way—to me and to his son. He was also a religious fanatic." Her eyes searched the ceiling. "Making a bowl of popcorn for a snack and being forced to say grace before you could take a bite of it? Hard to believe, isn't it?" Her deep inhalation sucked most of the air from the room. Then she let it out in a shaky sigh. "Nobody deserves getting killed, not even Cordis. But I can't cry because he's dead. The income will dry up—I'll have to sell this house, and I won't be able to afford Cord going to college. But I hated my life and hated my marriage. So there you are."

I nodded. "You could have divorced him."

She shook her head vehemently. "He was too damn smart—and he'd have the whole church backing him up. Most of them are bigger nuts than he was. I would've had to move away from here or they'd make sure I was—shunned."

"Shunned? Isn't that an Amish expression?"

"Get the Baptist church of Queenstown mad at you and you'll find out pretty damn quick what 'shunned' is." She looked away. "It would have been tough on Junior, too."

"I thought he didn't like his dad, either."

"He *didn't* like him," Gwen Poole snapped. "But him being a—what do they call it these days?—a child of divorce? Humiliating, especially in a small town. Cord has his pride." Then sadly, "He didn't get that from me."

She slid off the stool and went around the corner to the refrigerator. "Want something to drink? We don't have liquor in the house, but if you want a Pepsi or a fizzy water—"

"Nothing, thanks."

She showed me a cold can of lime LaCroix. "No calories," she said, opening it, and took a sip. Then she sat at the counter again, absently fluffing her hair. "I have to start looking halfway decent again. I can't remember how long it's been since Cordis even touched me. In the bed, sure, with all the lights off. But never any other time. Not even a kiss good morning or good night." Big, elaborate shrug.

"No affection?"

"Not for—well, damn near never."

I approached my next question with trepidation. The subject was dangerous. "Ms. Poole—is that why you were having an affair with Paul Fontaine?"

Her eyes opened wide, and she actually gasped. Though she wore no makeup, her cheeks flamed red.

"I don't judge you," I assured her. "Just getting facts in order."

"Oh, shit," she said, suddenly exhausted. "I knew that'd come out eventually. In this little pissant community, do *anything*, and within twenty minutes everybody knows about it."

"It's just between the two of us."

She snorted. "So far."

"Mind telling me how long this was going on?"

"I didn't exactly write down the date! Sometime in late winter or early spring, I guess."

"From what I hear, Fontaine was quite the playboy."

"Like I gave a damn. Whenever we did get together, he treated me well—with affection. Kindness, you might say. That's something I missed for most of my life." She took a healthy swallow of La Croix. "Hell, I'd even sleep with *you* if you kissed me first and cuddled me afterwards."

Now *I* blushed. "I'm—involved."

She nodded sagely. "With that Cleveland police detective I talked to. I know."

"So," I said, "within two weeks you lost a husband and a lover."

It was blunt, but I'd meant it to be. Her eyes widened, she gulped noisily, and the tears came. She wept for almost a minute, whimpering as she went through three sheets of tissue from a box on the counter. Then she sniffled. "I'm not that broken up about either one, to tell the truth. I didn't love them or anything. The way you put it, though, sounds a lot worse than it really is."

"Did you go to Paul Fontaine's place, or did he come here?"

"Motel," she said, wiping her eyes with a fourth tissue. "Probably the same motel you're staying in now—by the freeway."

The same motel. For all I know, the same room, the same bed. I tried not to think about that. There've been more people who'd banged away at each other in the bed where Tobe and I were now sleeping than I could probably count.

That's one of the main reasons motels exist in the first place.

I wondered if Philo Ackerman knew about it, too. He, the Fontaines, and the Pooles were all members at the Baptist. That must have been awkward—nodding pleasantly to him on Sunday morning and then checking in for an assignation the next morning. They all shared secrets.

"The management at the motel didn't notice you?"

"Of course they noticed! You think anyone would say something? Spread it all over town?" Her laugh was an angry staccato. "How long d'you suppose a motel would stay open if they blabbed around about who's screwing who?"

"You have no idea why anyone wanted your husband dead?"

"Not specifically. But he was no saint."

"Does the same go for Paul Fontaine?"

"Paul was an even bigger shit than Cordis—even if he was good in bed." She blushed. "Not that I know anything about being good in bed—but lousy at everything else, including his business, his own marriage, his religious intensity. I had no use for him, except for the physical. But as far as I know, nobody hated him enough to kill him."

I created a scenario in my head. Perhaps Gwen Poole herself had stabbed Paul J. Fontaine in the heart because he, with whom she was cheating, was probably cheating on both her and his own wife with more than one other person. And she might have killed her own husband two weeks later when he found out about it and possibly tried to hurt her, as he'd done before. Extreme religiosity is often accompanied by a fearsome temper.

Unlikely, I admitted, but not impossible.

I said, "Not even you hated him enough to kill him?"

That didn't surprise her. "Not even me," she said. Gwen had lived most of her life shy, quiet, and obedient, but gained strength and guts even as we spoke. "Are you suggesting I killed them both? And Annie Jokela, too? Good luck with that. Other than saying hello, I barely knew Annie. Why would I hurt her? I had nothing against Paul personally—and as far as my husband is concerned, the insurance he left won't keep me for the rest of my life." She wrapped her fingers around her can of fizzy water and tapped it noisily with her fingernails. "I'm a lousy suspect, and I'd really appreciate being left alone—at least until I figure out what's waiting for me down the line."

Then she looked at me and laughed, and this time the laugh was genuine. "And frankly, Mr.—" She glanced down at the business card I'd given her, and stumbled over my last name. "Mr. Jacovich, I don't give a damn whether you believe me or not."

I finally got outside, slid into the Queenstown police loaner car, and massaged the back of my neck. My most recent hostess was tiny, hovering right around five feet zero, but perhaps anger had changed her life and her motives. Considering her relationship with Paul Fontaine and his own scandalous reputation as a playboy, the fact that his fly was open provided a distinct possibility for her stabbing him to death. It's plausible that rage had made her strong enough to cave in her husband's skull and then roll him out of the car and into Conneaut Creek. She'd offered no alibi as to where she was when the murders were committed. And she might have lied about her distant relationship with Annikki Jokela.

Murderers lie. All criminals lie. She might indeed be a suspect, but if so, I needed proof. Tobe, who'd probably solved more cases in her lifetime than the fictional Ellery Queen, was better at finding proof than I ever hoped to be.

It was past lunchtime, and it occurred to me that both Tobe and K.O. had been busy that morning, too, and it might be nice to sit down and exchange notes.

First I called K.O. and learned what he'd picked up at the *Messenger*. "From everything we know," he said, "John Aylesworth is right up there at the top of the suspect list. Violent guy—and when they suspend a prison employee because he's *too* violent, that's saying a hell of a lot. Besides—and I love this one, Milan—he hauled off and sucker-punched the Baptist preacher."

"Urban?"

"Decked him, publicly, in the parking lot of Pizzi's Pizzeria in Conneaut."

"Damn!" I said.

"What?"

"I keep hearing good things about Pizzi's, but with one thing and another, we can't seem to get there. Let's make it tonight. Set

up a lunch date with Tobe for half an hour from now, then call and
tell me where we'll meet."

"I'm on it," K.O. said.

I decided to drive back to the church. I wanted to find out *why*
John Aylesworth bloodied the Reverend Thomas Nelson Urban
Junior's nose. I rolled down the car window so I could inhale
whatever Lake Erie could offer up in this remote corner of a state
overwhelmed by big cities like Cleveland, Columbus, Cincinnati,
Toledo, and Youngstown. East of US I-71, of course, were flat
farms and prairie. The small towns of Ashtabula County were part
of a world all their own.

I was driving peaceably down Lake Road, the neighborhoods
changing with almost every mile, when K.O. called me back—and
then things weren't so peaceable anymore.

CHAPTER TWENTY-FIVE

K.O.

"I couldn't reach Tobe's cell phone," K.O. said, "and I didn't get kicked over to voice mail, either. I dialed it three times."

Milan drove with one hand, holding his cell with the other. A niggling fear tormented his insides. "I dialed it, too. Tobe never goes anywhere without her phone—or her gun."

"Maybe she forgot to recharge the phone."

"That'd be like forgetting to put her clothes on before going to work. Besides, we both recharged when we went to bed." Milan looked out the window; the sky was sunny, but the lake was choppy. An insistent wind blew hard, whitecaps peeking their way out from beneath the waves like the nose of a dolphin, just coming up to look around and see what's going on. "I'll call the motel and see if she's in the room."

"Did that," K.O. said. "Feelo answered. He rang the room—no answer, of course—and then told me she hasn't been there since this morning, when we were all cheesing him off drinking coffee in his lobby. Should we contact Koskinen?"

Eino Koskinen. The Prophet, Elijah Jackson. The meth chefs of the McInerny family. All connected? Maybe too much connection? "No," Milan said, "we don't call Koskinen."

"How about the state police?"

"Tobe has been missing only a few hours. No cop gets bent out of shape about that. She visited Bobby Jeff McInerny this morning. Let's start there. Meet me at the motel and we'll go together."

"Right." Pause. "The McInerny family have guns."

"I know."

"Neither of us has one, Milan."

"Tobe has one."

"Yeah—but Tobe's phone isn't working. Maybe her gun . . ."

"Well," Milan said, more worried than he sounded, "I guess we'll just have to speak to the McInerny boys very sharply."

Both of them broke the speed limit heading back to their motel. Milan sat in one of the uncomfortable lobby chairs and tried locating Tobe on his iPad, but failed to get a response. His heart hammered in his throat.

K.O. got there moments later. Philo Ackerman looked surprised to see them at this hour of the day. He nodded brusquely.

They were clear across the lobby from the front desk, but K.O. leaned close to Milan's ear and spoke in a whisper anyway. "Should we ask Feelo if he knows anything about the McInernys?"

Milan shook his head. "He might know them too well—and call to warn them we're on our way."

"Good thought."

Milan waved bye-bye to Philo Ackerman as they went back out to the parking lot together. Ackerman just sniffed audibly and turned his head away, Pinocchio nose aimed at the sky.

"Some people are just assholes," Milan said, "but they ought to put Feelo in a frame."

K.O. laughed as they approached their vehicles. "Should we take my car?"

"No. In case there's shooting, it's better we get the Queenstown cop car shot full of holes rather than yours."

"I learn more from you every day, Milan."

They drove south toward Geneva, the sun in their eyes, but even though they flipped down the sun visors in the car, they had to squint, as neither carried sunglasses. Two native Clevelanders, they rarely bothered with sunglasses, even when they should. Wearing sunglasses is not a Cleveland thing—unless you're an egomaniac.

"She'll be all right, Milan," K.O. said in a "There, there" tone, hoping he sounded as if he believed it. "She's one ball-buster of a cop. I don't think she's ever been in real danger, has she?"

Milan gritted his teeth. "Not since she's been in Cleveland. Before that—in Raleigh or Cincinnati—she doesn't talk much about her jobs, and I don't ask her." He rolled down his window partway; the wind rushing by made it more difficult for them to hear each other. "Maybe I should." A missing cop would worry anybody—but for Milan, his relationship with Tobe meant this went far beyond "worrying."

K.O. knew he'd fret even more if *his* lady love was missing. She worked in a cosmetics store and studied public relations at night; she was no cop, and didn't carry a gun. She probably didn't even know how to use one.

"How long till we get there, Milan?"

"You sound like a five-year-old."

Milan drove for a while longer. Then he said, "We're unarmed, and they have guns. We shouldn't just march in there together."

"Okay. What's your suggestion?"

Milan cleared his throat, preparing to tell him.

Milan parked the car about a quarter of a mile from the long, rutted driveway that snaked its way from the road through the trees and over a few minor hills to the McInerny home. He trudged along the side of the highway by himself, the prospect of seeing one or all of the meth-cooking family forming an acid lump in his stomach, and mentally kicked himself because one of his handguns was locked in the drawer of the desk in his office on Collision Bend in the Flats in downtown Cleveland, and the other was on the top shelf of his apartment's coat closet. He had a license to carry, but Tobe had insisted he not be armed while in Ashtabula County with her, reminding him not for the first time nor the tenth that she was the only true cop assigned to this job.

K.O. had also headed off-road on foot, rummaging through a thick forest, thistles and tall, relentless weeds tormenting his legs as he pushed away the hanging tree branches that snapped back and hit him in the face. There was no path where he was going; he was making a trail of his own.

Five minutes later he was atop a ridge overlooking the river. It wasn't nearly as muddy-brown as the Cuyahoga in the city, but it wasn't a cool mountain stream, either.

The ridge sloped downward like a modest hill—so when he spied a long, sturdy tree branch on the ground, he figured to use it as an alpine walking stick. He picked it up, broke the small branches off, and pared down the rest of it with his Swiss Army knife. Wrapping his hand around it made him feel good—strong and fearless. Sturdy and not too light, the staff was the perfect solution—an aid to walking on uneven ground, and a weapon should he need one. For a brief moment he felt like Gandalf in the *Lord of the Rings* movies, leaning heavily on his staff as he plodded along.

Instead of reclasping the knife, he slipped it into his belt, blade open. He might need it—and no fair asking the McInernys to wait until he fished it out of his pocket and clawed it open before they attacked him.

If they attacked him. Why would they? Milan Security couldn't arrest them because what was done in their kitchen was none of their business. They might just be on a fool's errand, too—looking for the absent Tobe who might not be missing after all, but sitting in some fast-food burger joint near the motel, drinking coffee and trying to get her dead-battery phone to work.

He moved on, noticing it grew chillier the closer he got to the river. A complete stranger to the area, he worried he'd get lost out there, that he'd be unable to find the McInerny house coming around behind it, or even to find his way back to the road, but would be stuck in the woods forever until the birds came and covered him with leaves.

Glancing skyward at a light covering of clouds dimming the rays of the sun, he noticed gray smoke floating almost straight upward, as there was little to no wind that afternoon, and figured it must be coming from Bobby Jeff McInerny's kitchen.

Bobby Jeff and Jimmy John, K.O. mused. Here they were, as far north as one could get in Ohio, and the McInerny men boasted three names—or at least two of them did—like many Southerners. It made K.O. wonder if Wyatt McInerny only got one first name because he was being punished, or if his middle name was somehow *too* bizarre to be spoken aloud.

And that made him think of his own middle name. He never used it, never even used the initial, and preferred being called K.O. instead of "Kevin." But—"Cillian"? Pronounced "KILL-ee-an," which virtually no one could say properly? Kevin Cillian O'Bannion? Milan didn't know Cillian was his middle name, nor did Carli, probably because they had never asked. Perhaps, he mused, Cillian wasn't so bad after all. It sounded much better to him than "Bobby Jeff."

Moving along, he wasn't sure what he was supposed to do when he finally arrived there. Plodding through thistles and briar and sharp branches had put it out of his mind. He had to chuckle. Maybe it was "Irish Alzheimer's." An elderly Irishman will forget everything, they say, except grudges.

He and Milan had no arrest responsibilities, they weren't there to bust up a meth lab, but were simply looking for Tobe. He veered from the path he'd chosen and headed toward the smoke, his makeshift walking staff digging deep into the dirt.

As he got closer, the odors hit him. A hospital smell, first. It stirred up a memory from a surgery, when the juvenile corrections center had ordered an operation on his right knee. He'd told them he'd accidentally fallen down the stairs and wrenched it. The truth was he'd been in a fierce battle with two other inmates and had knocked his knee completely out of joint by kicking one in the head.

Nearing the McInerny compound, he caught a whiff of ammonia, and another scent—like over-the-counter cough and cold medicine one could buy at any drug store.

Whatever it was, K.O. was certain the McInernys were cooking meth. Home meth labs in people's kitchens and trailers and garages exploded and blew to smithereens on an almost regular basis, and he hoped if it did happen on this particular day, Tobe wouldn't be anywhere near it.

Nor the dog, either. An ugly dog, admittedly, but the last time K.O. had been there, Bobby Jeff had kicked the old dog in the ribs for no reason at all. The poor overgrown animal suffered enough without having to be blown up by criminals, too.

Although the property had been cleared decades ago for a house, the land around it was heavily wooded with oak and beech and pine that formed an impenetrable curtain. K.O. almost passed a stand of trees without seeing, out of the corner of his eye, the left bumper of Tobe Blaine's Cleveland cop car not hidden quite well enough.

And that meant Tobe must be there against her will.

CHAPTER TWENTY-SIX

MILAN

I headed for the McInerny "estate," if that's what it was. Despite the several-acre spread in the woods, it wasn't a farm, either, because nothing was grown on it except a few chickens.

It was, however, dusty as hell. There aren't many places to walk in Cleveland where you'll kick up the dust with every step, much of it winding up in your shoes or in your nose. The outskirts of Geneva, Ohio, hardly resemble Cleveland, only an hour's drive away—here I was, sleeping in a racist motel, investigating three murders, mixed up in a meth distribution scandal that stretched farther than I could imagine, and now walking through a dust bowl John Steinbeck might have written about, searching for the special woman in my life, who was "missing in action."

I estimated the length from the road to the McInerny house was probably one-third of a mile. Turning a corner in the rutted driveway, I could see the run-down house, and smoke billowing from the chimney. On warm May afternoons, few people heated their homes with such fervor. I was used to the clouds emerging from the Cleveland steel mills that often darkened the sunlit sky, but the McInerny smoke smelled strange and different.

I've run into a drug peddler or two in my profession. They all played hardball, although the ones on the Cleveland streets were such low-grade hustlers that whenever one of them got pushed even slightly, he ran crying to the middle-management guys, who indeed have hired muscle just hanging around waiting to be asked. I'd never dealt with the manufacturing end of illegal substances, though, until it shouldered its way into my current Ashtabula adventure. The McInernys were no high-level drug kingpins pocketing money hand over fist, or they'd live in a somewhat nicer place than this. I wasn't even certain they could read. But they were connected to the powerful Elijah Jackson—the Prophet of the Conneaut prison—and perhaps with Chief Koskinen.

Were the McInernys responsible for three killings? I guessed probably not. They had firearms, but I doubted they'd do more with them than sit on their brokeback porch and shoot rats. Nonetheless, looking for Tobe, I walked in there feeling naked and defenseless.

I had my fists, I suppose—my sixty-year-old fists. I could still throw them pretty well—but the sore muscles that propelled them had been issued along with my AARP registration card.

I had "hired muscle" of my own—my studious assistant, K.O., who could fight with the best of them, and had. He was half my size, half my age, and twice as rough. I'd sent him around to approach the house from the back, although I had no solid knowledge if Tobe was there or not. There was always a chance that K.O.'s barely controlled temper might flare up—but even so, a solid right uppercut doesn't move nearly as fast as a bullet.

The slight breeze changed direction, and the big dog chained at the foot of the porch caught my scent, lunged to his feet, and began barking—low and deep from that massive chest.

It alerted Bobby Jeff McInerny. He plodded out through the bent screen door, wearing what looked like the same pair of overalls as the other day, scratching his armpit and frowning. When he saw me coming up his driveway, he moved to the edge of the top step, put his fists on his hips à la Yul Brynner, and waited until I was close enough to hear him over the barking.

"Sumbitch," he said, efficiently changing four words into one.

"Mr. McInerny." I nodded back.

"You here again? What's the deal, man? You people botherin' the shee-it outta us." He *added* a syllable that time. Creative guy.

I approached Bobby Jeff carefully. He didn't seem to be armed, but that didn't mean one or both of his boys weren't lurking around inside the house, peeking out the windows, their gun sights trained right on me.

At the bottom of the steps, just out of reach of the dog, I raised both hands to show him I wasn't carrying heat, either. I said, "I'm looking for a friend."

"Yeah? Which friend would that be? The young punk suckin' around after you like you're his longtime boyfriend? Or that smart-ass colored bitch thinkin' she's ten times tougher'n she really is?"

Colored bitch. Oh my! "I thought she might be here. She said she was coming to see you today."

"Well, she weren't here a-tall, so you just shit outta luck."

"Interesting. How would you know about *the colored bitch* if she hadn't been here before?"

Bobby Jeff cocked his head. "Whaddya think, we live at the bottom of a coal mine? We heard about all you the minute you hit town. But I tole you before, nobody here kilt nobody. We's just three men, we lives here by ourselfs, an' we minds our fuckin' bidness. You oughta do the same. Up here, we take care our own bidness. We don't need no help from Cleveland or someplace."

"I'm just here to find Detective Sergeant Blaine."

"An' what *she* come out here for? Spyin'? She spyin'on us?"

"You said before, you've done business with Paul Fontaine."

Jimmy John McInerny came through the screen door. Soiled jeans and grungy T-shirt were apparently the uniform of the day for him, although the shirt was worn outside the very baggy pants and didn't quite hide the pistol he had stuck in his waistband—an old-time Colt out of a Randolph Scott western. This time he was wearing what looked like Latex gloves, too. Quite an outfit.

"So?" Bobby Jeff said. "He mostly raised and sold horses." He waved a hand at his moth-bitten farm. "This look like a horse ranch?"

"Did he sell other things, too?"

McInerny shrugged. "This here's a poor county; we do what we gotta do to put food on the table."

"Like cooking meth?"

He shook his head. "That's gotta be three other people, Officer. Not us."

I made a big point of sniffing the air. "What's that you're cooking now, Bobby Jeff? Klobasa?"

He scratched his armpit again. "What's that klobasa stuff?"

"Slovenian sausage."

Bobby Jeff burst out into a big smile. "Why, that's exactly right. Slov—uh—" He struggled with saying "Slovenian." Finally he re-tooled. "It's Polack sausage." He cocked his head the other way. "I 'member your name from last time. You a Polack, too, right?"

I considered reminding him I was not Polish, but Slovenian, and that Polish people aren't Polacks, either, but the political correctness issue was so far down the line, I just ignored it. "Lots of smoke in the air now for sausage, don't you think?"

His nod was grudging. "It's a lotta sausage."

I took a deep breath. "I don't think it's sausage at all, Bobby Jeff. I think you're fooling me."

Bobby Jeff came down two of the four steps. Behind him, Jimmy John's hand crept close to his waistband weapon. It's hard to talk to one person and keep your eye on someone else's gun at the same time. "You callin' me out a liar?"

"Let's just say I know the difference between Polish sausage and methamphetamine." I moved toward the steps, close enough that I could smell his unwashed body. "And I know damn well Detective Blaine was here this morning."

"You're just guessin', copper."

If McInerny thought I was a policeman, I wouldn't disabuse him of the notion. "I only need one guess, Bobby Jeff."

"You guessed wrong, boy."

"Did I?" I looked around. "Where's your other son, then? Where's Wyatt?"

"He's a growed man," Bobby Jeff said. "I don't know where he's at, an' I don't care, neither. All I cares about is where *you* is, which I want to be anyplace else 'cept here. Now, best you git your ass on the road 'fore it gets shot off."

Jimmy John perked up, hearing the word *shot*. He came down to ground level, his jittery fingers hovering over the handle of his weapon like butterflies around a flower. Either that, or he was trying to hold his pants up.

"If you take that gun out of your pants, Jimmy John," I said, "you're going to eat it for dinner."

"Wooh!" Jimmy John said. It surprised me; I hadn't been sure he was even able to speak. "You a tough guy, huh?"

"Damn right I am."

Jimmy John snickered. Well, not exactly a snicker; I don't know what else to call it. Perhaps he'd tried swallowing an entire bagel whole, and it had gotten stuck in his throat. When he was finally able to talk again, he said, "You're a old man. Old men ain't so tough."

"Then try me."

"Ev'ybody calm down," Bobby Jeff said. "Ain't gonna be no shootin' round here today, lessen someone sees a big rat. Listen, Officer Pig—you axed if your partner come here today, and I say she di'n't. So that gotta be the end of it. As far as what we do here in our own home, that's nobody's bidness."

"It's hard not to notice the stink of meth you're cooking."

Bobby Jeff laughed. "You think we're all goin' to jail 'cuz of your nose?"

I immediately thought of Tobe's nose. One sniff and she can identify almost anything. "You'll all go to jail if you've harmed Detective Blaine. So I'll ask once more: Do you know where she is?"

"You're wastin' your time, an' mine, too. You took a long walk from the road to here for nothin'. Now take another long walk back."

"What if I come back with a warrant?"

"I'll wipe my ass with it. Now *move!*"

Jimmy John took another step toward me, hand dangling near his waistband. Were he even a third-rate cowboy movie actor, I could have taken him down easily. Since I didn't have a weapon, I was screwed—at least for the moment. I wasn't even sure I could *get* a warrant. Warden Glasser was on the pad, and so, I believed, was Eino Koskinen. I wondered if at least one honest judge lived in the county.

I bluffed anyway. "You'll see me again, Bobby Jeff."

"Come back any time, Officer Pig—'cuz you'll be wearin' a target on your back. An' we hardly never miss."

I was out of options, and even though I was certain the McInernys knew where Tobe was, I couldn't argue with a shooter. I'd have to figure out another way to find her.

I was about to turn and leave McInerny land, and then I stopped short and just stared.

I didn't want to miss the parade.

Leading it were the chickens from the jerry-rigged coop around behind the house, bustling ahead, clucking and squawking and flapping their wings, possibly to announce the main event, which was coming up behind them.

First in sight was Wyatt McInerny. He staggered as though completely intoxicated, but probably the cut in his scalp due to some sort of attack caused him to be a bit out of it. Blood from scalp wounds flowed as copiously as Niagara Falls, and the right side of Wyatt's face was a bright, sticky red. There was blood, already dried, that had come out of his right ear, too, and had trickled down into the collar of his dirty T-shirt. His limp reminded me of Chester on the old *Gunsmoke* TV show.

His hands were securely tied behind his back with what looked like chicken wire. There was another loop of wire, three layers thick, wrapped around his neck, forcing him to keep his head up. A trail of that wire, about four feet long, was wrapped tightly around the biblical-looking staff in the hands of Kevin O'Bannion, who marched behind him like a dog walker strolling a too-eager mastiff out for his morning constitutional. That wire looked as if it were pulled tight—possibly why Wyatt's eyes were bulging.

The front of his pants, starting at the crotch and descending all the way down his legs, was dripping wet.

Walking next to K.O. was Detective Sergeant Tobe Blaine. She carried Wyatt's ancient rifle at the ready, pointing it at Bobby Jeff while with her other hand she aimed her police-provided Glock right at the staggering Jimmy John. As she approached, I noticed a major swelling above her left eye—a blooming "egg" bruise, with the eye itself halfway closed. There were raw reddish marks and dried blood around her mouth. She tried a smile, but it didn't come off too well.

"Jimmy John," K.O. called out as he marched forward, "take that cannon out of your waistband with one finger and one thumb—careful, so you don't shoot off your own dick. Put it on the ground, and then step away from it and clasp your fingers together on top of your head. Mr. McInerny, you do the same. Piss me off just a little tiny bit—and one twist of this chicken wire's gonna take off Wyatt's head. You don't want to see it rolling around on the ground like a beach ball, do you?"

He laughed—one short staccato burst. "Or do you?"

CHAPTER TWENTY-SEVEN

TOBE

Four hours earlier . . .

When she maneuvered up the driveway, which was little more than a wide path in the sandy dirt, Tobe Blaine could hear a music system blasting from inside the McInerny house at top volume, so nobody heard her car arrive. She knew about rap and hip-hop, she knew plenty about rock and punk, and she was familiar with country music, even country rock. But she had no idea *what* she was hearing that apparently entertained the McInerny family with far too many decibels. She turned off her engine and listened for a moment, but couldn't even find a beat. It was just noise.

She hadn't come here to dance anyway.

Gray smoke poured from the chimney of the house, and it took only one sniff of her hyperosmia-ridden nose to tell her whatever was cooking in the kitchen was not food, only a combination of chemicals. She rubbed her nose vigorously, then shook her head as if to chase away the expected migraine.

The dog, chained to one side of the steps, noticed her but didn't seem bent on attack. Shifting his position, he made a soft rumbling sound in the back of his throat. Perhaps, she thought, he reacted differently to females than he did to males—because in his lifetime no *man* had treated him with anything other than either abuse or neglect.

She felt sad—she was not quite the animal activist K.O. was, but she felt worse about dogs chained up and all alone in their yards than she did about the scores of people she'd arrested over the years. At least *those* perps had deserved it. Dogs didn't.

Damn it, though, she couldn't rescue every dog in the world who needed rescuing. Nonetheless, she patted the Glock she carried on her hip, hidden by her jacket.

Just in case.

She carefully mounted the sagging steps to the front porch. The screen door was closed and latched. There was no doorbell. She rapped heartily, even called out, but the music from the rear of the house was too loud for anyone to hear her.

She didn't want to go back there, she didn't want to be anywhere near the stench. But she wasn't here about what Bobby Jeff was cooking. She was putting connections together in her head—Paul Fontaine and Chief Koskinen and the meth makers who owned this house. While she didn't think the McInernys were eliminating all the good churchgoing Baptists in Queenstown, they might reveal something to point her in a different direction.

She went back down the steps. The dog rumbled louder, his tail actually wagging. She squatted down and slowly extended a hand toward him. He didn't flinch. She stroked the top of his head, and his rumble turned into a happy whine. She took a few more moments to scratch his neck beneath the choke collar, and rumple his ears.

"Sorry, pal," she said, her voice soft as she straightened up. "Duty calls. Work before play."

The dog arose, too, tail whipping madly, and followed her as far as the chain would allow. He probably saw females rarely, and it was doubtful they even bothered talking to him. Tobe took one last look at him over her shoulder. God damn these people! she thought.

As she moved around the outside of the house, the music got louder and the smell more sickening. There was a back door, but no steps to reach it—only a few large, square bricks she had to climb so she could peer inside the screen door.

The gas stove had been converted into a Rube Goldberg–like contraption with a series of tubes, hanging containers, and temperature gauges, and whatever was on the burner bubbled merrily away with a nauseating miasma that made Tobe's eyes and nostrils burn.

Bobby Jeff McInerny and his son Jimmy John were doing the

cooking, or rather Jimmy John was, wearing Latex gloves and a full-length apron over his sleeveless undershirt and filthy slacks. His father was sitting nearby on a stool, watching and calling out instructions. "A skosh more ammonia there, boy. That's the way."

Tobe had seen meth labs before, but had never watched anyone actually use one. She wondered, now that Paul J. Fontaine was dead and buried, who would move the McInerny product to the waiting customers? The Prophet was still in prison, Warden Glasser only got meth money to pocket when he was able to get a piece of Jackson's, and Koskinen had nothing to do with any of it except discreetly looking the other way. As for the McInernys taking over the sales themselves, between the three of them they didn't have the intelligence to solve an eighth-grade crossword puzzle. Real selling was an art they'd be unlikely to accomplish.

So intrigued was she at what they were doing, she didn't knock on the door soon enough. Something hard hit her on the back of her head. Reeling, she tried turning around, catching only a glimpse of a young man whom she later learned was Wyatt McInerny. Again he swung his rifle butt at her, this time catching her just over her eyebrow.

Pain exploded inside her head and fireworks detonated behind her eyes. Everything went out of focus—and then went away altogether. She collapsed off the bricks on which she stood, falling—but she was unaware of it when she hit the ground.

Regaining consciousness, Tobe was immediately aware of the pain, as if someone had drilled a hole in her skull and poured acid inside. Focusing her eyes took a tremendous effort. A few moments later she realized she was on the floor of a chicken coop, her hands tied behind her, and another rope twisted tight around her body to keep her sitting up straight against a pole. Chickens in the cages behind her were making all sorts of clucking noises—but that's what chickens do. Between the stink of fresh droppings within a few feet of her, the chemical scent of the meth on the stove, the throbbing of the swollen bruise above her eye, and the exquisite agony of a headache that might have been either a migraine or a concussion, she realized she was not in good shape.

Wyatt McInerny was sitting on a bench across the coop from her, sucking on a cigarette, which also made her nauseous, and trimming his fingernails with a pocket knife. His rifle was propped up next to him. Abashed, she saw her own Glock was tucked into his belt.

When a cop loses a department-issued weapon, he or she might just as well turn in the badge and get a job pouring coffee and asking people if they want fries.

It wasn't until she tried to say something to Wyatt McInerny that she realized her mouth had been taped shut, probably with duct tape. Still punchy from the head blows, the first thing that popped into her mind was that everyone used to call it *duct tape*, and then someone had copyrighted the catchy title.

Whatever noise she made alerted Wyatt that she was now conscious. He stood and moved closer, looming over her.

"Thought you was gonna sleep all fuckin' day. Don't try talkin'. Not that I give a shit what any nigger's got to say, but Daddy wants your mouth shut so you don't make no noise."

Tobe glared up at him.

"Don't be givin' me no dirty looks, now, girl, else I rip off that tape an' shove somepin' else down your throat." And he cupped his own crotch with his hand. "Ain't a bad idea at that."

And I'll bite it off and spit it in your face, Tobe thought but did not say.

He grinned, leering at her. "Tonight, maybe, us'll have lotsa fun with you, 'fore we dump you in a hole an' leave you to rot."

Tobe massaged the thought in her mind. They'd kill her. She hadn't done a damn thing to them, had harbored no desire to do so.

Then *why?*

Racism is certainly alive and well in this country. But murder is a real reach, even for the most bigoted idiot, which made Tobe wonder why they'd chosen her, a police officer. Didn't they know that when a cop goes down in the line of duty, no matter where that cop is from or where he or she plies that trade, every badge-carrying flatfoot is going to come after them with guns blazing, and won't quit until that death has been avenged?

No, they *didn't* know that, being too damn dumb to know in

what direction the sun rises every morning. She strained at the cords wrapped around her wrists. She had to give them points for tying a solid knot.

Eventually Wyatt McInerny grew tired of glowering down at her, so he sauntered back to his bench, scratching between his buttocks as he went. Had Tobe been able to speak at that moment, "*Eew*" would have been her only utterance.

He sat down, leaned back, half closed his eyes, and began humming a tune that wasn't a tune at all. Tobe wondered if he'd go to sleep, as there didn't seem to be anything else he could do in the chicken coop. Part of her wished he would so she could try to escape, but she was bound too tightly, and her hands would lose what little circulation was left before she could free herself.

Her throbbing head made *her* want to go to sleep, too, but she remembered that with a concussion, falling asleep is dangerous. So she began running over things in her head that might distract her from closing her eyes.

The myth is that when you're about to die, your entire life flashes before your eyes, but Tobe didn't want to revisit all the arrests she'd made in her career, the three people she'd had to shoot, one of whom died. She wasn't that interested in her childhood, which had basically been without incident.

Except for one Christmas.

She'd been eight years old, and had desperately wanted a camera. She'd been bugging her parents for one throughout half the year. Not a big expensive camera; she was too young to figure one out. Just a simple Kodak—put in the film, look through the viewfinder, and click. She could hardly wait for Christmas morning. When she finally tore into her presents, her big main gift from her parents was, of all things, a ukulele. They were joyful, and told her they were anxious to hear her play it when she'd mastered the art.

She never picked up the damn thing again.

Move along, she thought, maybe ten years. Her first real boyfriend. They had met in American history class in high school. Tyrone, his name was, back when people didn't often name their kids Tyrone. Tyrone had given her her first real kiss, and later, her first sexual experience—a pretty dull one, as neither had had a clue as to what they were doing.

Other men, of course. Tobe flipped through them quickly in her mind—black, white, even an Asian, and she didn't bother rating their personalities, their looks, their sexual expertise. She was too anxious for her vivid memory bank to get her to Zan Bricker.

Zan. Alexander. Black mother, white father. North Carolina State University, ROTC lieutenant in the U.S. army for three years, then a cop, first in Greensboro, then in Raleigh, where they met. Both attaining the rank of detective, they were partnered for a while and worked well together, but had asked to change partners because they were falling in love. They'd been officially engaged for two months before Zan went out on a call to a reported shooting on the east side of town. Shortly after he arrived at the location, there were other shots fired. He didn't come back.

Too many memories in Raleigh, too much pain for Tobe to report for work every morning to look at that empty chair, that unused desk. She trolled around for a job in another city and was finally offered one in Cincinnati.

More arrests. A few men came in and out of her life. Not many, because a shattered love affair was why she left Raleigh in the first place. A few friends, and not many of those, either. A promotion to Detective Sergeant. Interesting baseball and football teams, a nice view over the river to Kentucky, and a pretty Fountain Square downtown.

Undisguised racism in a town that was far more postbellum than Midwest.

After a few years, she moved even farther north, to Cleveland. To a good job and a good division: homicide. To a great restaurant town, especially a few blocks from Public Square on East 4th Street and West 6th Street. A great music town, a great sports town. To a nice apartment on the West Side, two blocks from the lake.

And then to Milan Jacovich.

God knows why. He was fourteen years her senior, slightly overweight, long divorced, losing his hair, and working at a career most cops didn't really understand.

And now a temporary assignment in Ashtabula County, even though she was still mispronouncing it in her head, and to a chicken coop where she'd probably be killed by three mouth-breathing loony birds as soon as it got dark.

Distressing to think about. She had to go through other thoughts to distract her from the immediate future.

Songs. Songs that she loved, a major part of her life for as long as she could remember, started running through her head. She'd heard Nina Simone, and later, Billie Holliday, sing the depressing song "Strange Fruit," which was all about lynching Negroes in the South, where she'd been born and raised. Luckily she'd been born too late, or she might be swinging from a tree limb, too. She didn't want to deal with "Strange Fruit."

"Hit the road, Jack, and don't you come back no more." The great Ray Charles. She ran through a few more of his big hits, ending up with "Georgia on My Mind." She wondered whether Milan was a Ray Charles fan; they'd never discussed it.

They'd not discussed a lot of things in the time they'd been "keeping company," as some liked to say. From the beginning, race had never been part of their conversation. Of course, she was into many white singers, too. She had CDs of almost every Tony Bennett recording, which started her on "I Left My Heart in San Francisco," except she couldn't remember all the words.

Maybe, she thought, something with a little more bounce to keep her conscious and thinking. "And here's to you, Mrs. Robinson, Jesus loves you more than you will know." Hmm. The reference to Jesus kicked in a completely different thought that pushed all her favorite songs off to the side. Pastor Thomas Nelson Urban Junior, the parsimonious bigot, and his three devoted parishioners who'd been killed—the reason she was in Ashtabula County in the first place.

Wyatt was paying no attention to her. Secure that she wouldn't figure a way out of the ropes, his mind was elsewhere. And that was great for her, assuming she ever got out of this henhouse alive, because she needed time to think.

And the last one in the world she'd want to bother and distract her was Wyatt McInerny.

CHAPTER TWENTY-EIGHT

TOBE

She'd lost track of time. She was still wearing her wristwatch but couldn't see it, since both hands were tied behind her. She'd been trussed up here several hours, and her fingers were already numb. Wyatt, the son of a bitch, had drifted off to a nap, and listening to him snore had grown unbearably boring, even more so than just having to look at him.

She worried that eventually she'd have to pee. Since the McInernys had decided to eliminate her from the human race in a few hours, she'd doubt Wyatt was going to untie her and walk her back to the house, where she could use the bathroom.

And on the outside chance he *would,* her mouth was plastered shut with duct tape—she couldn't ask him even if she wanted to.

Well, she'd hold it. As long as she possibly could. If she were to die, she'd be damned if she'd piss herself first.

She fought valiantly not to go to sleep. Her shoulders ached and her butt tingled from not moving for so long. Her migraine had subsided into a slow, pounding headache.

Amazingly, she was still able to think.

If the McInerny clan planned to dispose of her remains when it got dark, she figured they would do the deed someplace else. She remembered nothing after Wyatt had knocked her silly. For all she knew, her car was sitting right there in front of the house. She imagined they'd relieved her of her keys to get the vehicle out of sight.

She shuddered, hating that they'd reached into her pants

pocket, touched her any way they wanted to while she was un-
conscious. Okay, she thought. When they were ready to kill her,
they would have to untie her from the post to take her someplace
where no one else would see or hear them. She thought she might
not survive. All of them had guns, and Wyatt McInerny had hers,
too. But deep down inside, where it mattered, she knew that she'd
definitely count coup before she died.

She disappeared into another montage of memories. Her training in yoga, in kung fu, in street fighting, in the "proper" police
chokehold that would immobilize her victim but not kill, and the
times she'd put those things to proper use when making arrests.
She'd worked long enough in the Cincinnati Homicide Division
that fellow cops and street criminals alike learned she was nobody
to fuck with. Thinking over the good old days, which weren't so old
at all, she realized nobody had ever gotten the best of her in a physical fight. She'd taken down men twice her size and weight. She'd
disarmed three or four with firepower in their hands. She'd taken
more knives away from bad guys than she could even remember.

She'd also worn a badge for twenty-some years, and every
officer knows each time they clip that shield on, there is a chance
they might not take it off, ever. It hadn't occurred to her when she
signed on for a loaner tour in rural Ashtabula County. But here
it was.

Regrets? Everyone has them. She was never close to either of
her parents, but she didn't mourn the distance that had widened
between them as soon as she had entered her teen years. She had
no children, and couldn't imagine herself as anyone's mother.
Never had a dog, even though she liked and cared about animals.
Never had three-way sex, though two Cincinnati cops had suggested it to her—but she'd sometimes fantasized about it, like everyone else in the world. Never spent a year or two in someplace
beautiful like the Greek islands or Barcelona or Fiji. Her truckload
of regrets didn't bother her. Her last thoughts before the McInernys killed her would not be those terrified shoulda-woulda-coulda
sorrows.

Scared of dying? Not exactly scared . . .

Everybody dies eventually. Not usually in their mid-for-
ties, in perfect health, more or less happy with their job, their

relationship, the way life was going—but eventually. She didn't worry she might not go to heaven but to hell instead, because her idea of death wasn't an afterlife, or being reincarnated as a butterfly or a dandelion or the king of England. Dead is dead; dead doesn't come back. Not frightened of dying, but it wasn't her first choice.

And what would she leave behind her when she was gone? She'd never made a will. Had she thought about it, she'd have arranged for whatever money was in her various savings and checking accounts and pensions—she wasn't sure, but thought it all added up to about $45,000—to be distributed to her favorite charities.

What *were* her favorite charities? Many charities supporting the victims of terrible illnesses rarely gave more than twenty cents of the donated buck to the people who needed it the most. The rest went for advertising, executives, fundraisers, and people who worked for these organizations just for the sake of a job.

She'd never discussed her own funeral with anybody. Failing her first choice of being set out at the curb with the rest of the trash on garbage day, she'd rather be cremated. Her parents were too religious to allow that to happen, so she'd be buried somewhere, with every cop she'd ever known all dressed up in their uniforms, standing around doing the stiff-upper-lip thing and wanting desperately to get out of that cemetery and into the nearest bar.

She wondered whether Tyrone would come to pay his respects. If they had been one another's fifth lover, or tenth lover, neither would have remembered the incident at all. But two high school kids both giving up their virginity, despite it not being much of a life-altering memory—well, that deserved a show-up at the funeral.

Milan, naturally. She knew Milan better at this time in her life than anyone else in the world. And one thing she was sure of: he wouldn't cry, at least not where anyone could see him. Grave, sorrowful, but no tears.

If, that is. *If* anyone found her body where the McInerny boys would dispose of it. Otherwise—no ceremony, no cremation, no gathering of mourners. Anyone who'd miss her would do it at home.

Shit! she finally thought, her breath coming faster through her nose, as her mouth was still taped. Why in hell was she spending perhaps her last few moments on earth thinking about wills and funerals and who was going to cry and who wouldn't?

She considered making a run for it as soon as they untied her, but dismissed it out of hand. Men like the McInernys probably went hunting once or twice a week, shooting birds, rabbits, probably even deer for dinner—too dumb to realize it was cheaper to go to a supermarket. Any one of them would nail her with the first shot.

Behind her back she flexed her fingers, and her knuckles popped, which awakened Wyatt McInerny from his afternoon snooze. He jerked awake, looked about as though scared of some unknown forest monster coming to get him in the henhouse. Snuffling, he stood and stretched himself almost luxuriously, groaning as he did so.

The loud fart was an afterthought—although it disturbed the chickens, setting them to clucking and rustling around in their nests.

Finally he looked at Tobe. His grin was nearly demonic. "Tick, tick, tick," he said. "Know what that is, bitch? Your life tickin' away. Ain't got much time left. Count those seconds. Tick, tick, tick."

He unconsciously felt for the gun in his waistband to make sure it was there. Satisfied, he hitched up his pants. "Your own damn fault, too, bitch. Pokin' your nose where it don't belong. Spyin' on us through our windows. If you ain't done that, there'd be no problem. But you were lookin' at us right through the back window, you seen what we was doin', which was none a your goddamn bidness! Nobody had no proof before, not till you come around. So now we cain't let you walk outta here and go to the tri-county cops, kin we?"

He strolled aimlessly around the coop. "You ain't the first one. Couple a years back, there's this one guy, used to move our product for us. He come back, said he delivered it, but he got mugged on the way back an' somebody stole our money. Now, if you was us, you think we're gonna b'lieve that? He wasn't really from around here anyways, so when we shot him in the fuckin' head and buried him out in the woods, nobody even noticed. Damn good thing you're not from around here, neither." And he made a pistol with his fingers, pointed right at Tobe, and said, "Pow! Pow!"

Tobe didn't blink.

"Tough, huh?" Wyatt said. "We gonna see how tough you are with a gun stickin' right in your eye." He patted her weapon again. "Think we'll shoot you with your own gun, too. Neat, huh?"

Tobe still didn't blink. Despite her immobility, and him with a rifle and her gun, she made him uncomfortable.

"Damn," he said, "they makin' me sit in here smellin' chicken shit all day! Jimmy John oughta come out and take my place a while." He looked at his wristwatch, the kind you get at WalMart for $9.95. "Shit!" he said again.

He unzipped his fly and took out his penis. "Get a good look, bitch," he said, vastly amused. "I bet you'd just love gettin' a piece a this, huh?" He waved it around like a miniature flag at an Independence Day parade, looking like the crazy uncle you keep locked in your attic until one day he gets near a window and waves his dick at the passers-by on the way to Sunday-morning church. "Ain't gonna happen, though, I got no use for nigger cooze. I'd rather spend twenty bucks on some skanky old whore than stick it in you for free."

He faced the opposite corner of the henhouse, spread his legs a bit, and urinated against one wall. Tobe wanted to look away, but wouldn't give him the satisfaction. She telegraphed her disgust through her eyes.

Finished, he shook himself dry and put himself back in his pants, then rezipped with a flourish. "You liked that, huh, bitch? Bet that got you all hot." He came back to stand over her, looking her over from top to toes. "My ol' man said I shouldn't facefuck you. But he didn't say nothin' about anything else." He squatted next to her, took both her breasts in his hands, and brutally squeezed them.

"Ha!" Wyatt said as he abused her, "you nigger bitches are butt-ugly—but you all have great tits."

Whoever had tied Tobe up in the henhouse, her hands behind her, her mouth taped shut, and another rope securing her upper body to one of the posts that held the roof on, had forgotten to disable her legs, leaving them free. So when Wyatt shifted position in his squat, she used her boot-encased heel to nearly shatter his knee-bone.

He reared back, bellowing in pain, toppling over onto his side, rolling around in the dirt, clutching his knee, spewing more obscenities and racial epithets at the top of his voice.

It took Wyatt a while to stop groveling in pain. Finally, leaning hard on the wall for help, he managed to stand up. His eyes on Tobe now were murderous eyes—psycho eyes. He took a few steps toward her until his hurt knee gave out and he almost fell again, unleashing a new set of profanities on her as he moved painfully across the floor of the henhouse, but this time they were said in a soft, vitriolic whisper instead of an angry rant—and this time Tobe felt a chill fear galloping up her spine.

"Goddamn cunt!" Wyatt hissed. "You kick at me when you can't even move a muscle? You were gonna die anyway—but now dyin's gonna be *hard*." And he unbuckled his belt and pulled it out of his pant loops. He ran his fingers the length of it, then grasped it from one end, the buckle on the other.

"You a-scared now, bitch? How long's it gonna take you to die when I start whuppin' on you with this? Huh?"

He began swinging the belt around his head, Tobe hearing the whistling sound it made. Up until this moment, she figured she'd have time before it grew dark and quiet and they disposed of her. Now she wondered how long it would be until she actually died from the beating.

"Hee hee!" Wyatt chortled, still swinging. "You *are* a-scared now, by damn! I see it in your eyes."

And he brought the belt buckle down hard on her left shoulder. Tobe saw it coming and turned her head to the right to protect her eyes as the metal buckle cracked into her collarbone. She was still wearing her lightweight jacket, but there was little or no padding to protect her—and the agony reached to the ends of her toes in milliseconds. She couldn't scream, of course, as her mouth was taped, nor would she have even if she could. A groan sprang to her throat, though, whether she wanted it to or not.

The sound made Wyatt smile broadly. "Oooh, yeah!" he breathed. "I think I'll go for the tits next."

He raised his hand again and took aim. However, the belt

buckle never landed. Because the door to the chicken coop burst open, and Kevin O'Bannion blasted through it, already swinging the heavy tree branch he'd turned into a walking staff, and laid it across the back of Wyatt McInerny's head with an almost sickening force.

Wyatt went down on both knees, blood already spurting. As he tried to drag himself up, K.O. landed on his back with both knees, driving every bit of breath from his body, and making him lose control of his bladder—apparently he hadn't finished the first time. Still straddling him, K.O. delivered two hard overhand punches to the side of his head, one striking his ear, which put Wyatt into dreamland.

He stayed straddled for a moment, catching his breath. Then he arose and moved quickly to Tobe. "Sorry," he said, "I was about fifteen seconds too late." He squatted down and put his hand to her face, fingering one end of the duct tape. "This won't feel good when I pull it off. Slow and careful?"

She shook her head no.

"One fast yank?"

She nodded.

He sighed. "Hang on," he said—and did what he said he'd do. The ripping sound was more awful than the damage it did.

Tobe winced. The area around her mouth was chapped and bleeding. She took a deep breath.

K.O. frowned at the egg-shaped bruise above her eye. "Jesus, Tobe! Did he hurt you?"

"Does a bear shit in the woods? Get me out of here!"

He took out his Swiss Army knife, already unclasped. It took him a few minutes, sawing at the ropes binding her hands behind the post—but eventually Tobe was free.

"Give me a hand, will you?" she said, and K.O. easily lifted her to her feet. She rotated her head around on her shoulders, stretched, and groaned. "Oh, God, it feels so good to stand again. I've been tied up for . . ." She looked at her wristwatch. "Four hours at least." She touched the top of her shoulder where the belt buckle had bitten into her and sucked in a breath between her teeth. Then she said, "Thanks for showing up, K.O."

"Milan's here, too."

"Not surprised."

"He's up at the front house, keeping them busy. He sent me around the back way so nobody saw me looking for you."

"They have guns."

K.O. turned, picked up Wyatt's rifle from where it had fallen. "Good, now so do we."

Tobe fingered her lips and winced. "That's my service revolver in his pants. Grab it and we'll have two."

K.O. did so, and handed it back to Tobe. "Will we have a shoot-out?"

"Somebody might get killed," she said, shaking her head. "I've got a better idea. Where's that knife of yours?"

K.O. gave her the knife. "Are you going to kill Wyatt?"

Tobe opened it and started carving away at the chicken wire that kept the hens from running away, glancing only momentarily at the slumbering Wyatt McInerny. "Don't tempt me," she said.

CHAPTER TWENTY-NINE

MILAN

For a while, I feared Jimmy John would start shooting. That was a scary thought, considering I was the one person there, besides Wyatt, who wasn't armed.

But Bobby Jeff—the McInerny daddy—figured out that one twist of K.O.'s walking staff would kill Wyatt in a moment. He put down his gun, nodding to Jimmy John to drop his on the ground, too.

Eventually, all three of them were trussed up. We left the chicken wire wrapped around Wyatt's hands and neck, I tied Bobby Jeff's hands behind him with clothesline rope, and Tobe clapped Jimmy John into the handcuffs she always carried with her. I couldn't help noticing she clicked them on very tightly.

Then while Tobe and I stood guard, K.O. trudged back through the woods to where he'd seen Tobe's hidden car and drove it into the front yard. Tobe retrieved her camera from the trunk—police detectives never go anywhere without a camera—and went inside to take photographs of the kitchen and all its meth-cooking paraphernalia.

Bobby Jeff said to me, "You people got no right here. That colored woman got no right takin' those pitchers. It won't stand up in court, neither, cause she got no warrant to take 'em."

"Watching too much *Law and Order*, Bobby Jeff? You assaulted and kidnapped a police officer, and threatened to kill her."

"Aw," Wyatt whined, even though the chicken wire was practically choking him, "I was just teasin' her."

"Tied her up, taped her mouth shut, and beat her with a belt buckle—to tease her? You're quite a kidder, Wyatt."

He shut up. I turned back to the old man. "As far as pictures are concerned—right, they won't stand up in court. But when we take them to the Tri-County Drug Task Force, they'll *get* a warrant and come marching back in here to look for themselves. And since you and your Rover Boys are going to be in jail anyway for what you did today, you won't be able to do a goddamn thing to stop them."

"Yeah—but at least we didn' kill nobody. An' that's why you come around here in the first place." Bobby Jeff shook his head sadly. "You should give us a break here—cut us a little slack."

"You would've killed Detective Sergeant Blaine!"

"We was gonna, but we didn'! You cain' put nobody in jail for what they's thinkin'."

I got very close to him. I was bigger than him and outweighed him by almost a hundred pounds, and my face inches from his scared the hell out of him. It made it worse when I said, "If they jailed people for what they're thinking, Bobby Jeff, I'd be on death row."

The air seemed to go out of him with a sucking rush, and he became smaller and more vulnerable, hanging his head. "You're a bad man, sir. You're such a bad man."

While we were piling the family into cars, K.O. found his way over to the dog, who growled and arched his back. K.O. knelt beside the animal, murmuring soft words, his head down so as not to make eye contact. It took about five minutes, and Tobe and I, watching him almost as closely as we were our prisoners, grew anxious to get the McInerny clan behind bars as soon as possible. Finally K.O. was able to touch the dog, scratch his neck and rumple his ears, which earned him a tail wag in return. He stood up and came back over to us.

"We can't leave him here. There'll be nobody here to feed him or give him water."

"We can't take him," I said. "I've got Herbie, and I don't have room for another one. And you can't just waltz back into Carli's place with a dog that size trailing along behind you."

"Shit!"

I knew him well enough to understand when he was furious—

usually it was about animals. I said, "He doesn't relate to anyone because they leave him tied up out here. Can you imagine what'll happen when you surprise Rodney with him?"

That shook K.O. a bit. Rodney, his cat, was the love of his life—well, Rodney and Carli—and he hadn't thought about Rodney co-existing with this giant, bad-tempered dog. Finally he said, "We've got to take him somewhere. I'm not abandoning him." His glare at Old Man McInerny could have cut through diamonds. "They treat him like shit here anyway. They kick him."

"We'll take him to the state troopers along with our three pals here," Tobe said. "They'll know what to do with him."

"They'd better," K.O. murmured.

We finally got straight who would go in which car. Bobby Jeff was loaded into the back of the Queenstown cop car, K.O. next to him. The dog—no one seemed to know his name—shared the front seat with me.

The two younger guys were in the back of Tobe's car. We might have changed seating arrangements, for safety if nothing else, but Tobe was the one who had all the guns. Besides, Wyatt was in no condition to do much of anything. When Tobe bent him low to put him in the backseat, she took the opportunity to drive her knee up, hard, between his legs from the back, which put him flat on his face on the backseat, screaming in agony and threatening "Police brutality! Police brutality!"

Tobe leaned in, grabbed a fistful of his hair, and bent his head all the way back so he could see her face, and she shoved the rifle muzzle against his throat. "Open your fucking mouth once more, Wyatt, and I'll show you what police brutality is."

Jimmy John crawled beside his brother, not daring to speak a word. Tobe got into the front, started the car, waved good-bye out the window at me, and tore off toward the highway in a cloud of dust.

The dog perched next to me, nearly filling up the entire front seat, was snuffling, drooling, and leaving sticky nose prints on the window. His breath cried out for a Tic Tac.

"I hope," Bobby Jeff said, "you're gonna make sure that dog is okay. I got him out of the pound, y'know. I really love dogs."

"Is that why you kick him?" K.O. said.

"Hey, you gotta train a big sumbitch like that to behave, lest he gonna chew off your dick."

"Maybe," K.O. said, "the cons in the jail you're going to will want to train *you* how to behave. Most of 'em really like dogs. So you better watch out for those ribs, you skinny old fuck. They'll probably snap like twigs."

"Maybe," Bobby Jeff said, "but we didn' kill nobody."

"Not today," I said. "We showed up before you got a chance."

"Well, I didn' kill no Paul Fontaine, I swear to God I didn'. Maybe if I got pissed off at him a few years back, I'd key his car—or pour sugar in the gas tank. That'd get his attention, make him pay up what he owes. But I wouldn' kill him. Not those other people, neither. Didn' even know 'em. I don' hang out with nobody who got all that religion. Hey!"

The Ohio state police in Ashtabula were at first startled but eventually delighted when we arrived with our cargo. All the stories that needed telling were told, especially Tobe's. Everyone wanted to see the photos she had taken of the meth kitchen as if she'd just come back from two weeks in Jamaica and was showing off her vacation pictures. As the McInernys were being escorted downstairs to their cells, one of the troopers, a strapping-looking young female named Jayna Willis with thick hair braided down her back, happened—just *happened*—to accidentally trip Wyatt McInerny so he fell down the uncarpeted steps. He was hand-cuffed behind his back, and he had no way to break his fall. Too bad for Wyatt. His last words of the day, bellowed around some broken teeth and a heavily bleeding nose, were "Police brutality" until the steel door slammed shut in the basement.

Tobe was by the water cooler, soaking a towel in cold water and pressing it against her eye. Tobe might be the bravest person I know, and once she was cut loose from the henhouse she didn't complain or whine even a little bit at what she'd gone through. But now that the meth chefs were locked up, I could tell she was in pain.

I walked over and put my hand on her waist. "Okay, Tobe?"

"Barely okay, but hanging in there."

"Bad day," I said.

"Not many good days for a cop." She moved a bit closer to me so

I could snake my arm completely around her waist. "Good nights, though—with you."

I started to say something, but she shook her head. "Uh—if I were you, I wouldn't plan on any festivities this evening."

"Gee, and in such a beautiful, romantic motel, too." I squeezed her gently and then let go.

K.O. was on a bench against the wall, the big slobbering dog at his feet. K.O. hadn't been able to find a leash for him, so he was using his own leather belt to keep the creature from running away—not as if the dog was in any hurry to go someplace.

One of the troopers we'd met before, Brian Hollinger, walked by K.O. and stopped to pet the dog's head. "What're you going to do with him?"

"We're hoping *you'd* know what to do with him," K.O. said.

The trooper thought for a moment. "I can get him to a shelter. Not the pound—that's pretty terrible. He's an old guy, and he's not gonna win any beauty contests. Nobody'll adopt him anytime soon."

"You gonna take him someplace where they're gonna kill him?"

"I wouldn't do that," Hollinger said. "I know a no-kill shelter. They'll take care of him." The trooper pointed to his badge. "They pay me to be honest, kid. I'll give you the shelter's phone number. You can call and check on him whenever you want. What's the dog's name, anyway?"

K.O. was startled. "Uh—hell, I don't know."

"You're inside out over a dog and you don't know his name?"

"It doesn't matter. He's a person; he deserves to live."

Hollinger scratched his head. "A person, huh? Well, that's a new one on me, buddy." He walked to the desk, tapped on a computer keyboard for a minute, and printed out the shelter site's home page.

"Here you go—info and phone number of the no-kill shelter." He looked down at the dog. "I'll get this—person—there first thing in the morning."

K.O. stubbornly jutted out his jaw. "What're you gonna do with him tonight?"

"I'll take him home with me. I've got three dogs of my own, and plenty of food and water. And I know my dogs' names." He sighed. "I hope this big mean-looking son of a bitch doesn't eat them."

When Hollinger escorted the dog out of the room, I moved over to K.O. "He took your belt with him."

"I can hold my pants up until I can buy another belt tomorrow."

Tobe was still treating her eye with the cold-water towel and looking askance at K.O. "K.O.—you said this was the first animal you've ever seen that you didn't like," I reminded him. "But you just told the trooper he was a *person*. What's with that?"

"I've met a hell of a lot of persons I don't like. That didn't mean I wanted 'em euthanized."

I jammed both hands into my hip pockets and processed K.O.'s thought. Finally I said, "I guess you've got a logical point at that."

CHAPTER THIRTY

MILAN

Tobe came out of the bathroom fresh from a shower, wrapped in two towels, one around her hair. The egg-shaped bump above her eye hadn't gone down very much, and the eye itself was swollen out of shape. The bruise on her shoulder from the belt buckle was a dark purple color on her coffee-with-cream skin, and there were raw red circles around her wrists from the ropes. The area all around her mouth was reddened from the duct tape.

"Feeling any better?" I said.

"Still hurting, but I'll get over it. The main thing is, I think I washed off most of the chicken shit smell."

"I don't smell anything except you." I leaned down and kissed the ugly bruise on her shoulder.

She smiled weakly. "Is that supposed to heal it?"

"Just absorb the kiss, and you won't feel a thing."

"Taking two aspirin might have been more effective. The kiss felt kind of good anyway."

"A sandwich will make you feel better, too." There was no way I could get Tobe, in her present condition, to attend a restaurant sit-down dinner with a cocktail, so I'd sent K.O. for takeout food.

"I don't feel like eating."

"I don't blame you. But you have to eat something."

She shrugged off one towel, keeping the other wrapped around her head, and crossed the floor, nude, to get her robe. "They would've killed me," she said, as matter-of-factly as if she had been commenting on the weather. "I've been shot at, threatened with knives, had rocks and furniture and empty bottles thrown at me, I've ducked a hell of a lot of punches—and there were a few I didn't duck. Several people I arrested tried biting me, including one guy that, I found out later, had AIDS and wanted to infect me with it. It comes with the job. I knew it the first time I pinned on my badge. But I didn't need time to think about it. Any good cop's best weapon is quick reaction." Her sigh was shaky.

"You should make an appointment with the department's shrink when we get back home."

"The department shrink is a pain in the ass," she said. "He keeps asking cops about their mothers! Besides, you only see him when you shoot somebody. I didn't fire my weapon today."

She touched her "egg" bruise. "You know why Wyatt McInerny would have beaten me to death with his belt buckle? I damn near kicked his kneecap right off him!"

"Bad idea when you were tied up like that."

"He was squatting down groping my tits."

"Jesus, Tobe."

"He wasn't going to rape me. He thinks if he sticks his dick into a black woman's pussy, it'll fall off or something." She chuckled—once. "Besides, it would have been too much trouble for him to get my clothes off, anyway."

"You didn't mention that."

"Not to you. I did mention it to that state trooper, though—I think her name was Jayna something—and that's why she threw him down the stairs."

"Hats off to Jayna, then."

"The trouble is, Milan, we're no closer to finding the killer of those three people yet."

"I might've been given a clue by accident," I said.

"What?"

"Let's wait until K.O. gets back with the sandwiches. I hate having to repeat myself."

"I better go put some clothes on then. I'm not wearing anything under this robe."

"I noticed."

*   *   *

K.O. returned ten minutes later, juggling three bags from Subway. "I had to guess what you guys liked—so I had them put every veggie on these sandwiches. Hope nobody'll get mad at me."

Tobe said, "You saved my life today, so I won't get mad at you until a week from Thursday—at three o'clock in the afternoon."

He grinned. "Feeling better?"

"Sore all over, but I'm not dead. What've you got there?"

K.O. opened the packages and gave each of us a foot-long sandwich—salami, with all the vegetables and honey mustard dressing, and six bags of potato chips, in case we were still hungry. "I can run out to the machine and get Cokes if you want me to."

"Thanks for not getting chicken sandwiches—I had enough of chickens this afternoon to last me a lifetime." She watched K.O. open his own bag. "Your sandwich looks different from ours."

K.O.'s ears turned pink. "Uh—it's an all-veggie sandwich."

"What's that all about?" I said.

He lifted his shoulders, then dropped them. "Don't feel like eating animals," he said.

"Just tonight?"

"Well—kinda heading in that direction."

"Have you told Carli about this?"

He shook his head. "Not—yet."

"Is it okay," I said, "to discuss our current case while you're eating vegetables?"

"Fire away," he said, sitting at what the motel called a desk and taking a big bite. I began carefully picking some veggies out of my own sandwich. I like vegetables—but not raw tomatoes and not raw onions. Then, that's just me.

"No McInerny killed Paul Fontaine or Cordis Poole or Annie Jokela," I said, "but the state police can hang them for just about everything except the Lindbergh kidnapping."

Tobe said, "They *didn't* do the Lindbergh kidnapping?"

"When I was driving Bobby Jeff to jail, he didn't stop talking. Remember, K.O.?"

"I wanted to stuff my fist in his mouth to keep him quiet, but the frail little fart would've died or something."

"He made a comment that got me thinking, though."

"About religion?"

"Not exactly," I said. "Lots of people don't like religion."

K.O. raised his hand like a first-grader in school. "Me, me!"

"Maybe. But is there anybody around here who actually hates the Baptist church and the people in it?"

"Well, Feelo Ackerman goes to church for business reasons," Tobe said, "when he's not busy behind the hotel desk disapproving of everyone. But I don't think he's the most religious guy in town."

"Bobby Jeff was right when he used the word *hate*. That's a frightening word."

"What about John Aylesworth?" K.O. said. "The prison janitor. He's very vocal about church-hating, more than anyone I've run into."

Tobe sneaked a glance at the tiny digital clock on the night table between beds. "It's almost eight o'clock," she said. "Do you know where he lives, K.O.?"

"I've got his address written down."

"Well, let's go see him, then."

"You're not going anywhere, Tobe. You had a lousy day, you need to rest."

Tobe tilted her head. "Did you ever hear of a homicide detective letting a killer wander around because she's *tired*? You guys, go sit in K.O.'s room for ten minutes while I get ready."

"Damn it, Tobe," I began, but she interrupted me.

"Where's your badge, Milan?" she said, her tone heavy. "I know where mine is, and where my weapon is, too. Now go!"

I went, K.O. with me. Every so often, especially when it comes to her being a police officer when I am still a civilian, Tobe makes me feel like I'm five years old.

We headed down to the other end of the motel. K.O. stopped at the drink machine for a Mountain Dew. "You have to wash all those vegetables down with *something*."

We hung around outside in the rapidly cooling evening. It was one of the few times I wished I had a cigarette to smoke; lacking a gym, or even a place to run, smoking a cigarette helped to calm the nerves, even though it's as unhealthy as anything one can do, and it makes your home, your furniture, your walls, your clothes, and your hair stink from the tobacco. I had smoked since I was fifteen, but I had managed to kick the habit a few years earlier.

K.O. and I stayed quiet, listening to crickets rubbing their legs together to attract female crickets—almost sounding like a Saturday evening at a thirties-and-under singles bar.

I said, "We've all talked to John Aylesworth. Is he our man?"

"Maybe. He's full of hate for everybody. Maybe some self-hatred, too, because his son hung himself."

"*Hanged* himself, K.O. A picture is *hung* on the wall; a man is *hanged* in the garage."

"Yeah, I'll remember the proper word the next time I'm at a lynching. Meantime, we should go alone. Tobe had a bad day."

"Cops all have bad days. Homicide cops? That's a full-length portrait of a bad day."

K.O. shook his head. "You love the woman, don't you? I mean, really love her?"

I had to think carefully before I answered. Then I took a deep breath and said, "Yes. I really love her."

"But you weren't all that upset when you saw her this afternoon. You just shrugged it off?"

"No. If she'd really been hurt, or . . ." I couldn't manage to say it. "Yeah, I'd be crying and rending my garments, ready to kill anyone who even moved funny. But she made it through today only a little the worse for wear, and if I'd fussed over her, she'd have been mad as hell and maybe dumped me for good."

He shook his head sadly, jamming his hands into the pockets of his jacket. "Damn, I couldn't do that with Carli, Milan—like if anything bad happened to her. I love her too much."

"There's a different kind of love for every person on the planet. I don't know Carli as well as you do, so I don't know how she'd take your coming all undone if she got hurt. That's the trick. If you love a woman—really love her and want to keep her around—you'll learn to love her the way she wants to be loved. Otherwise, wave bye-bye."

"Does that go the other way around, too? A woman has to love you the way you want to be loved?"

"Devoutly to be wished," I said. "But it doesn't always happen that way. You have to adjust."

"Maybe you didn't adjust so good," K.O. said. "Before Tobe, you went through a long list of relationships with women."

"Not such a long list."

"So you didn't love them the way they wanted to be loved."

I wanted to slap the little shit silly—because he was right. I thought of my ex-wife, Lila; of my first postdivorce love, Mary Soderberg, who had dumped me worse than Lila had. Of Nicole Archer and Connie Haley—dynamic women who had loved me once and then quickly outgrew me and my lifestyle. Great times for a short while, and then dreams crashed and burned, me burning with them. "That's what I meant," I said. "The older you get, the more you learn."

Tobe came out of our room, fully dressed, wearing a jacket that was long enough to hide the Glock on her hip. She waved at us to congregate at her car.

"You guys solving the problems of the world?" she said.

"Not even solving the problems of Queenstown," I said.

"Well, let's not ruin the evening just for Queenstown." Tobe unlocked the car and opened the driver door.

"You're okay to drive? No migraine?"

"Not a migraine, just a headache. It'd be better if the killer dropped by our room and confessed. But a cop's gotta do what a cop's gotta do." She slid behind the wheel. "Let's ride, cowboys."

It took us twelve minutes to get to John Aylesworth's house. Much of Queenstown was built on rolling hills near the lake, and some streets were only a block long, so all three of us were pressed against our windows, looking.

We found it on the wrong side of the railroad tracks. That used to be a joke all over the country, when railroad tracks were ubiquitous, and depending on your bank account and your social standing, you lived on one side of the tracks or the other. Apparently it wasn't a joke at all in Queenstown.

Interestingly, the house wasn't run down; the lawn was cut, the paint wasn't peeling, and none of the steps were cracked or broken. But someone who stared at the Aylesworth house for an hour would have no memory of it five minutes after driving away.

There are people like the Aylesworth house, too. Sometimes you take one look and remember them for the rest of your life. Sometimes you forget what they look like as soon as they turn their backs.

There was a one-car garage, and no vehicles in the driveway. We parked on the street and made our way up the walk. The TV was loudly playing a Cleveland Indians baseball game. There was no doorbell, just a knocker, and Tobe used it with the authority that only comes with a gold badge.

John Aylesworth opened the door. Lounging around in his own home, he wore a long-sleeved black T-shirt and wrinkled khaki Dockers. His sockless feet were in flip-flops, and there were three beer bottles on the table next to his easy chair—two of them empty.

"Are you bothering me again?" he snapped instead of greeting us, once more crossing his arms defensively across his chest, hiding the crooked hand. "Goddammit, why don't you leave me alone? I answered enough questions already from you people. I *work* in a goddamn prison. I'm one of the good guys, remember?"

"If you're a good guy," Tobe said, "why don't you invite us in?"

"This is my home," he whined, "where people go when they want to be private—and safe."

"People get murdered in their homes," I said, "so sometimes homes aren't safe at all."

"We're the police," Tobe said. "We're not here to kill you."

"Well, I got nothing to talk about."

"We'll see."

Aylesworth stayed at the door for one beat too long, trying to decide if he should let us in or not. Finally he said, "Got a warrant?"

"Come now, Mr. Aylesworth," Tobe said easily, brushing past him into the living room. "We're the good guys, too."

He looked more flummoxed than upset, but he did step back so K.O. and I could enter as well. The living room was tastelessly furnished in tacky Value City Furniture chic, but then my Cleveland Heights living room isn't exactly *Architectural Digest* material, either. What struck me was the unusually large number of photographs and awards on the walls, the mantel, and nearly every flat surface. There was one, obviously taken at least a decade earlier, of Aylesworth and a pleasant-looking woman who must have been his wife. Another recent one, encased in a black frame, was of a skinny young man, about eighteen years old, smiling into the camera but looking vulnerable and uneasy. I had to assume it was his son, Tate, who had taken his own life.

The rest of the photos and memorabilia on display were almost a tribute to his daughter, Mia. Athletic photographs of her with her volleyball team, in her gymnastic uniform, in a baseball uniform, in a competitive swimsuit, and a raft of trophies she'd won for her prowess. She was smiling triumphantly in every photograph, the smile of an effective and almost unbeatable winner.

She'd been a middle school and high school superstar until her brother's death. After that—nothing. Tate Aylesworth had given up on life, and Mia had given up on practically everything else.

"Nice pictures of your daughter," K.O. said.

Aylesworth grunted.

Tobe studied the trophies on the mantel and raised her voice to be heard over Tom Hamilton calling the Indians–Red Sox game. "Successful athlete. A real credit to your family, Mr. Aylesworth. You must love her very much."

"Of course I love her! She's my daughter!" He reached out his good hand and touched one of Mia's photos, and his raspy voice quivered. "She's all I got left."

I moved to Tate's photograph. "Your son?"

He just nodded.

"Did you love him, too?"

"Dumb-ass question!" he growled. "Why you comin' around asking dumb-ass questions? He was my son, I loved him. Didn't really understand him, couldn't figure out why . . ." He looked away.

I said, "I have two boys myself, both grown. Very different. Milan Junior has his mother's personality, and her looks, too. Stephen—well, he's a lot like me. So we love our kids equally, for different reasons. Is that about right, Mr. Aylesworth?"

"So what's the deal here? The three of you *invade* my home in the middle of the evening to chat about parents' love?"

"You love your kids," Tobe said. "But you're carrying around a lot of hate, too."

He made a scornful sound like "Pffft!," his eyes dark. "I work forty hours a week in a prison. How can you not hate?"

"My week is chasing and busting bad guys," Tobe said. "I don't drag hate around with me."

"Your daughter Mia," K.O. suggested, "has a lot of hate, too, and she doesn't work in your prison."

The man chewed on his lower lip. Then he gestured at Mia's photos. "Does that look like hate to you? That big grin when she's on top of the world? On cloud nine, waving around a trophy?"

"That was a while ago," I said.

K.O. added, "Before her brother died."

"Who does she hate now?" I asked. "Who do *you* hate?"

All Aylesworth's bones seemed to liquefy at the same moment, and he backed up into his easy chair, fumbled on the table for the TV remote, and clicked off the ballgame. Then he waved us into seats as well. Tobe and I took the sofa, K.O. an uncomfortable-looking straight chair against one wall.

"Since Tate was fourteen years old," he said with great difficulty, "I knew he was a—a homo." He caught himself quickly: "A homosexual. Naturally, I didn't like the idea much. It didn't make me stop loving him, y'see, but it was awkward sometimes. I mean, he wasn't fruity or anything. If you didn't know him well, you wouldn't've guessed. And nobody did, until his junior year in high school. All those kids at that age, y' know—sixteen, seventeen— they were all macho, chasing girls, screwing girls, lot of sports and sneaking beer. And every other word out of their mouth was the f-word. So when they noticed Tate didn't smoke or cuss or chase girls, they figured it out for themselves."

"They bullied Tate?" I asked.

He reached for the half-full beer bottle, then thought better of it. "Not then, anyway. They teased him. Taunted him. It was stupid, but I wouldn't of called it mean. Until . . ."

None of us said anything.

"One Sunday," Aylesworth continued, "when Pastor Urban took me aside after his sermon—a sermon spent trashing gays and lesbians, by the way, saying that they were the spawn of Satan—and he said . . ." He took too long a moment to get emotional control. "He said it'd be better, since Tate was part of our family—that we would be more—comfortable finding another church."

K.O. ran his fingers through his hair. Tobe hugged herself as though she'd grown cold. I swallowed too loudly.

"Tate had stopped going to church a while back, but me and

Mia kept on until that day. But that was sure as hell the end of it. We never did find another church, probably because we didn't even look. That washed it up for us."

"Where is Mia tonight? Out on a date?"

"I don't know where she is. She's a grown woman, she doesn't have to answer to me or anyone. She goes out by herself a lot in the evenings. Maybe she just drives around, goes all the way to Mentor to see a movie. She doesn't date anybody, though. And she sure as hell isn't doing evening activities at the Baptist church. We're not Christian no more. Don't know what to call us, but it's not that."

Tobe and I exchanged glances. She shook her head for me not to ask a question right now.

"Anyways," he said, "a couple new things happened about the same time. The kids both had computers, but before the business with Urban, they'd both gotten onto—I think they call it Facebook—and Twitter, too." He looked expectantly at each of us. "Are any of you on Twitter?"

I said, "I'm on Facebook, but not Twitter."

"Well, Tate started getting some ghastly things on Twitter. 'Get out of town, you stinking cocksucker.'" He grimaced. "Oh, excuse me, Officer, I didn't mean to repeat that. I didn't want to offend you."

"Not offended," Tobe said. "Go on."

"And other stuff. Threats—bad threats, like Tate was gonna get beaten to death, or shot. Or even worse, I guess, that he should kill himself and do everybody a favor. Do God a favor, too."

"Who sent these?"

"Phony names. We never knew who they were for certain. Maybe Mia knows. But it was kids, that's for damn sure."

"Like Cord Poole?" K.O. said. "Jason Fontaine. Cannon, or whatever his name is? Other kids from the same high school?"

"Probably. There were some girls, too." His chin dropped to his chest and he stared at his own knees. "Tate never did a damn thing to any of them. Why are kids that cruel? Why do they hate?"

"Kids aren't born hating," I said. "They have to learn it from somewhere."

Tobe leaned forward. "Did you teach your kids about hating?"

"No!"

"Really? You love everybody and taught Tate and Mia to love everybody, too?"

Aylesworth sounded defensive. "I don't love everybody, Detective. Nobody loves everybody."

"So where did you learn to hate?" I said.

"I work in a prison—cleaning up after scum every day. I hear what they say and I see what they do."

"You taught your kids to hate convicts?" Tobe bored in. "Most of the inmates are black, aren't they? Black or Hispanic?"

"When one guy cuts off another guy's ear right after breakfast one morning, well, if I gotta mop up all the blood on the floor, I don't know what color he is. And I don't care."

"You don't know whether these kids that wrote bad shit to Tate were black or white?"

"I don't know, Detective!" he sputtered. "But if they were all from that high school . . ."

K.O. finished for him. "That high school is all white, isn't it?"

Nobody spoke for a few moments. Then I said, "Nobody's tried to eliminate all those kids. Yet."

"No," K.O. said. "Just their parents."

"Annikki Jokela didn't have children," Tobe said. "But she worked in that school. She talked to high school kids all the time." Her look at John Aylesworth was sad, sympathetic. "Your son was picked on because he was gay, or some people thought he was gay. Maybe they learned that kind of hate from grown-ups."

She turned to me. "We hear about hatred of homosexuals every day. In some places, they've actually put laws on the books that are flat-out discrimination hidden behind their tired old 'religious freedom' bullshit." Leaning back against the sofa, she wondered, "Where do you suppose they all learned to hate gays in this simple little town, Milan? A hatred, maybe, that's getting them killed."

I looked at my wristwatch. It was nine fifteen at night. "Maybe," I said, "we should pay a little evening visit to Pastor Thomas Nelson Urban."

"Junior," K.O. said.

CHAPTER THIRTY-ONE

MILAN

The streets in Queenstown are darker at night than the inside of a raven's ear. Rural, to say the least. There were no cheerful street lights like the ones found at Playhouse Square in downtown Cleveland, or at Cedar Fairmount in Cleveland Heights, where I've lived for the past quarter century. Maybe it's one way to tell Queenstowners they're not supposed to go out at night.

Tobe's eyes are better than mine. Of course they are; she's younger than I am. But she still drove carefully to find her way to the Baptist church. Squinting ahead into the spread of illumination from the headlights, she said, "I wonder if Mrs. Junior will talk at all now that it's nighttime." She chuckled. "Maybe she's like Dracula—she only comes alive in the dark."

"If she's Dracula," K.O. said, "maybe she's the killer."

"Let's see," I mused. "Stabbed in the heart, bashed on the head, drowned in a spa—but nobody's neck got sucked. No vampire."

Tobe said, "I wish guessing was covered in the cop-training handbook. Since it's not, we shouldn't be guessing. But Urban's wife could be the bad guy here. Anybody could be. Ackerman at the motel, that newspaper woman both of you talked to, Nowicki with the horse that's got asthma, or even the county assistant coroner."

"Maybe," I said, "it's that family who glared at us while they held hands and said grace at the restaurant where we had dinner."

"You might be right, Milan." Tobe clutched the steering wheel with both hands as we traversed the road running along the lake.

It was hard to see the stripes painted on the road to tell us what lane we were in. "Damn, there are no clues. It's all guesswork."

"Think Urban knows more than he's told us?" K.O. said from the backseat.

"This time *we'll* do the preaching and he'll do the listening. And we won't have to say grace ahead of time, either."

The Baptist church, no surprise, was on a dark, quiet street. Next door at the parsonage, the only light was on the second floor, off to one side. Lights were turned on in the church, too—not many, but enough to make the stained-glass windows stand out prettily in the blackness. I put together that Mrs. Urban was probably in an upstairs bedroom.

"Which door should we knock on?" Tobe said.

"Likely the pastor's in the church. Let's try there first," I said.

We parked across the street from the church under a low-hanging weeping willow tree, and Tobe cut the engine and turned off the lights. Before any of us could get out of the car, the church door opened and Pastor Urban came out slowly, followed very closely by a tall young woman. She was silhouetted against the light so we noticed her almost military hairdo—more of a Mohawk.

"Holy shit," K.O. whispered. "That's Mia!"

"Mia Aylesworth?" Tobe said. "From McDonald's?"

"She hates this church and the preacher, too. What's she doing with him now?"

"Let's sit here," I said, "and find out."

The two descended the three church steps and headed for a small, perky pickup truck parked in the driveway. It was peculiar that they both entered the truck on the driver's side. Urban went first, sliding under the steering wheel to the other window, and then Mia Aylesworth, who started the engine. We were too far away to hear, but apparently there was an argument between them, because I saw Urban waving his hands, his mouth open wide as if he were yelling.

And then Mia Aylesworth took a swing at him. Urban's head jerked back fast, he hurled himself as far away from her as he could, and a gout of blood spattered onto the windshield.

"Move out!" said Tobe as she lunged from the car. However, as in all automobiles, the overhead light went on, illuminating us, and Mia saw it, because she quickly slammed her truck into drive and sped off down the street, laying rubber behind her.

"Goddammit!" Tobe cursed. She got back into the car, turned on the ignition and the headlights, and took off, nearly jolting me out of my seat.

I thought Mia would head for the I-90 freeway, but she pointed her truck the other way, toward Conneaut and eventually the Ohio–Pennsylvania border. By the time she got onto Lake Road, she was doing ninety miles an hour, and we were behind her by about a quarter of a mile, driving at pretty much the same speed.

K.O. said, "Can't you go any faster?"

"Sure I can," Tobe said through gritted teeth. "I can run her off the road into a tree or into Lake Erie. That means maybe she dies. Maybe Urban does. Is that your choice? Or are you in a hurry because you have to pee?"

"No, ma'am."

"Then fasten your fucking seat belt—and don't call me *ma'am* ever again."

He clicked his seat belt and said, "Yes, ma'am" again. Very softly.

We were moving at almost double the speed limit, and though there were several stoplights on Lake Road, our vehicle sailed through them as if they weren't there at all. The county is mostly rural, and there were few cars on the road, especially this late in the evening, so none were endangered when we zoomed through the intersections, and those driving on the same road did their best to get out of our way.

I said, "You have a siren, and a rooftop bubble light that flashes red. Why don't you use them?"

"It won't slow her down. She's running from us, not out for a warm spin with a man three times her age whose teeth she just knocked out." Tobe's voice was tight and intense as she studied the road disappearing rapidly beneath our wheels. "And the siren would wake up half the people in the county. So both of you—shut up!"

I watched Mia's taillights bouncing along ahead of us. Where were they going, and why? What made Urban get into her truck at that hour of the night, with his wife upstairs in the parsonage next door? Something made Mia hit him in the face; was it what he said to her, what he did? Would she could hit him again?

Tobe looked grim. She'd seen enough violence that day at the McInernys' chicken coop to last her for a while. And now this.

Was Urban the serial killer we'd come looking for, picking off members of his own flock at leisure? And why was an angry young woman like Mia getting involved with him?

After less than two minutes, which felt more like half an hour, Mia's truck lurched off the main road, tires and brakes screeching, and headed onto a narrow, winding road encompassing both hills and valleys. Tobe took a deep breath, said, "Hang on," and almost flew off Lake Road, two wheels leaving the ground. I actually did hang on, clutching the edge of the dashboard in front of me. We landed hard, and I caught my breath as we hurtled past comfortable-looking homes whose inhabitants were already asleep for the night. For moments at a time we lost visual contact with the truck.

I asked K.O., "Is there anyplace around here like Tinker's Hollow where she could disappear?"

"How the hell would I know?" he snapped. "I don't even know where we are right now!"

Ahead of us, Mia hit the top of a hill and her bright red taillights dropped out of sight as though she'd gone off the edge of a cliff. We still heard the thrum of her engine and the bumping of her tires on earth and not pavement. Following, we crested as well, looking down the hill to a marsh-like beach, a quiet, mysterious-looking Lake Erie hovering dark in the distance. Mia's truck headed down to the sand—a strip, I learned later, that was semi-officially called the Sand Bar, although most local residents refer to it as the Mud Hole.

Well known all over the county for the plethora of ducks there, the Sand Bar was quiet at a time when ducks were sleeping elsewhere. A good thing, too, because Mia's truck barreled out onto the beach and made a 180-degree stop-and-turn, the sand rising into the air like a dry fountain. Headlights, nearly blinding us, were turned off. There wasn't much of a moon out, and the only illumination now was our own headlights as we approached the littoral coast.

The driver's-side truck door opened and Mia got out, turned, and gave whatever she had in her hand a powerful yank, and Pastor Thomas Nelson Urban Junior came tumbling, heels over head, landing on all fours in the sand. Wrapped tightly around his neck was a chain approximately six feet long, and when Mia gave it another jerk, he raised his head and sat back on his heels. His mouth was bloody.

We left our headlights on and got out of the car, starting toward them until Mia waved her end of the chain at us and shouted, "Don't come any closer or I'll wring his goddamn neck right in front of you."

Urban tried to say something, sounding as if a ladleful of steaming hot Cream of Wheat was in his mouth. Several jagged broken teeth were getting in his way. It was easy to figure out what he was trying to say. His eyes showed unadulterated fear, and he really meant, "Help me!"

Tobe took a few steps closer. "Come on, Mia. You can't do this. Not to another human being. We aren't like that, you and me."

"Speak for yourself, whoever you are."

Tobe waved her badge, but they were too far apart for Mia to see it. "Detective Sergeant Tobe Blaine of the Cleveland Police Department. We're here to help you."

"Go home!" Mia said. "That's how you can help me."

K.O. stepped forward. "Hey, Mia—remember me? K.O. We've talked before a few times at McDonald's—and I know what a good person you are. I like you. You're a lot like me—pissed off all the time—but when you get down to it, we're pretty sensible people."

"Would you be sensible," Mia said, her voice sounded close to bursting into tears, "if you found your brother hanging in your garage, knowing it's because of this miserable bigoted shit and all the people who follow behind him, kissing his ass and doing whatever he says?"

Urban tried saying something, clawing at the chain around his neck, but instead just gurgled. Mia paid no attention to him—nor did we.

"Those kids who bullied my brother," Mia continued, "the kids I went to school with, the ones I knew all my life . . ." She sobbed, once, and pulled tighter on the chain. "It wasn't their idea. They teased him at the beginning. And the teasing was mean. All teasing is mean. But then—"

"Mia," Tobe said, "put down the chain; then we'll talk. Pastor Urban is choking."

"Good! It was his fault. He started all this anti-gay stuff at church. Every Sunday the same thing. Hate abortions. Hate abortion doctors. Hate gays. He never stopped. Some kids quit church, like Jason Fontaine. He quit sending teasing stuff to Tate, too, because some kids can spot evil when they see it. Or hear it.

"But their parents didn't quit! Ms. Jokela didn't." Now she was loud, practically screeching, and on a roll. "They repeated everything Urban said to their children. At school, at dinner, every goddamn minute! They were the ones who convinced their kids that gays don't deserve to live in this town—and to tweet that to my brother.'"

Another sharp jerk of Urban's chain. He groaned and coughed, and another gout of blood spilled from between his shattered lips.

"Urban," Mia shouted, "and Fontaine and Poole and Annie Jokela killed my brother just as if they held a gun to his head and pulled the trigger. I lived with that for two years! I cried myself to sleep every night, and now I won't live with it anymore. Those— *haters* deserved to die. And so does this miserable piece of shit!" She tightened the chain, looping it around her wrist one more time. "So shoot me, lady," she said to Tobe, "because I don't give a damn anymore. But he's going first."

Tobe shook her head and reluctantly removed her Glock from her holster, holding it down at her side. "Just put the chain down—please." Mia shook her head violently. "Don't make me shoot you, Mia," Tobe sighed. "Please don't make me."

"Easy, Tobe," I said softly, but Tobe ignored me.

"Hold on a second," K.O. said, moving closer to Mia and her gasping prey, speaking softly. I could barely hear his whisper. "It feels like you stepped in shit, right, Mia? I get it. I've been there. For real—and paid the price. I had to figure out the hard way to keep my chin low and how to get clean, stay clean, and still give the bad guys what they deserve." He looked toward Urban, dripping with contempt for the preacher. "If you kill this son of a bitch in front of us, there's no going back. Then we can't help you, Mia— and believe me, we want to help you."

"I don't need your help," Mia said, her voice vibrating with real fright. "I don't need anyone's help. They deliberately talked their kids into killing my brother. With words. With cruelty. Well, now they won't do it to anybody else. And nobody's gonna listen to this fucking bigot telling them to hurt and kill gay people, either!" She tightened the chain again. Urban gagged.

"Easy, Mia," K.O. soothed. "You'll get through this. We'll get through it together; I'll help you. You're smart, you're beautiful. There's a life ahead of you. The rest of the world isn't like Queenstown. People will love you. Accept you. Respect you."

One mirthless staccato laugh. "Respect? Yeah, right."

"I respect the hell out of you, and I respect what you've been doing, even if it's wrong. Other people will think so, too. Trust me."

She shook her head. "I don't trust anybody."

K.O. nodded. "I get that. But if you don't trust somebody, you're lost." He held out his hand. "Give me the chain, Mia. Let's get Urban to a hospital and you someplace to get help."

"And what if I say no?"

He shrugged sadly, nodding toward Tobe and me. "Then Detective Sergeant Blaine will have to shoot you."

"Let her!"

"Okay, but the thing is, she won't kill you. She'll shoot you someplace where it'll hurt more than you can imagine, just to make you put down the chain. And then you'll still be in trouble, but you'll be in agony, too." He took one step closer and held out his hand. "Work with me, Mia. For a change, do something for yourself."

"So I'll limp in jail for the rest of my life. Ask me if I give a damn!"

K.O. ran his fingers through his hair. "Give a damn about your father, then."

That stopped her momentarily.

"He hates his job, and he's counting the days till he can move out of Queenstown with you and go somewhere happier. You both need to start over. He lost his wife and he lost Tate. Don't make him lose you, too, Mia. He loves you. He needs you."

"He doesn't need me." Mia was crying now, tears trickling over her perfect cheekbones and dripping off her chin. "Nobody needs me."

"Everybody needs somebody," K.O. said. "Otherwise they become the loneliest people in the world." His face was a study in sympathy. "Don't make your dad the loneliest man in the world." He extended his hand, palm up.

She sniffled, thinking it over. "I don't want to hurt my father . . ."

K.O. nodded.

"Your friend there won't shoot me, will she?"

K.O. looked back at Tobe, who still held her Glock at her side. He said, "Not if you cooperate."

Nobody seemed to pay any attention to Urban. Now he clawed the chain away from his throat by a bare half inch and croaked, "Shoot her, goddammit! She's gonna kill me! *Shoot the little bitch!*"

Mia had almost changed her mind, but Pastor Urban ruined the moment—as he'd apparently done with many other moments. She whirled toward him, snarled something unintelligible, and gave a mighty wrench to the chain. Urban screamed.

And K.O. moved.

Two quick steps forward and he grabbed the chain about eight inches from Mia's hand and tugged on it. Mia took hold of his wrist and began twisting it. Urban choked and sputtered.

"Let go, Mia!" K.O. said.

"Fuck you!" She shifted her weight, twisted some more, and flipped him over her hip. Startled, K.O. lost his own grip on the chain and landed hard, flat on his back in the sand, with most of the breath knocked out of him. The look on his face was one I'd never seen before. He was stunned, and totally taken aback by a young woman flipping him around like an overcooked pancake.

By the time Mia Aylesworth turned away from him, Tobe was on top of her, the gun pressed firmly against the side of her head. Mia took a moment to think about it, then dropped the chain and didn't move a muscle. In the total darkness of the Sand Bar, illuminated only by our headlights, she froze like a statue.

"That's about enough, Mia," Tobe said. "It's all over."

CHAPTER THIRTY-TWO

MILAN

A week later, we were back in Cleveland, where I feel comfortable. This is my town. My home.

I'm sure there are many nice, decent law-abiding citizens up in Ashtabula County, where I spent the better part of a week—people who work at a job and pay their taxes and watch their kids play football and soccer, and see movies and TV shows that make you smile and sometimes even make you think. But while doing my Queenstown job, I spent more face-to-face time with pond scum.

When I thought of my case in Ashtabula—which wasn't really my case at all, but one in which I played backup to Detective Sergeant Tobe Blaine—the nicest local was Mia Aylesworth, a pretty, slim high school graduate with a modified Mohawk do whose many athletic activities had blessed her with the strength of three men, and who had killed three people and was taking aim at an entire congregation of churchgoers.

I had no idea what they were going to do with her. Tobe officially turned her over to the Ohio state police, as she had little faith in Queenstown's police chief Eino Koskinen—and I think she mentioned to the state cops that Koskinen's involvement with the booming Ashtabula County meth trade should be looked into.

Pastor Thomas Nelson Urban Junior, who had come within minutes of finally shaking hands with the Big Guy in Heaven, if that indeed was where he was headed, which is doubtful, was relieved no one who knew him personally witnessed him being hauled around at the end of a chain like a recalcitrant stray dog at a shelter. He was even more delighted that the three of us who'd been present, K.O., Tobe, and I, were headed back to Cleveland and would probably not think about visiting again.

I never learned the assistant pastor's name, but Urban had her announce to his parishioners that he was called away on business and wouldn't be back for at least two weeks, which was long enough for him to visit Pittsburgh and a skilled dentist who could rebuild his fragmented mouth and teeth and not tell any locals about it.

Pastor Urban would hopefully take those few weeks to think about what he might have learned when he was just moments from dying for his sermons of hatred and intolerance. My guess is that someone like Urban would, at the very least, adjust his judgments a bit.

Of course everyone in town knew, anyway; unless one happens to be a devout Buddhist thinking only good thoughts, there is a plethora of nasty, juicy gossip in every corner of the universe. Those who faithfully attend Urban's church, however, would never, *ever* mention it. In truth, some of them wouldn't care one way or the other.

K.O. and I were in our office in the Flats, just across the river from Progressive Field (which is still called "the Jake" by everyone in town). It was late in a midweek afternoon, floor-to-ceiling windows open to capture the cool breezes off Lake Erie. Too soon, it would be time to close the windows and turn on the air conditioner.

I was writing checks to pay off utilities and other expenses incurred over the past month. K.O. was doing clerical work, too, typing up reports and things, just in case someone wanted to ask us questions. He had an elastic brace around his right wrist, which was sprained when Mia Aylesworth had tossed him over her hip on the Sand Bar near Conneaut as if he were a sack of dirty laundry.

He was embarrassed about getting slammed on his ass by a young woman, but he had great sympathy for her and wished she'd not been the killer we wound up catching and turning over to the authorities.

I had a certain amount of sympathy for her, too.

When Tobe showed up at our office, finally done for the day and feeling wrung out—an occupational hazard, as most police officers feel used and diminished at the end of their shift—she suggested we repair for a drink somewhere close where she could unwind. It sounded like a great idea—until I asked her the wrong question:

"How was your day?"

"I've been up in Ashtabula since this morning," she said. "With the Ohio Bureau of Criminal Investigation inspector. I told him things he didn't know, and he told me a few I didn't know."

"Can you put the two of us in the loop, too?"

Tobe took out her notebook. "K.O., you remember Mia told you how mad she was at all the teenage boys who texted and Twittered and Facebooked her brother to kill himself, but that she wasn't really that mad at Jason Fontaine?"

"I remember," K.O. said. "After talking with him, I thought he was a pretty decent guy, too."

"There was a reason she wasn't mad." She flipped over the notebook and found what she was looking for. "He'd texted Tate things like 'You shouldn't wear a yellow shirt on Thursdays,' and 'Come to a football game sometime so no one will think you're queer.' But when the other tweets and texts got vicious and threatening to Tate, Jason quit sending."

"Because he is a decent guy," I said.

"Partly."

Partly? A chill ran down my spine. "What's the other part?"

"Just about that time," Tobe said, "Mia Aylesworth went to a women's clinic just outside Columbus and had an abortion. Jason Fontaine was the father. He paid for everything out of his own pocket. He and Mia were the only two who knew about it—not even their parents or best friends."

K.O. said, "Wow!"

"They stopped seeing each other after that," Tobe continued, "but I guess they remained friends. And he stuck by her after Tate's death, even when a lot of other kids from high school, both male and female, dropped her like a hot rock."

"I understand her rage," I said, "but those kids sent the damaging tweets that drove her brother to suicide. Why didn't she go after them, and not the adults?"

K.O. said, "She told me the kids were too damn dumb to come

up with that on their own. They listened to their parents, or to Annie Jokela."

"Tate killed himself two years ago. Why did Mia wait until now?" K.O. wondered.

"She lived with it eating away at her gut," Tobe said. "But she watched her father get more and more depressed, more and more miserable, and she thought that if they had to stay there another few years until he could retire, they'd both go ballistic.

"But then, one morning at McDonald's, Paul Fontaine, Jason's father, stopped in for coffee, and made some pretty heavy moves on her. Forget about her Mohawk haircut, she's very attractive. Paul didn't know about the abortion, according to Mia, but he did know she and Jason had dated for quite a while, and weren't together anymore."

I shook my head, more in sorrow than shock. "Hitting on his son's ex-girlfriend. Paul Fontaine must've been some piece of work."

"What with all the fury and hatred from what had happened to Tate, Paul's coming on to her pushed Mia over the edge," Tobe said. "She arranged to meet him that night at Sunset Beach. In his car, he moved over from behind the wheel because, he said, he needed more room. He told her to go down on him, and when he unzipped his fly and displayed his package, she stabbed him in the heart."

We were silent for more than a minute. Then K.O. asked, "Did Cordis Poole try to hook up with her, too?"

"No. By that time, she went after him. She got in touch with him and said she wanted to talk about the church. She picked him up in the church parking lot and brained him with a hammer. Then she drove down to Tinker's Hollow to dump him."

"Two questions," I said. "First, what the hell must the inside of her truck look like? Blood and brains all over the place?"

"She said she'd driven twenty miles to WalMart and bought a load of towels and two spray bottles of Fantastik. After she cleaned up her truck, she disposed of everything in a Dumpster in Conneaut. All that stuff was taken to the landfill and by now it's covered with several feet of other garbage."

"Won't the police find traces of gunk in her truck?" K.O. said.

"The state cops are investigating that as we speak." Tobe's shoulders lifted and then relaxed again.

"Okay," I said. "Mia weighs about a hundred and ten pounds, give or take. The late Cordis Poole weighed in the vicinity of two-forty. So she killed him in the church parking lot with one blow, as the assistant coroner said, which means she hit him awfully damn hard. Then she drove all the way to Tinker's Hollow, and managed to get him on the ground and roll him down the hill into the creek. How did she manage to do that? Did she have help?"

"I can answer that, I think," K.O. said, holding up his taped wrist. "She almost ripped my arm off with one hand. She's stronger than all of us; she's been doing serious sports since she was a little girl. Handstands on the horse, hanging from the rings, volleyball, push-ups, chin-ups, even wrestling. She probably couldn't lift Poole out of the truck, but she managed to pull him out and then roll him over the top of the hill and watch him bounce down until he hit the water."

"If she was that strong," I said, "it wasn't hard for her to hold Annie Jokela's head under the water in the hot tub until she drowned."

"According to Mia," Tobe continued, flipping over a notebook page, "when she was still in high school, every time she got to talk to Ms. Jokela in the school office, the woman said horrible things to her about gays—especially about women who spent all their time doing sports that should only be done by men. *Real* men!"

"That must have been a gut punch," I said, "her suggesting to Mia that she was a lesbian."

"Jokela also suggested Mia should look very carefully at her own brother, who, as she said, walked a little light in his loafers."

"Well, at least we showed up in the nick of time to prevent another murder," I said.

"Right in front of us," Tobe said. "I talked to the assistant D.A., too. He'll call all three of us as witnesses at her trial."

K.O. stood up, fast. "A trial on what charge?"

"What do you think, K.O.? One charge of attempted murder, on Urban—and three counts of aggravated murder."

"Jesus Christ!" K.O. said bitterly. He turned and walked to the window to stare out at the river lazily drifting past the back-to-back stadiums where the Indians and the Cavs play.

"K.O.," I said, "Mia admitted to everything."

He didn't make eye contact. When he spoke, it was obvious he was gritting his teeth. "They're going to fry her, aren't they?"

"They won't 'fry' her at all," Tobe said. "And if she's nailed with a death sentence, there are many years of appeals before any execution. Besides, she's all but pleaded guilty."

"So that means life without parole, doesn't it?"

I said quietly, "They haven't even tried her yet. Relax, K.O."

His hands, hanging at his sides, were doubled into fists—painful, I'm sure, considering the sprained wrist. He finally said, "I won't be a prosecution witness! I'll testify for the defense."

"Testify to what?" Tobe said. "You'll be asked what you saw and heard that night—just like Milan and me. What will you do, lie? That's a crime right there. You'll be sworn in court to tell the truth."

He turned around quickly. "I'm not swearing on any Bible! I don't believe in God, so that'd be lying in court."

"Will you swear on the United States Constitution?" I asked him. "I assume you believe in that."

K.O.'s mouth almost disappeared, as if he was tightly holding anger inside his mouth. Finally: "I wish we never went up there! I wish we hadn't busted her in the first place!"

"She committed cold-blooded murder three times," Tobe said as kindly as she could. "You might think she's a good person—and in many ways, she might be. But we can't just politely ask her not to kill any more people and let her walk away. Good, bad, or indifferent, everything people do has its consequences."

"K.O.," I said, "you always made it clear you wanted to be a cop, and being a private investigator is your second choice, which is great. You're damn good at your job, and you were terrific up there with us in Ashtabula County. But you've got to come to terms that the law is the law. It's not your job, or mine or Tobe's, to decide who gets away with murder and who doesn't. I know you like Mia very much—and we all agree that the people who goaded Tate Aylesworth into hanging himself were not worth the powder it'd take to blow them to hell. But we're not judges. *You* aren't a judge—and you can't just decide to be one whenever it takes your fancy."

"When you're on the stand," Tobe said, "you tell the truth about what we saw that night. If you can't do that, and if you *won't*, you might as well pack your suitcase, put your cat into his carrier, say bye-bye to Carli, and head out of town, far away. Change your name, get a job, and hope to God you aren't recognized, because if you lie under oath, nobody will ever trust you again."

We all were silent for more than a minute—a tableau instead of three people just talking. Then it was as if all the air went out of K.O. His shoulders slumped, his chin flirted dangerously with his chest, and he melted miserably into his chair, pouting like a seven-year-old kid whose father wouldn't let him take some photographs with his six-hundred-dollar camera.

"They're going to lock her up forever," he said.

CHAPTER THIRTY-THREE

MILAN

In the good old days of Cleveland, one of the classiest jewelry stores in town was Cowell & Hubbard, in the middle of Playhouse Square. I couldn't afford to shop there, but I've never been much into jewelry, anyway. When I got married, I bought Lila a plain gold band, and another one for myself—only a little larger and thicker, purchased at a discount jeweler somewhere in Collinwood. That pretty much sums up my jewelry-buying experience.

Cowell & Hubbard, the upscale jeweler, is long gone, but in the same space a classy, dramatic restaurant opened a few years ago, actually keeping the name Cowell & Hubbard. Zack Bruell, the owner, is one of our town's foremost creative chefs, and the place caters to theatergoers, especially those going to the Cleveland Play House, almost next door at the Allen Theater, and the Great Lakes Theater at the refurbished Hanna, right around the corner on East 14th Street.

It was where Tobe and I decided to have dinner that evening, after her long day in Ashtabula and the stressful afternoon for both of us trying to make K.O. feel all right about catching a multiple killer—even one who was young and pretty and could probably kick his ass in a wrestling match. Tobe's bruises from her afternoon in the McInernys' henhouse had faded enough that she could cover most of them with make-up, so she felt pretty good about going out and "being seen." It was our first real date since before we went north.

"You never know," Tobe said after we ordered cocktails. "The

ADA is an even bigger jerk than the assistant coroner, which shouldn't surprise you. He's considering putting her on trial for aggravated murder, but the defense will push for temporary insanity. She grieved quietly for two years, and then something inside her snapped—" and she snapped her fingers—"like a too-small rubber band you put around your wrist."

"Which means they'll put her in a cracker factory instead of prison."

"It'd be a hell of a lot better than an eight-by-six cell."

"Unless," I said, "the hospital is run by Nurse Ratched."

"If the doctors determine at some point that she's cured—however a murderer gets cured—they can sign a release for her at any time."

"We did a lot of work," I said, "going all the way up there and catching her—and both you and K.O. got knocked around while we were at it. But if she gets released with a wrist slap, it'd be almost like her skating free. Would that piss you off, Tobe?"

"Piss me off? The mayor of Cleveland called me this morning! He thanked me for all my help in Queenstown and will put something into my record saying what a hell of a wonderful human being I am. The chief of detectives wants this to go all over the newspapers and on TV about my catching a bunch of crooks along with a killer, which will make the department look good, make me famous for about fifteen minutes, and get the chief mentioned at least a dozen times." She looked around for the waitress. "Where the hell are our drinks?"

"Coming," I said. "So what will you do about this big local news story?"

"I told him if my name appears anywhere in the paper or on TV about this, he can have my badge, and I'll tell him exactly what to do with it."

"I'd hate for you to give up such a good job."

"A good job." She looked at the ceiling. "My job isn't determining guilt or innocence or anything in between, Milan. I catch bad people. What judges or juries do with them—well, as a snotty waiter might say, that's not my table."

"What about your feelings?"

She sat back, perusing some of the people seated around us.

Playgoers, probably, which meant they were comfortably well to do, as legitimate theater tickets are not inexpensive. And theater lovers are relatively bright. After a moment, she said, "There's more than one person in this room right now who would be thrilled to pieces knowing that Tate Aylesworth was driven to suicide by bullies because he was gay. Some in here hate black people for no other reason than their skin shade and think they should still be slaves, because slavery turned a huge profit for the plantation owners, just like the huge profits of almost every big corporation and hospital and oil company in America today—including privately owned prisons. If I were in a different mood, I'd tell you I hate their guts. I don't know which ones they are, but I have nothing but contempt for them." I noticed that her hand on the table across from me had knotted into a fist.

"But much as I'd like to, Milan, I can't just pull my Glock and blow them all away, or I'd end up on the wrong side of the cell bars."

"Maybe they all learned hatred from people like Pastor Thomas Nelson Urban Junior."

"From him, from their parents, from God knows where," she said. "Hate is like weeds. It grows everywhere, and it's a full-time job for the rest of us to pull it out of the dirt and get all the roots before it eats up the world." She leaned forward and offered a sort of whisper. "I had a moment out there on the Sand Bar—just a moment, mind you—thinking I should let Mia choke Urban to death with that chain."

I put my hand over her fist and squeezed gently. "He made that town as corrupt as he is."

"Maybe, but I doubt it. For every hater he created and egged on, there must be twenty other people up there in Ashtabula County who are nice, decent, and kind. Regular people living regular lives."

"How come we didn't run into any of them?"

"Because," Tobe said, "we were looking for a murderer. Haters are the cost of doing business." She turned her hand over and squeezed mine in return. "I'll bet if we did in-depth interviews with everyone in America, we'd find more nice people than serial killers."

"Like Pastor Urban?"

Her chuckle was nearly silent. "I probably never mentioned this, Milan, but my parents were churchgoers. I went to a mostly black Baptist church in Raleigh, every Sunday morning. I sang all the hymns very badly, and I believed like crazy."

"Why did you stop?"

"College. Wearing a badge. Deciding to shit-can religion altogether. But when we take a bad guy, or girl, in this case, off the street, we're helping people who'd be in deep doo-doo if we hadn't showed up."

The waitress arrived with drinks. I was a beer drinker most of my life. Now, Tobe has introduced me to classier libations that are more expensive and that hit harder. Not that I don't enjoy a Stroh's in the summer, watching a ballgame, but few beer guzzlers ever find their way into upscale restaurants like Cowell and Hubbard. On this particular evening I was drinking a Maker's Mark, neat. Tobe taught me one single ice cube, or one teaspoon of water, brings out the flavor of good whiskey.

She'd ordered a Bombay Blue Sapphire martini—always gin— with three olives. The only time I ever consume olives is on a pizza.

"Before you dive into that martini," I said, "shouldn't we say grace? Like those people in the Ashtabula restaurant?"

Tobe laughed. "Saying grace in downtown Cleveland over booze? Probably not. Not for us, anyway, Milan." She held out her glass, though. "Instead—how about 'Here's mud in your eye'?"

"Slainte!" I said.

And we clinked.

ACKNOWLEDGMENTS

My thanks to Kathy Pape, Library Director at the Conneaut Public Library. So much of this book was inspired by her treating me to an amazing tour of the county, a great lunch at the Covered Bridge Restaurant, her marvelous stories (and *double* thanks for the "Chocolate Jesus"), and her great feeling for this beautiful part of the country. I named one of the characters in the story after her—though Kathy herself is *not* an eighteen-year-old blond ditz.

Thanks, too, to Pulitzer Prize–winning journalist Connie Schultz, for sharing so many of her memories of the city, Ashtabula, where she was born and raised.

I've visited Ashtabula County many times, and invariably met people who are kind, funny, welcoming, and helpful. Unfortunately, a mystery novel about kind, funny, welcoming people would never get off the launching pad, so a big hug to all of them who were not much like the characters I created here.

A tip of the hat to dear friend Police Chief James T. McBride (retired), who knows more good cop stuff than anyone else.

To Jack and Jenifer Warren (one *n*, please), who took me on another tour and told me more Ashtabula County stories that drove me forward in writing this book.

And as ever, to Dr. Milan Yakovich and to Diana Yakovich Montagino.

There is no "Queenstown" in Ashtabula County. That's what we fiction writers do sometimes—we make stuff up.